A]

By Eric Bahle

Cover art by S. A. Hunt

To my wife for her love and belief

The Post

"Hey mister. You headed west?"

The tall man didn't stop what he was doing. He continued checking the horse's girth strap, but his grey eyes flicked over the saddle to the man who had spoken. The man who spoke was short but burly. He had long, greasy hair and a great bushy beard, sandy blond, except for the brown streak where he spat his tobacco juice, an act he performed at that very moment.

His dress didn't give away much, for he wore a plainsman's long buffalo hide coat against the cold, as did the tall man himself. But this fellow wore it belted on the outside with his pistol, an old fashioned Colt dragoon, thrust through at the ample belly. He did wear gauntlets and had a long whip coiled and slung over his shoulder; a wagon driver then, what the frontiersmen called a mule-skinner.

"Could be," said the thin man to the fat man's question.

Satisfied with the cinch of the girth, he pulled down the saddle skirts and began checking the stirrups.

"Why do you ask?"

"Oh, I been askin around town for someone headed west. The hostler said you might be, mister."

The man's tone was deferential, though it seemed somehow the man didn't often speak in such a manner. It was annoying, but the tall man was patient.

"Well, I am headed west," he said, "but I say again. Why do you ask?"

"Well, mister, I run a freight line," the shaggy fellow said. "Hadley's Freight and Post. I'm Hadley. Bill Hadley."

Hadley touched the brim of his battered hat.

"Nathaniel Caine at your service, Mr. Hadley," Caine said.

He slid the Henry home in its scabbard and moved to the pack animal, a stolid mule. Caine would have to cross the mountains, and wasn't sure of the grazing. The mule carried extra fodder and a few bundles of wood, as well as most of Caine's food.

"Anyway, Mr. Caine," Hadley went on after an awkward pause, "since you was headed west, I was hopin you might do me a favor. I'd be able to pay you for your trouble."

"What sort of favor?" said Caine.

"Well, like I said I run a freight line, but I'll take post and parcels and the like," Hadley said. "You know a place called Hartsburgh?"

"Never heard of it," Caine said. "I haven't traveled overmuch in these parts. I was planning on taking the Carson Pass and making for Kensington. It's in my mind to see the mountains."

"Well, they're somethin to see and no mistake," Hadley said. "But here's my problem and my proposition. There's a town, more or less on your way, called Hartsburgh. If you take Elkhorn Pass and follow it into the valley, you'll hit Blackfoot Creek. Follow the creek south for about a day and you'll find the place."

"It sounds as if it's rather more out of my way than less," Caine said. "But I still haven't heard your problem or your proposition, Mr. Hadley."

"Well, it's like this, Mr. Caine."

Hadley held up a pair of large saddle bags.

"These are bound for Hartsburgh. Mostly letters, but a few parcels and the like, and I need to get 'em to Hartsburgh. They're already pretty late."

"Well, you do run a freight and post line."

Caine's Yankee twang sounded unhurried, but he wished Hadley would get to the point.

"That I do," Hadley said with an obsequious nod. "But the passes are hard this time of year for a mule team. Still under snow most like. There ain't no freight goin, just these. So it ain't worth it to send a wagon. Usually I can find a rider I know, but I been comin up dry."

"And so you want me to take them?"

Caine was ready to refuse. Normally he wouldn't have objected to the task, he had no real destination in mind or purpose other than travel itself, so the detour wasn't a problem. The problem was Hadley. Caine disliked the man, though he couldn't say precisely why.

"I'll pay you for your trouble, Caine," Hadley said and thrust a gauntleted paw into his coat pocket.

It came out with a leather pouch, which Hadley shook to make the coin ring. The gesture struck Caine as vulgar, and he opened his mouth to refuse when Hadley went on.

"Twenty dollars in silver and the quartermaster will give you twenty more when you get there."

"Quartermaster?" Caine said.

"Yup. See there's a fort there," Hadley said. "Just a small outpost under a Colonel Hayes. Most of these letters are for the soldiers there. A letter from home can mean an awful lot to those boys."

"I know it well," Caine said.

The money didn't interest him, although his purse was getting pretty light lately. But Caine had seen himself how important a soldier's correspondence was. On occasion, he had personally gone to some lengths to see that his men got their mail in the War. Greater lengths than taking on an extra set of saddlebags.

"Very well, Mr. Hadley."

Caine took the saddlebags and the money. He secured the bags on the pack mule and mounted his horse. Hadley continued to thank him, but Caine just set spurs to the gelding, eager to be away from the unctuous wagon driver.

Caine took the gelding to a trot. He glared as he passed the hostler, displeased that the man had told Hadley his intended destination. The hostler dropped his eyes and Caine wondered at his own anger.

He had made no effort to hide his intentions, and it wasn't unusual for folk to ask such favors out here in the West. There was no real post for vast stretches of territory and people were usually willing to help out. Yet angry Caine was.

He tried to tell himself it was just his dislike for Hadley, but he slowed as he neared the edge of town and the jail. The town marshal, a spare man by the name of Roarke, stepped out the door as Caine reined up. Caine and the Irishman had hit it off somewhat and had spent more than a few nights at cards while Caine stayed in town.

"Like to get an early start, eh Caine?" Roarke called with a cheerful grin.

Roarke always had a cheerful grin, but that grin rarely took the steel out of his black eyes. It was an unwise troublemaker who mistook the cheerfulness for weakness. Roarke kept law and order with fists or gun and didn't flinch from a fight. In truth, Caine thought he might be a little unhinged, but that hadn't stopped them from getting along. Caine trusted him.

"Indeed, Roarke," Caine said, "the curse of the Protestant."

Roarke laughed and crossed himself, not bothering to put down the tin coffee cup he held.

"Tell me, Roarke," Caine said, "what do you know of Elkhorn Pass?"

"I thought you were going through Carson's Pass."

"Well, I was," Caine allowed, "but I've taken on a side job as a postman."

"That shaggy bastard Hadley, I reckon," Roarke said.

Caine nodded, and Roarke spat and swore, then spat again.

"Don't do it, Caine. I don't like that mule skinning son-of-a-bitch, and I don't trust him as far as I can throw his fat arse."

"Well, I didn't like him either, and I'm glad to hear it's not just me," Caine said. "Unfortunately, I've already agreed and taken payment. It's just a bundle of letters and parcels."

"Elkhorn Pass is wild country," Roarke said. "Bandits, and road agents, and Indians."

"But I thought there was a fort out there."

"Faugh!" Roarke spat again. "One troop against the whole Blackfoot? Plus Crow, and Flathead, and who knows how many red devils."

"Only a troop?" Caine said. "I expected a regiment. Hadley said there was a Colonel in command."

"That's as may be," Roarke said, "but there ain't more than fifty soldiers. It's just an outpost really. Don't go Caine."

Caine nodded but said nothing. It was clear Hadley had been less than honest, and Caine felt no obligation to the man. He could still turn around and return the money and parcels, and take the southern pass. Nevertheless, Caine found his gaze following the line of mountains north to where Elkhorn Pass must lie. Roarke saw the direction of that gaze.

"Damn it, Caine," he said, "don't worry about that dirty freight driver Hadley. I'll go box his ears this minute and that'll be an end to your deal."

"I'm not worried about Hadley, and I've ridden in lawless land before," Caine said.

He wondered why Roarke was so set against it, and asked just that.

"There's more, Caine," Roarke said. "There's…some kind of trouble out there in Hartsburgh."

"What kind of trouble?"

"Well…"

Roarke tossed the remainder of his coffee in the street and threw the cup angrily against the wall of the jail.

"No doubt you'll think me naught but a superstitious Celt."

Caine had never seen Roarke flustered in any way. He was tempted to laugh but feared the lawman would take offense. In his current state he might even lose his temper, so Caine tried to set him at ease.

"Come, my friend," Caine said. "It's true we've only known one another a short time, but we've shared too much good whiskey to hold back with each other."

It must have been the right thing to say for Roarke's grin returned instantly.

"There ain't no good whiskey in this town, buck," he said, "but I take your point."

He looked up and down the street and kicked at the post. Roarke sighed and reached inside his coat for a cigar. He bit the tip and spat, then started fishing again in his pockets for a match. Caine sat the gelding patiently while the marshal got his smoke going. Finally, Roarke blew a great cloud of smoke into the cold air.

"It's like this, Caine," Roarke said. "Hartsburgh is haunted."

"Haunted?" Caine said.

If Roarke expected mockery he would not get it from Nathaniel Caine. Caine had more than once found himself treading outside the normal pale. In fact, he had glimpsed things that Roarke, superstitious Celt or no, would find hard to believe.

"Haunted by what?"

"Well, I can't say," Roarke said. "Not for certain anyway, for I haven't been there myself in more than a year, mind. There was something brewing then, though I couldn't put my finger on it. Just a feeling, but trusting those feelings has kept me alive in a dangerous business."

"I've seen your instinct at work, Roarke," Caine said. "I've no reason to doubt you. But what sort of trouble?"

"At the time it was just a feeling, as I say," Roarke went on, puffing at his cigar. "The folk were polite, but close. Like they were hiding something. They were nervous, too. Some folk'll always be nervous around a lawman, but this was different."

"What did you do?"

"Wasn't much I could do," Roarke shrugged. "I went to see the marshal and sound him out. A Texan by the name of Rollins. No sense of humor in that man, but a good lawman and I trusted him."

"Past tense?" Caine said.

"He acted the same as everyone else," Roarke said. "He didn't exactly give me the bum's rush, but he wanted me out of there. When a lawman wants you out of his town, you go or you fight. I didn't have any cause to fight."

"What about the fort?" Caine said. "This Colonel Hayes?"

"I couldn't really say," Roarke shrugged. "I never met the Colonel. He was up in his fort, I suppose, and the troopers all keep to themselves."

"All well and good," said Caine, "but how do you go from a town behaving strangely to a town being haunted?"

"Well, at first it was just strange talk. From the wagon drivers mostly," Roarke said. "That lot complain without end, of course, no matter how easy the run is. Mind you, Elkhorn Pass is not an easy run even in summer.

"But they started complaining about the town, as well. First there weren't enough whores nor whiskey. Nor enough people for cards.

"Then the town folk were openly hostile. They would shut everything up at sundown, even the saloons. They started getting hit by road agents and neither the marshal nor the Army gave a damn.

"The town started to get an empty look and there was rumors of…something taking them."

"The pox?" Caine said.

"No, Caine. I don't mean they just died," Roarke said. "I mean they were *taken*."

"Hm. As you say," said Caine, "but taken by what?"

"No one's sure," Roarke admitted. "At first I would have it out with someone, insist they were exaggerating. That it was natural. A bear that had turned man killer or summat."

"What changed your mind?"

"Well, bears don't hunt in winter for one thing," Roarke said. "And anyway these people were taken at night in town. Right out of their houses, it's said. No animal would do that."

"In any case, someone certainly would see it," Caine said. "See it and shoot it."

"Just so. And now we get to it," Roarke said.

Caine noted his friend's voice start to fall into the natural storytelling cadences of the Irish.

"The tale is that folks *have* seen it. Seen it and shot it, or tried to. They speak of a creature that walks on two legs. Like a man, eh?

"But too tall and bulky to be any mortal man. It comes out of the shadows and darkness of night, quick as a ghost. It must be more than spirit, though.

"Men have tried to fight it, townsfolk and soldiers, aye. Bullets shatter and bounce off its hide as if it were made of stone. It rends and kills all that try to stand before it.

"Well, not all. If they speak true, it leaves the women and children. Even so, the town is supposed to be all but abandoned, for anyone that stays there will bring the monster down upon them."

"Only at night?" Caine said and Roarke nodded. "Curious. What do you think it is, Roarke?"

"Who knows? A devil from Hell?"

Roarke made the sign, and his cigar traced a hazy cross in the air. It hung for a moment before the cold morning breeze scattered it.

"Maybe something older."

"Older?"

"My granda' knew many stories of Ireland from the days before Patrick brought The Christ," Roarke said. "Tales of the old heroes. They sometimes fought monsters with their spears of bronze. No one has brought Christ to these Red Men, or to great stretches of this land, Caine."

Caine listened and nodded slowly. But again his gaze went to the mountains and grew distant. It seemed to him he could see the road stretch out before him; over the wooded hills and up the rocky slopes to the windswept pass, where winter's grip was still fighting to hold. Beyond the pass to the people who watched the sun sink with growing terror before they must huddle and wait through the night.

"So it's like that, eh?" Roarke said.

"I don't take your meaning, Roarke."

"You have a wolfish look about you this morning, Nathaniel Caine," Roarke said. "I can see it's in your mind to take the pass despite what I've said. Damned if you don't want to go *because* of what I've said!"

"I mean to have a look, at least," Caine said. "If I can determine what bedevils these folk, perhaps I can help them."

"I'll come with you then," Roarke said. "You'll not go after this creature alone."

"No, my friend," Caine said. "I think I *shall* go alone for this one."

"This one?" Roarke said. "Meaning you have experience with this sort of thing? I'm no coward Caine!"

"I didn't mean to imply you were," Caine hastened to reassure the marshal. "It's just a feeling perhaps, but sometimes we must listen to them as you yourself said. Besides, your responsibilities lie with this town. I'll ride to Hartsburgh." Roarke's mustache bristled, but he seemed to accept Caine's wish.

"It'll haunt me, wondering what's become of you," he said. "How will I know if you've come to a bad end?"

"If you don't hear from me, things will not have gone well," Caine said. "But if I make out alright, I'll send you a letter by the post."

Roarke spat and sputtered a bit, rankled by Caine's laconic humor. Finally, he nodded and reached again into his coat. This time he came out with a silver flask, which he unstoppered.

"It struck me when we met, Caine," Roarke said, "that there was more to you than meets the eye. I see now that's so, it's a fey road you ride. Here's to reaching the end of that road hearty and hale. God watch over and keep you."

He tipped the flask and drank and passed it to Caine. Caine drank and passed it back before shaking Roarke's hand. The men nodded to each other and Caine shook the gelding's reins.

He rode off at an easy pace, leading the mule, and didn't look back. Roarke watched Caine's receding figure. He spat into the street and thought Hadley better not cross his path today.

Elkhorn Pass

Caine tried to work fast, for with his gloves off, the cold of the mountain quickly stiffened fingers and robbed them of dexterity. He needed dexterity to use the flint and steel. He used the flint and steel because he tried to save his Lucifer matches for emergencies. Or at least for smoking his pipe on the trail.

Caine was glad to see that the pass didn't climb above the timberline, though hardwoods had turned to beech and aspen in the foothills, then given way totally to mountain pines. It was a stout pine branch he was using to fashion a torch now. There wasn't much pitch flowing at this time of year, but he shouldn't need the light for long. He settled for a dry limb with some green needled branches wrapped quickly around one end.

The flint scraped and skittered, and the tinder sparked, caught and flared. Caine kept his gloves off and stood with the torch in his left hand. Before him was a black triangle in the stone wall of the mountain. The entrance to a cave.

His right hand disappeared under the heavy coat and reappeared with a revolver. The rifle would serve better against a large animal, but the light outside was already fading. Caine would rather have a pistol and light to shoot by than two hands on a rifle in the dark.

Caine meant to use the cave for shelter tonight. He also meant to make sure nothing else had the same idea. There were no tracks in the snow, so Caine didn't expect wolves or panthers, but there might be a bear sleeping away the winter.

Caine advanced with the torch before him and his thumb on the hammer of the Smith and Wesson. The entrance was fairly narrow, but widened into a slant-roofed cave, dry floored and sheltered from the worst of the wind. Caine swept the torch near the ground. There was no sign of animal occupancy, recent or otherwise. No tracks or spoor, and no bedding.

So the cave was empty, but it was also small. If he brought the horse and mule in it would be close quarters. He doubted they would be the best roommates, but there was no real shelter out in the pass.

Caine held the torch up high and swept it about while taking a few steps into the cave. A shifting shadow caught his attention and he walked the few yards to the back wall. There he discovered a cleft in the stone that went back at an angle, farther than the light of his torch reached. He turned an ear down the tunnel and listened for a few long moments. He heard nothing, so he ventured into the cleft.

This passage was narrow, much too narrow for the animals, and low enough that Caine had to fold his tall frame almost double. Caine's torch wouldn't last long, but he didn't want to sleep in the outer chamber if something could come on him and the animals from deeper within.

He didn't have to worry about losing the light, for the tunnel only went about thirty feet before opening into another cave. This was smaller than the outer chamber, but dry with a sandy floor and completely out of the mountainous winds. The outside could serve as a stable for the gelding and the pack mule, and he could sleep comfortably here.

Apparently, at some time, someone else had the same idea. There was a small ring of stones in the center of the chamber, blackened from many fires. Wood, too, was laid up in neat piles along the wall. It was dry and brittle, obviously old. Caine wondered how long it had been since a human had been in the cave. He set the torch in the ring and used some of the wood to build a fire.

Caine returned to see to the animals. In the short time he had been in the cave, night had almost fallen. He led them in and relieved them of their burdens. In the last bit of light, he gave them both a quick rubdown and put on the hobbles, though why they would venture into the cold dark of night, he couldn't imagine. Caine spread some fodder on the cave's floor and, satisfied that the animals would be warm and dry, returned to the inner cave.

Caine found that the fire was burning steadily with very little smoke. What smoke there was did gather a bit at the ceiling, but Caine saw it streaming away through a fire blackened crack—a small crevice that must reach outside to form a natural chimney.

Protected from the wind with fresh air vented from outside, the little chamber was ideal. Even with the cold and wintry night in the mountain pass outside, it was already comfortable and warm in here.

In fact, despite the modest size of the fire, Caine was too hot in his buffalo coat and shrugged it off. Caine had traveled through much of the Southwest territories and maintained, for the most part, his Yankee dress. Coat and weskit over a white shirt and more often than not, a cravat. Not flashy, but well made and well tailored.

These high plains and mountains, however, had necessitated a change of apparel. The heavy buffalo hide coat he had just shed, for one. For another, the thick woolen shirt he wore underneath. It was bib fronted like a soldiers, though he had taken care not to get a blue one. It was a rusty red with horn buttons, not brass.

The cave was not only too warm for the coat, but Caine undid the front of his shirt and set about making his supper. He was a spare man and generally ate sparingly, but long days on the trail built an appetite, and Caine ate accordingly. That business attended to, Caine leaned his back on a smooth boulder, made rather comfortable by draping the buffalo hide over it, and began to pack his pipe.

Caine had, on occasion, resorted to smoking the tobacco the cowboys used for rolling their cigarettes. It was dry and harsh and burned too hot. Caine gave it up, fearing it would foul his prized meerschaum, and went without if he couldn't find good pipe leaf.

Fortunately, tonight he wouldn't have to go without. Roarke's little town was well supplied, and the pungent odor of a nice black cavendish reached his nose when he opened his pouch. He dipped in the meerschaum and his fingers took over the ritual until the bowl was well packed. Caine fished out a suitable branch and got his pipe burning, then stretched his legs out before him.

This wasn't just for an after-dinner smoke, but for contemplation, a task for which the pipe was second to none as an aid. He was worried about what might lie before him in the haunted town of Hartsburgh. Haunted, Roarke had said, but not by a ghost. And if not by a ghost, then by what?

There were plenty of haunted houses where Caine was from. Some among the newly educated men scoffed, but many swore they had seen or encountered spirits, even these educated gentry. Caine's own education had done nothing to dispel a belief in the otherworldly. Quite the contrary, in fact.

Caine regarded the ring on his right hand and thought of Shaw with the usual mixed emotions. The heavy silver ring was in lieu of a fraternity key. Caine and several of his fellow students held the silly social clubs, as they thought of them, in disdain—beneath true men of learning. Never mind that these men were little more than boys, and the little society they formed was its own kind of fraternity.

There was plenty of brandy and cigars at their meetings and more than one 'feat of immortality' that usually amounted to nothing but a schoolboy's prank. These misdeeds could be forgiven, for they were just letting off steam. They were generally serious about their studies and had among them some brilliant minds.

Of these, Shaw was by far the most brilliant and, perhaps not surprisingly, the most troubled. Were Gibson Shaw still here, Caine knew he would have several theories on what might be haunting Hartsburgh.

A Nathaniel Caine Adventure

It was Shaw who, many years ago now, had convinced Caine to accompany him to England. Shaw was making an exhaustive study of the ghostly black dogs that many places in the isles claimed as local legends. That was a pleasant excursion, long before Shaw's voracious curiosity drove him to such dark and dangerous paths.

Caine wasn't particularly given to ironic bents of thought, or he might have wondered how he himself had walked a few of those paths and come out the other side. No matter, it was no quaint Black Shuck in Hartsburgh. But one of Shaw's stories did sound similar.

Caine had never been to the Pine Barrens of New Jersey, but Shaw had told them over brandy one night of a fell creature there. The Barrens were apparently a wilderness full of rough and clannish folk. The woods were harried by a winged monstrosity they called the Leeds Devil, after a woman of that name who was an admitted witch.

Shaw had of course, been there himself and talked to as many 'Pineys' as he could. He thrilled his audience with all the versions of the legend. Some of them were rather comical and there was table thumping at the best parts.

When asked if he had seen the creature himself, Shaw grew serious—or rather, more serious. Shaw wasn't given to light moods. Instead of answering directly, he continued to lecture. He informed them that the Piney legends were merely assimilations of an older creature.

The Indians that used to live in the area had their own legends of just such a creature. This devil seemed tied to one location or at least a territory, and Caine suggested it was merely a natural creature that had been improperly identified. In response, Shaw showed them a sketch from his field journal and dared Caine to name an animal that could be mistaken for the beast recorded in the drawings. Of course, the winged and fanged brute with bulging eyes was like nothing any of them had seen in the woods.

The other young men laughed and raised their glasses at Shaw's jest. Caine knew Shaw better than that, and knew his friend's smile wasn't indicative of humor, but satisfaction. Shaw *had* seen the creature and the sketch was a record of that encounter.

Caine blew out a long plume of pipe smoke. The blue-white smoke hung in thick wisps about his head. They suited his growing melancholy. Looking back, Caine saw how early the signs of Shaw's doom had been apparent. Caine felt dormant pangs of self-anger and guilt reawaken.

He knew now, of course, that Shaw probably couldn't have been saved, for it was his own nature he needed saving from. Wisdom gained in the intervening years told him the truth of this, but did little to ease the loss of his brilliant friend. It might help him on the path ahead, though.

Roarke believed something more than natural harried Hartsburgh and it's folk. It might still turn out to be something more ordinary, but Caine's intuition said otherwise. This didn't particularly frighten him, but the creature's reported immunity to weapons was worrisome. Caine was well armed and well practiced in the use of those arms, but if they would not harm the creature, how could it be overcome?

Shaw and his damned books would undoubtedly have methods set down in uncomfortable detail, but Caine had recourse to neither. He would have to rely on Yankee ingenuity and earthly stubbornness. With that Caine laid back, his weariness grown suddenly heavy, and closed his eyes.

* * *

The fire's flickering flames seemed to reach out and touch the walls of the small cave with burning fingers. Caine watched as the fingers danced over the walls in dizzying patterns. The patterns were not random, but took on aim and intelligence until it seemed they were painting figures on the wall.

The flames drew back until the fire was just a fire in the ancient stone ring. Yet still the small chamber pulsed with livid light. The light revealed the cave paintings, primitive but beautiful and potent.

Caine wondered how he had missed them earlier. The fitful flickering lent the etchings a sense of movement. As Caine watched, the pulsing became more rhythmical until the cave paintings' movement became purposeful, like images in a zoetrope.

The figures of people were primitive and representational, almost childlike: simple black lines for limbs and a circle for a head atop triangular torsos. The animals these intrepid stick men fought, though, were rendered in immediate detail with gorgeous strokes and deep color. With spear and bow, the tiny men strove and hunted against beasts both recognizable and fantastic.

Bears of monstrous size and mammoths with gargantuan curving tusks. Antelope and bison he knew, but also leopards. There were tawny cats with huge fangs and wild kine with long horns.

He saw the people cross great waters in long canoes. Saw them dance around fires, and walk across grasslands to the forested mountains where they hunted the great red elk.

The scenes showed much Caine didn't understand. A huge winged bird with lightning in it's beak swept over the figures in their hide tents. The people danced beneath a smoking mountain which erupted in flames. The tiny people fled the fiery debris, but one figure climbed the volcano and strove with a monster at the top.

The motion of the figures was inconstant, but still the reds and oranges that showed through the lava-man's hide of joined plates glowed with such realism, Caine fancied he could feel the heat radiating from the monster.

Other vignettes of hunting and dancing and unknown ceremonies flickered over the walls, but the pace seemed to be slackening. The light seemed to lose its lurid intensity, and the black figures slowed and blurred into a shadowy smudge.

The smudged outlines wavered, indistinct. As the witch-light finally settled into normal firelight, the outlines coalesced into a shadow. The shadow seemed to be that of a man with head bent.

Caine stared at the shadow, wondering idly what trick of light would cause the illusion. Then the shadow's head moved.

Caine whirled toward the fire, drawing his revolver and cocking it in one blurred motion. There was indeed someone sitting just feet away between him and the fire. How the man got past the pack animals and so close without rousing him was a mystery. Caine was a wolfishly light sleeper and not used to being taken unawares.

The man was hunched over and turned mostly toward the fire, and he reacted not at all to Caine's movement. The head and shoulders moved slowly in an attitude of inspection, as if studying something in his lap that Caine couldn't see.

"Who are you?" Caine shouted. "What are you doing here?"

The figure stopped and the head half turned, but the man didn't speak. Though Caine couldn't see the man's face, he got the distinct impression the man was amused.

"Speak, you bastard."

Caine was in control of his voice now, but control of his temper was uncharacteristically slipping.

"Speak and let me see what's in your hands. Move slowly, or I'll blow you to hell."

"I like your pipe, Caine."

The man didn't turn, merely raised his hands over one shoulder. He was indeed holding Caine's meerschaum, still turning it, the fingers inspecting the carvings.

"The work is exquisite. Wherever did you get it?"

"Budapest."

Caine wasn't sure why he answered. He had assumed the man was a bandit, one of the road agents he had been warned about, but there was something familiar about him.

"How the devil do you know my name?"

"The same way I know your purpose in these wild mountains, Nathaniel Caine."

The voice was perfectly reasonable, as if they were at tea in a parlor.

"I wonder, old fellow, do you know what these carvings mean? I speak of their true meaning, their *deeper* meaning, if you'll allow."

The man turned and placed the pipe between them. His face was still in shadow, and he moved a bit to one side so he might sit more comfortably. But before he leaned back into the light, Caine knew who he was. It was impossible, but the man's voice and that phrase 'if you'll allow' were ones he used to know well.

"Shaw?"

Caine almost couldn't bring himself to say it, afraid of what it might mean.

"Is that Shaw?"

"At your service as always, my dear Caine."

He leaned back and it was indeed the face of Gibson Shaw.

"You can put up your revolver, I believe."

It was Shaw just as he had been so many years ago. No, not exactly. His dress was the same, which was to say twenty years or so out of fashion now. High-waisted trousers and a tailed coat with a broad-cloak about his shoulders. He wore no cravat which had been a frequent habit of Shaw's.

Shaw's family had been from Baltimore which was as good as a Southerner to most of his New England classmates. That and his growing interests in the strange, even the macabre, had garnered him many comparisons to Poe. Caine had never agreed, thinking Shaw and Byron could have been brothers.

Shaw was never sickly as Poe had been rumored to be. Though not a dedicated athlete, Shaw was well made, the perfect fencer's body of quick strength and lithe grace. Indeed, he was one of a very few who could regularly get the better of Caine on the piste.

His face also was Byronesque, fine boned, but still masculine with large dark eyes. Those eyes lay in heavy shadow from the fire, but the face was the same. His hair was long as a libertine's, chestnut waves that fell over his shoulders and forehead, and drew women like iron to a lodestone. That hair was still long, but had gone white as bone.

Caine did not put up his revolver.

"What are you?" he said. "A ghost?"

"Well, if I am and you set off that piece, the ball will pass right through and ricochet all about this cavern." Shaw gestured to indicate the bullet's possible trajectory, and the fire light glinted off his silver society ring, a match to Caine's own.

"I'm no ghost, old friend. Well...I'm corporeal at least."

If ghost it was, it spoke true enough about firing in this space. The tone and manner were Shaw all over, so if it was some sort of doppelganger, it knew its mimicry well. Caine put up the pistol, lowered the hammer, and slid it back in the holster.

"It's not possible, Shaw," Caine said. "You can't be here."

"You should know better than most that what's possible is infinite, Caine," Shaw said. "However, if it makes you feel more comfortable, I'm not entirely sure that I *am* here."

This too, was a response so much in Shaw's character that Caine shook his head and almost laughed. Shaw just went on.

"This cave is special, old boy. Very old. From here I can feel the ancient veins of power in the mountain. The powers of the earth and the things that dwell in the deep."

"Why are you here?"

"I was summoned, Caine," Shaw said. "By you, if I'm not mistaken."

"I?" Caine said. "I have no such powers."

"Spare me the plain country squire speech," Shaw said. "You always had more power in you than you knew. I daresay it's what drew us to each other, despite how different we seemed. Granted, your stubborn Yankee pragmatism was an anchor. It kept you from being swept away by dangerous currents as I was."

"Shaw, I…"

Caine started to speak, maybe to apologize, but Shaw cut him off.

"Not everything is rational though, old boy," he said. "You always knew that, but never wanted to accept it. There are times when intuition is far superior to intellect."

"What lies ahead, Shaw?" Caine said. "What monster haunts Hartsburgh?"

"No monster, I think. Though you must understand, I have a very different perception of monstrosity these days." Shaw's voice broke a bit on the last words and he made a sound. It could have been a laugh or a sob and he covered his face with his hands. Caine started to reach out but his friend dropped his hands and went on, his voice normal again.

"But there has been *something* unleashed. As I said, I can feel the ageless veins in the bones of this land. They have been disturbed, savaged. Someone has tapped into them, for what purpose, I know not."

"How do I fight it?" Caine said.

"What's to say you can? You can't always fight," Shaw said. "You can't save them all, Caine. You couldn't save me."

Caine bowed his head and it was his turn to cover his face.

"No, my friend," Shaw said, "I don't mean you *failed* me. You just *couldn't* save me."

"That's as may be," Caine said. "But I'll go anyway to this town, and I mean to save them. So I ask again. How do I fight it?"

"Not with your pistols, or even with this very curious knife you're carrying."

Shaw's hand dropped to his side and his fine boned fingers played over the gleaming blade. Caine started and his own hand went to the empty sheath.

Caine would have sworn that the knife was in its proper place when he woke. He didn't bother asking how the trick was managed. He knew Shaw would not answer. Shaw was silent for a long moment and gave a heavy sigh before he went on.

"You're headed for a trial, Nathaniel Caine. An ordeal," Shaw said. "You are a skilled man at arms, but you are headed for a combat where those studies will not be enough. You will need your instinct and your spirit. I'm afraid for you."

"I thank you, old friend," Caine said, and he may have bristled a bit. "I may be stronger than you give me credit for."

"You are not hearing me, Caine!"

Shaw leaned forward into the light and Caine drew back. His friend's eyes were no longer dark chestnut, but pale white like polished ivory and they gleamed with unimaginable madness. That madness was made more horrible by the seemingly normal and even pleasant tone of his voice.

"You cling to your rationality, even now in an irrational space. When this is over you can keep clinging and convince yourself it was a dream and no harm done. However, cling to that rationality when irrational sorceries are upon you, and you will be blasted to nothing."

There was the sound of screaming and for a disorienting moment, Caine thought the screams were his own. But no, it was the shrill whinnies of a terrified horse.

Caine snatched up his rifle and chambered a round. He moved toward the cleft but turned back at the entrance. Shaw said nothing, his eyes were closed, mercifully hiding the chilling white orbs. One hand was splayed before him on the ground, so that only the fingertips touched. He held the other up and open, but whether in supplication or warning, Caine could not discern.

Caine moved into the narrow passage and all was blackness. No light came from the inner cave or the outer, and Caine's consternation grew. There should have been some moonlight from without. The moon was waxing and the night had promised to stay clear.

Caine's first worry had been of a hunting puma after the animals. Shaw's supernatural visit and the lack of any light put the possibility of unearthly dangers in his head, and his heartbeat quickened with unaccustomed fear. He edged forward on his knees and found at least the reason why there was no light from the outer cave.

The horse was giving voice to its terror by neighing and prancing about the cave mouth as if it wanted to get out, but couldn't bring itself to brave the entrance. The more sensible mule was keeping quiet, but had edged as far back into the cave as it could and blocked the narrow cleft. Caine moved him back with a gentle hand to its chest and there was indeed a silver light from the moon without.

As he watched, the horse ceased its caterwauling with one last snort and stood quivering with head lowered. Caine knew not what silenced it. It was quiet, but not calmed. Whatever had spooked it was still out there.

Caine eased into the outer cave and moved toward the mouth, edging along the wall. He kept his eyes fixed on the triangle of light, ready to fire at anything that presented itself. Nothing did and he found himself at the edge of the mouth looking into the wintry night.

The moonlight played over the snow so that the pass glowed with silvery light. It was a tricky light, though, making distances hard to judge and making black slashes of impenetrable shadow.

Caine saw nothing at first. Neither animal nor man presented itself. But still the animals were scared and Caine himself could feel the menace, palpable in the cold air. Caine stood motionless, only his eyes moving as he scanned the pass for anything out of place.

There!

The keen grey eyes caught something moving among the rocky crags. It appeared to be about fifty yards out and heading away, down the pass. It was hard to be sure, for its movements could only be judged as shadow within shadow.

It was stalking through the tall outcroppings; not hiding but moving from rock to rock in a curious fashion. The shadows of the stony ground seemed to twist and melt with the night walker, and there was the illusion that the rocks themselves were marching. Presently the shadow detached itself and Caine lowered the rifle in shock.

The thing was no beast, for it appeared to go on two legs. Caine could make out no details, only the bulk of the thing,. There was the impression of great, blocky weight, and Caine wondered that he heard no footfalls. It moved out a few more ponderous steps, still just a black mass, but there could be no mistake that the hulk was bipedal.

A Nathaniel Caine Adventure

Caine was also certain that the thing was not human. The monster that stalked Hartsburgh then! Caine moved forward, raising the rifle back to his shoulder, when he heard a voice. Perhaps in his ear, or only in his head.

Do not step out of the cave!

At first he took it for Shaw's voice, but it was barely above a whisper and he couldn't be sure. It seemed he could be sure of nothing on this witchy night. Caine froze, one foot on the threshold. A change came over the hulk outside. It stiffened and tensed, and human or not, Caine felt a sense of intelligence from the thing.

The shadow moved in its bulky and unnatural way, and Caine realized it was turning. Before that thought was even fully formed, Caine backed up a step, then another. It *was* turning, for presently Caine saw what could only be its eyes, though they were like none he had ever seen. Twin red orbs, misshapen and asymmetrical, glowed dull red like a blacksmith's forge.

More than intelligence burned from the red flares. Malevolence washed over the pass where those eyes roved, and Caine could feel it like a blast of heat from an open stove. The red eyes moved mechanically, scanning the ground of the pass before settling on the cave.

How long it stared, Caine couldn't say, but finally it moved and it was coming closer. Caine stood, mesmerized. Despite the unhurried gait, the monstrous shadow was soon quite close, and now Caine could hear the thudding tread of its feet. Still, he was rooted to the spot when again the voice came.

Back! Into the chamber!

His paralysis broke and Caine darted back to the mule. He couldn't see the cleft and had to run his hand over the wall. He fought the urge to look back and finally found the crack. He scrambled into the narrow passage, taking care not to let the rifle strike the wall lest the scrape of metal on stone give him away.

Caine stopped and turned. He could see nothing but the faint light from the cave mouth, nor could he hear anything. Suddenly, the light vanished and Caine knew the moon had been eclipsed by the monster's great bulk.

He strained his ears and at first heard nothing. Then, loud in the sudden silence, the breath of the monster. It was slow and labored and Caine heard unnatural grinding sounds. He held his own breath unsure of his next move.

The thing was evidently examining the outer cave, so he just crouched there listening to the bellows-like breathing and stony grunting. Caine was, on one hand, glad to hear that breath—the monster was no ghost at least—but dismayed at what kind of creature would make such sounds. There was a final snort and then a heavy tread as the thing walked away. Caine allowed himself to breathe again. He stayed where he was until he counted fifty of his own breaths. Even then, he decided not to risk the outer cave and crawled back into the deeper sanctum.

Once there, Caine could only stand in bewilderment. Shaw was gone. There was no way he could have gotten past Caine in the passageway, and Caine had searched this cave for other tunnels before retiring. Nevertheless, he went and knelt by the fire ring.

A Nathaniel Caine Adventure

When he left moments ago to spy the beast, the fire had been burning high and the chamber well lit. Now it was just a bed of red coals, as if it had burned down for hours. Caine threw on fuel and quickly rekindled the blaze. When he had a brand, he reexamined the back walls of the cave.

Of course, Shaw coming from a hidden passage was just as unlikely as Shaw coming in through the front door. Caine searched anyway, including the smoke stained ceiling and found nothing but solid rock.

Caine also found no cave paintings, no stick men or fantastic beasts, though he peered so closely that his nose almost scraped stone. He grunted and stepped back to throw the torch into the fire.

Just a dream after all, then, he thought.

But it had been so vivid, more solid than any dream he could remember. Even the weird, uncanny visions on the cave wall hadn't felt like dreaming. The fire glinted off an object on the ground. Caine hunkered down.

His pipe and his knife both lay on the stone floor, but it wasn't these that had caught his eye. It was what lay between them. Caine looked at his right hand to find his ring missing, and it was silver that glinted in the firelight now.

He picked up the ring and read the motto, *Videre Verum*, before slipping it on. Or trying to, for the ring was too small for its accustomed finger where it had ridden for so many years. Caine thought of Shaw and his fine boned hands, and put the ring on his little finger.

The Ambuscade

Caine spent the better part of an hour that morning searching for sign of the monster he had seen. He started at the cave's mouth and walked in ever increasing arcs. Caine found nothing. He puzzled over this while walking back and forth across the pass.

The wind never really stopped up here, but it had been relatively calm when he saw the brute. The wind could have picked up sometime between then and now and erased the tracks; indeed the signs of his own approach were mostly scoured away. But only mostly and the creature he had encountered in the night had seemed huge and heavy.

Caine stood in silent debate. He was unused to doubting himself and he was sure he had seen *something* in the dark pass. Reason and cold feet argued to chalk it up to a weird dream and get back on the trail. Yet Caine stood, stubborn and implacable, and finally moved off to the rocky outcroppings where he had first seen the thing moving. Perhaps the rocks had sheltered footprints from wind or might bear some other sign of the beast.

In the night the crags had a sinister aspect of sharp-edged columns and concealing shadows, and Caine recalled the illusion of movement. They were still now and solid to the touch. Solid, but not cold.

Caine put his hand on several of the stony fingers. All of them were warm. It was faint, as if they'd merely been under the sun for awhile, but definite.

Caine found no prints. There were a few wide depressions that *might* have been prints, but they were too scattered and indistinct for him to be sure.

Finally, Caine left the strange stones and stalked back to the cave. He resisted the urge to examine the inner chamber again and instead readied the animals for travel. He didn't know how far he had to go to Blackfoot Creek, and according to Hadley he had a day after that. He wanted to get moving.

He walked the animals into the pass and through some of the deeper drifts. Neither showed any sign of whatever terror was on them in the night. Caine mounted and set off.

The snow allowed little more than a walk. Caine's head swung to and fro, still searching for the tracks of the monster. He saw no monster tracks, nor any of beast and bird for that matter. Whether this was good or bad, Caine couldn't say and eventually gave it up to study the land around him.

Rocky and austere as they were, the surrounding peaks nevertheless struck Caine with their beauty. They jutted up, proud and savage, to challenge the winds and the clouds. The cave and the strange fields of stone must have been the highest spot of the pass, for presently the trail began to descend.

The way widened and turned to follow the mountain. Soon enough he was riding through tall pines. Here and there, the call of a bird came and the icy solitude of the high passes eased.

A Nathaniel Caine Adventure

Caine still couldn't decide if his visit from Shaw had been a dream or something else. When he returned to the fire and found him gone, Caine thought he might have trouble getting back to sleep. But he had lain back and fallen asleep instantly, and this time there were no dreams of any kind. When he woke at dawn he felt tired still, and neither mountain air nor hot black coffee had really woken him up.

So now as he rode, Caine swayed in the saddle to the motion of the plodding hooves. Eventually, he drowsed with head bowed. His left hand with the reins rested on the saddle horn, and the right rested on his thigh with the mule's lead. It was the mule that kept Caine from dying on that trail.

Maybe the mule heard or smelled something he didn't like, or maybe he had no reason at all. But he stopped. The horse moved on for a few steps, taking up the slack in the lead, and the mule tossed his head.

Caine came out of his drowse and twisted in the saddle to gather the mule. That's why the bullet meant for his heart tore through the meat of his shoulder instead.

Caine felt the impact first, heard the shot second, and then felt pain bloom and spread through his shoulder and arm. The horse screamed and pranced. Caine sawed at the reins to keep him under control. His head snapped back and forth to assess the situation.

The ambush spot was well picked. The trail was already narrow and steep here. It narrowed further up ahead where one side was hemmed in by large boulders, the other a precipitous drop down the mountain. He assumed the shot came from these boulders, and the choice was turn and run or continue down the trail.

If he turned, the horse would be too slow up the slope and an easy target. To go on was to fly into the teeth of the ambush. Caine was doubled over, hiding as well as he could behind the horse's neck, and his hand went to his gun butt, thinking to fight. Ahead in the rocks, the road agents stood up, close to a dozen men with rifles.

There came a cry.

"Let 'im have it boys!"

Caine reacted instantly. He forgot the pistol and sawed around again on the reins. He pointed the gelding at the treacherous drop and dug in his heels. Man and animal plunged over the edge of the trail to escape the deadly volley of bullets. Of course, this ride might prove just as deadly, but it was a better chance than the bushwhackers' rifles.

Caine gave the horse his head, hoping its own self-preservation would serve better than reins. At any rate, the horse was sliding and falling more than running. Caine had to lean so far back in the saddle he was nearly lying on the horse's rump.

Pine boughs whipped them both and Caine was blinded by stinging needles and flying snow. For a time, there was only the heavy breathing of the horse, and Caine hoped the bandits had given them up. The crack of gunfire disabused him of that notion.

Rifle balls whistled through the air. Caine flinched when a bullet hit a tree near his face and showered him with splinters. He took up the reins and turned the horse this way and that in an effort to make them harder targets.

Caine wanted to know how far behind his pursuers were, but he didn't dare turn in the saddle. Instead, he kept his eyes ahead, hoping to find a level spot or track to turn the horse. They couldn't keep this pace or footing without injuring the animal.

No sooner had the thought formed than the horse lost purchase with its front hooves. It kicked madly with its hind legs and pitched forward with a high scream. Caine was catapulted from the saddle.

He had enough time to think '*from bad to worse*' before he hit the ground and started rolling. He lost all sense of direction, and before he had a chance to try and gain control of his flailing body, he slammed hard up against a tree trunk, directly on his injured shoulder.

Caine let loose a bellow of pain and fury. He scrambled to his knees and righted his hat, marveling that he hadn't lost it entirely. He shook the snow and dirt from his eyes to see the horse above him rolling crazily. Caine had a brief vision of being pounded to jerky between the gelding and the tree.

Fortunately for the both of them, the horse gained its legs. It appeared uninjured, for it kept running and swerved. Before Caine could grab at bridle or stirrup, it was past, galloping down the mountain and taking the Henry with it.

"Worse to worser," Caine muttered at the horse.

He started to turn and see how far behind his pursuers were, but a bullet tore into the tree he was leaning on. Before the fresh splinters hit the ground, Caine was up and running again.

The Road Agents

"Hold the line, goddammit!"

Elisha barked at his men, knowing most of them wouldn't listen. It wasn't that they were particularly disobedient, just stupid and undisciplined. Elisha Cullen had been many things in his miserable life, and he'd been a soldier on multiple occasions. This band of scum and curs would have been whipped, hanged, and shot out of the worst regiment.

Elisha led them, not through his experience as a soldier, but by being the meanest and cruelest scum and cur of the lot. So he wasn't surprised when what should have been a skirmish line degraded into a rabble, running and shooting wildly at the fleeing rider. He wasn't even disappointed. Although if their quarry escaped, he would loose his fury on the worthless villains, perhaps even kill one to make his point.

"Sonuvabitch is off his horse!"

This cry came from Pete off to Elisha's left. The kid took aim, fired, and swore loudly when he missed. Elisha's mouth twisted in a grimace that was the closest thing he had to a smile.

Pete was his nephew somehow. One of his cousin's bastard sons, but kin nevertheless. What little favor and fondness Elisha had, he showed the boy. Pete set off, but Elisha paused to take stock of the situation.

The rider's luck had saved his heart from the first bullet. It had also saved him a broken neck from his desperate plunge down the slope. Now he had lost his horse. His luck had run out.

Elisha had sent two riders down the trail to try to cut the man off on the switchback. They would surely beat him now. Elisha broke into a run. He saw the men spreading out and thought if he got ahead and around, they might drive the rider into him like hounds with a hare.

* * *

Down slope Pete ran, high stepping through the snow and holding his rifle at an awkward high port arms. Pete wanted to be the one to catch the rider. Pickings had been pretty slim lately. Mostly due to the winter weather, but the situation in town sure wasn't helping.

Elisha was already meaner than a bushel basket of badgers, but the poor trade had put him in fouler humor than usual. Whoever brought this quarry to ground would make Elisha happy. If the man got away…well…he'd better not, that was all.

Pete saw movement right ahead and shouldered his rifle. His finger was on the trigger and actually pulling back when the figure in his sights let out a whoop. Pete recognized Bill Stevenson's voice and hastily lowered his weapon.

Bill let off a shot and whooped again. Pete wondered how he didn't know it was Bill right off. You could hardly miss him with that stupid neckerchief he wore, a huge thing of red silk.

A Nathaniel Caine Adventure

Nevertheless, Pete had almost blown a hole in Bill's back. Pete looked around to see if anyone had witnessed his close call.

The woods had grown closer as the hunt descended, and the light that came through was unreliable. It made for strange shadows, and where it shone it could blind as easily as reveal. Pete could see figures where the other bandits ran, but he didn't recognize anyone. There seemed to be no plan or purpose to the pursuit.

Some let out wild yelps like Bill Stevenson, but they were wordless and came from all directions. More like a pack of wolves than men. Pete didn't think of it in exactly those terms, he lacked the imagination, but it was unsettling all the same. He had a feeling, almost a premonition, of bad things about to happen.

Then Bill fired another shot and let out another yawp. Pete watched him run off again, and his premonition was forgotten as he followed. Pete must have seen the man, and it was a race to get him first. He scanned the trees down slope for movement and thought he saw some, but it was gone before he could even take aim. He lowered his hammer to half-cock and took off.

There was sporadic firing from other quarters, but Pete couldn't tell if anyone had the guy or if it was just wild shooting. He tried to take an angle on Bill and head him off, but it was clear he wouldn't beat him. Bill, at least, thought he had the right trail, and he was moving with superhuman speed. Pete settled for trailing him as fast as he could.

The steepness of the slope softened a bit, so they were running along the top of a short ridge and Pete started to gain on Bill. He saw Bill stop and raise his gun. There was a small clearing, and Bill had stopped just at the ring of trees. Pete followed the line of the rifle barrel, and there was the man at the other side of the clearing. Pete saw the black hat and long hide coat, and thought the man must be injured. He appeared to be leaning against a tree, but his arms were held in an unnatural fashion.

Bill fired and Pete slowed to a walk, for surely the chase was over. The clearing wasn't even twenty yards across, so there was no way Bill could have missed. The man didn't fall and Bill worked the action on his rifle, a Spencer like Pete's. Bill walked forward and pulled the trigger, but the hammer fell on an empty chamber. The metallic clink sounded too loud in the cold air, harsh and unnatural, and Pete flinched a bit as he hadn't from the gunfire. Bill just dropped the rifle and pulled out his revolver, firing as he walked forward.

Still the man stood, and Pete wondered if he had died leaning against that tree. Old Bill Stevenson just kept walking and firing until he was close enough to reach out and touch the man with his pistol barrel. Then that hammer also fell on an empty chamber.

By now, Pete had almost reached the edge of the clearing. Bill stood behind the man, both figures wreathed in white smoke from the spent powder, and pulled his other pistol. That struck Pete as an odd thing to do, for surely the man was dead. Before Pete could form the thought, let alone say anything, the bad thing of his premonition came to pass in an explosion of blood and snow.

* * *

A Nathaniel Caine Adventure

As Caine ran, he was glad to see the trees start to close in and offer more cover and concealment. Shots continued to ring out, but they seemed to be everywhere. Some were close and others further away, even in front of him. He chanced a stop to crouch behind a tree and assess the pursuit. He came to a similar conclusion as Pete, had he known it, but they weren't wolves to Caine. They were just a pack of dogs, crazy with blood lust, running wild and undisciplined.

Caine revised his plan of flight. With the line of pursuit so spread out, he might be able to double back and slip through. He would have to abandon Hartsburgh and go back up the trail, but if he bought enough time before they realized their error, he could gain the pass.

But not yet. A knot of figures was moving this way, and Caine thought he might have to lay an ambush of his own. He turned and moved down the slope, staying low and trying to keep trees between him and the men behind. It wasn't more than fifty yards or so when the slope leveled off a bit, and Caine found the clearing.

Finally Fortune had seen fit to give him a glimmer of Her favor. A small break to be sure, but Caine intended to seize the opportunity. He ran across the small space shrugging out of his coat as he went.

A blind man could follow a trail through the snow, and Caine's wound scattered scarlet here and there on the white. Caine had no time to hide the trail, so he intended to use it to his advantage. An easy trail could make a man overconfident, likely to see what he wanted to see.

Caine drew his knife and chose a low hanging pine bough. The broad blade lopped off the branch, and Caine shoved the sleeve over the remaining piece so the coat hung with its back to the clearing. He placed his hat so it sat over the collar, and had a fleeting instant to curse the pine pitch he knew would be all over his clothes.

Taking the cut branch, he swept a trench near the base of the next tree over. Caine had been working quickly, mindful of the close pursuit, but here he had to be careful.

He put the knife in his teeth and grasped the end of a snow laden branch. He held the cut bough over his head and shoulders with his left hand. With the live branch in his right hand, Caine eased onto his belly. He shook the live bough and the snow gathered there dropped over him.

More fell when he let it go, and Caine wriggled into the snow as far as he could. He then lay perfectly still and slowed his breathing. He didn't have long to wait.

It was less than a minute before a bullet tore through his coat. The shot was very close, within the clearing, and Caine steeled himself not to flinch. He almost flinched anyway when the next sound was the hammer fall of an empty weapon.

Still Caine waited, and now he could hear the crunch of a man's boots in snow as the coat was subjected to a barrage of pistol fire. The man's legs came into Caine's narrow field of vision, and there was again the flat metal clack of hammer on empty chamber.

A Nathaniel Caine Adventure

Caine struck.

He gathered his legs beneath him and leapt forward, blinding the bandit with a spray of snow. The man instinctively threw up one hand to protect his face, but the other held a pistol that was trying blindly to find the source of the attack.

Caine was faster and hacked at the hand with the questing pistol. The revolver and several fingers dropped to the ground, and Caine slashed the bandit in the gut. He kept moving behind the man, and stabbed him again in the kidney. The man emitted a mewling moan of agony, and dropped to his knees in the now scarlet snow. Caine swung his blade in a flat arc and divested the bandit of his head.

Pete stood rooted in horror and awe as the killing of Bill Stevenson unfolded before him. He had seen men die before, but it was usually loud and chaotic affairs of roaring guns. The silent and businesslike knife-work had shocked the boy. He stared, paralyzed, while Bill's blood dripped off the wide-bladed knife in the tall man's hand.

Pete was holding his breath until he realized the lean killer hadn't seen him at the edge of the clearing. He shouldered his rifle and put the front bead between the knife-man's shoulder blades.

Pete was still holding his breath, and the rifle began to tremble, but there was no shot. Pete realized the piece was still at half-cock and it was his undoing, for he lowered the rifle to cock it.

The man's head whirled and the cold eyes widened. Pete shouldered the rifle again and fired. As the carbine roared and bucked, the man dropped and made a curious movement with his right arm.

He finished up on one knee with his arm straight before him, the hand spread wide, and Pete thought of a traveling actor he had seen in a melodrama. Before the incongruity of that thought took root, Pete's belly caught fire with pain.

He started to hunch, but that only intensified the hurt and Pete looked down. He didn't want to believe that the thing quivering there was the hilt of the tall man's knife. He didn't want to believe it was the blade of the tall man's knife that was now tearing his insides up. Pete dropped his rifle and drew a shuddering breath to scream, but it hurt too much. Pete started backpedaling as if to escape the pain and the steel.

"Oh, God," he said. "Oh, Jesus."

Pete kept repeating the words as he backed up, panting out his tiny prayer until his feet slipped out from under him. The jolt of his backside hitting the hard winter ground was too much. Pete finally let loose with a ragged and high pitched scream.

His eyes were shut tight against the flare of agony. When he opened them, the tall man loomed over him. The man's face was impassive except for his eyes—flint grey and just as hard. The man raised a pistol, and the black hole of the muzzle was like staring down a deep well.

"I'm sorry," Pete said.

He raised his hands in a useless gesture of protection against the coming gun blast. But that blast never came.

* * *

Elisha had been able to move fast once he gave up on his men and struck out on his own. He ran down the slope on his scrawny legs, staying low and darting from tree to tree. Not just to avoid letting the rider see him, but to avoid being shot by his own fools who continued to fire wildly.

Elisha would deal with those fools when this was over. Ammunition, like most supplies, was scarce in town owing to the weather and the situation. With Spring so close, Elisha hoped to cash in on his stake in that situation, but first things first.

Elisha stopped and knelt behind a pine tree. He had looped around and reckoned he was now in the path of the fleeing stranger. The tree was big enough to hide him if he remained still, but narrow enough that he could use either side to rest his rifle. This gave him a wide field of fire. Elisha cocked the piece, so there would be no betraying sound when his prey came into view.

Elisha was panting hard from the sprint and forced his breathing to slow. He knelt, motionless but for his roving, predatory eyes. Still and calm he appeared, but he was anxious to tie this up. The man had appeared easy prey, asleep in the saddle and oblivious to his surroundings. Yet things had gone wrong with the first shot.

Elisha should have seen him stretched out right there, or in the hail of bullets that followed. Elisha should have kept his men back after the man's wild plunge down the slope. He was wounded and in the bandits' territory, and they had the mule, after all. But any valuables were undoubtedly in the man's saddlebags, and those were on the horse, and the wildness had taken the dogs instantly.

No matter. All would be put right.

Except it didn't feel right.

Elisha felt the man should have shown himself by now. He made himself give a slow count to fifty, in case he was just being impatient. He only got to twenty-seven when shots rang out close—fifty yards maybe—up the slope. He was moving toward it without thinking and scanning the trees which grew thicker at a level spot up the way.

Elisha still moved from tree to tree, and now he heard the quick thunder of a pistol. Elisha froze and raised his rifle, but didn't fire. The form that had at first looked like a man was just a coat hung on a tree branch.

The quarry had set his own ambush. Elisha scanned the trees for danger. Elisha's first thought was that their hare had taken to climbing. He scanned the tree branches above eye level.

If he had scanned the ground first, he may have spotted the hasty blind in time to save Bill Stevenson. As it was, he no sooner spotted the snowy boot heels before the tall man sprang into action. The slope and the tree line meant the combatants were out of Elisha's view in an instant.

He reckoned the man was using a knife since there was no more pistol fire, which meant the fellow had brains *and* sand. Brains to lay the ambush and make a silent kill; he undoubtedly hoped to slip through the line and escape on his own back trail. Sand to lure a man in close and use a knife against a pistol.

Elisha himself remained silent, biting back the curses that rose up, and moved up to put an end to this fiasco. He kept low and knew by the giant patch of blood that one of his men was dead. Elisha moved from cover just in time to see his nephew Pete take a knife in the belly.

Indeed, Pete's last shot, which missed the crouching knife-man, almost killed Elisha. It was close enough that his wild beard was ruffled in the wind of the bullet's passing. Elisha didn't flinch, for he had gone cold all over and rage ruled him.

As the tall man rose up and advanced on the whimpering lad, Elisha lowered his rifle. He didn't drop it, just held it in his left hand, for he didn't want the sound of it hitting the ground to alert his foe. His right hand grasped the bone handle of his bull whip and he began uncoiling it.

Someone observing him would have thought him quite calm. He didn't hurry, his breathing was slow, his hands didn't shake. His eyes, though, were close to glowing with murderous fury.

He drew back his arm as the tall man drew a pistol to finish Pete off. Elisha would have none of that. His arm swung forward in a casual arc whose grace echoed the knife-man's throw a moment ago.

The whip struck out and the leather wrapped around the tall man's neck. Elisha's movements now were quick as lightning. He dropped the rifle and yanked back on the whip with both hands. Pete's killer went flying backward and landed hard, knocking the wind out of his lungs and the fancy pistol out of his hands. Elisha left no slack, just hauled at the whip like a fisherman bringing in his catch.

The man fought gamely. He wasted no time grasping for the lost pistol, but reached instead for a second revolver. He got it out and cocked, and pointed it back along the line of the whip. Elisha would have none of this either.

With one more jerk on the line, he brought his catch close enough to stamp the man's hand into the ground. Elisha ground his boot and was rewarded with a dull snap. The tall man's face twisted in a brief grimace of pain, but he didn't cry out. Of course, he may not have had the air, for Elisha pulled without mercy.

His quarry's free hand was clawing at the ends of the whip, trying to loosen the cruel braid. It was too late; the lash was too deep. The man's hands went limp and dropped as he lost consciousness. Elisha kept on the pressure for a few more moments to make sure the fellow was out. As he stood there, his curs began to gather around the clearing.

They made low sounds of inquiry among themselves, but no one actually spoke. They knew their leader's moods well, and cold murder shone out from Elisha like a beacon of doom. One by one, their eyes went to the mewling figure of Pete lying in a spreading pool of blood. Elisha removed the whip and coiled it as he walked to his nephew. Pete lay supine, staring at the hilt protruding from his belly. His hands convulsed as if he wanted to pull it out, but couldn't bear to touch it. Elisha knelt by the boy and placed a hand on his chest. Finally, Pete looked away from the bloody steel and clutched at his uncle's arm.

"Uncle 'Lisha," he said. "I'm kilt, sir. I'm dyin."

His voice cracked in a few short sobs.

"Shhh," Elisha said. "You ain't dyin."

"But it hurts bad. It hurts so bad."

"I know, son," Elisha said. "I know it does, but you'll be fine."

"Promise?" Pete said.

"Of course, I promise," Elisha said. "You'll be laid up for a spell, but you'll be alright."

The bandits in the clearing looked at one another in disbelief. None of them had ever heard Elisha sound so gentle, had never imagined he had any kindness at all in him.

They also looked at the gaping hole in the lad's belly, and knew he'd never make it off this mountain. Elisha just patted the boy's head, gentle as a doe with her fawn, and told him he'd be fine.

"You just lay back now," he said. "Rest easy and we'll get that shard out of you."

"Oh God, please don't touch it," said Pete. "It hurts like a sumbitch."

"I know it hurts, boy. That's why we gotta get it out."

Elisha smoothed the boy's hair off his forehead. "Don't worry, son. You're my blood, ain't you? Cullen blood. We'll get it out, and it'll stop hurtin. Close your eyes and I'll give you a good count of five. You hear?"

Pete nodded and laid his head back and closed his eyes. Elisha continued to smooth the boy's hair with one hand, slow and gentle.

The other hand moved quick as a rattlesnake, pulled the .44 on his belt and blew Pete's brains all over the snowy ground.

A few of the men jumped and a few looked away. One of them just whispered the name of Jesus. After a long moment one man, Frank Smith it was, looked at the unconscious form of Pete's killer. He walked over and pointed his rifle at the man's face, thumbing the hammer.

"Hold."

Elisha's voice was quiet, but all trace of gentleness was fled. Frank held his finger and looked over at Elisha. Elisha didn't look up from Pete's corpse when he spoke.

"He's mine," was all he said, but Frank hastily backed away and lowered the hammer on his weapon.

"Nobody kills him."

"What are we gonna do with him then?" Frank said.

Elisha sighed and holstered his revolver. His head turned slowly to the knife, and he reached out to grasp the hilt. It came out of the body easily, and Elisha hefted the weapon in his hand. He'd never seen its like before.

The hilt was carved of a hardwood he didn't recognize. There was no guard, but the haft hugged the hand like a saber grip. The blade itself was heavy yet well balanced, wide and full bellied, but tapering to a wicked point.

He wiped the steel on Pete's trousers and inspected the edge. It showed neither nick nor ding after hacking through first pine boughs, then Bill Stevenson's hand, followed quickly by his head, and finally opening Pete's belly. Elisha tuned over his left hand

and passed the knife edge over the coarse black hair. It came off easy as if he'd used a freshly stropped razor. Finally, Elisha got to his feet and turned to face Frank Smith. It crossed Frank's mind that Elisha might think he had been questioning his leadership, an unwise action at the best of times. He backed away from the fallen man, who was starting to stir.

"I was just wondering what your orders were, I meant," Frank said. "You know. Whatever you wanna do to him."

"*We* aren't gonna do anything to him," Elisha said. "We're gonna leave him for the Grinder."

The Ordeal

Caine struggled up out of blackness with a roaring in his ears and a fierce ache in his head. He knew he was in danger. His eyes opened and he saw blurry forms gathered about him.

The road agents!

Caine didn't know why he wasn't dead yet. He tried to fight, to lash out, but his hands were bound. Just as he was about to gain his feet, a rifle butt smashed into his kidneys, laying him low again.

"Get him up."

The voice was low and mean, the growl of a hungry animal. Rough hands pulled at Caine, and he tried again to stand.

"No, no," came the same voice. "On his knees'll do just fine."

There was another blow and Caine grunted from the pain, but managed to keep his feet. The hands pulled at him, and someone swung the barrel of a rifle across the backs of both knees. Caine went to his knees with head bowed.

He jerked his head back up and shook the hair out of his eyes to glare at the man who now loomed above him. Rangy and wild-eyed with a long, unkempt beard, the man oozed hatred and menace. Caine didn't need to hear the man speak to know that it was his voice giving the commands.

Caine noted the long stockman's whip on the shoulder and matched it to the burning of his swollen throat. That was one mystery solved—how he had been taken. The mystery of why he yet lived remained.

"A proud one, are you?" the wild man said. "Not fond of kneeling?"

Caine only glared and tried to heave up again. He fought against the bandits on either side, and the leader let him struggle for a few moments before kicking Caine full in the crotch. Caine went down like a felled steer and breathed heavily into the churned mud and snow.

"Kilt two of my men."

By his tone, the wild man might have been remarking on the weather.

"Ayuh," Caine said, face still in the muck. "I'm going to kill you too, you thieving whoreson bastard."

He matched the bandit's casual tone, though he had to suppress a groan for his aggrieved testicles. Again, Caine was hauled up and now the bandit hunkered down, eye to eye with his bound quarry.

"Many have tried, my young pup," he said. "Many and many, but Elisha Cullen yet draws breath."

"Cullen, eh? Nathaniel Caine is my name. I don't usually enjoy killing, Cullen, but I'll smile when I do for you."

"Hm. Like I said, proud."

Elisha spat in the snow and jerked his chin at one of the corpses Caine had made this day.

"Bill I could forgive. It was a child's ambush you laid for him and he walked right into it. But him…" Elisha jerked his chin at the boy. "…Pete was my kin and just a boy. Him I can't forgive."

Caine looked at the boy's body. In truth the lad's age, surely no more than fifteen, was troubling. But Caine had little time to mark the lad's age while staring down a rifle barrel. It seemed wildest luck the boy hadn't been the victor.

Caine had learned the underhanded throw from the same man who had given him the knife, but had never used it on a live target before. He had thrown in the same instant the boy shot. Caine's conscience was clear.

"Man enough to ride with a pack of thieving curs, and man enough to shoot a rifle."

Caine shrugged.

"Still, kin is kin. If it's satisfaction you require, I'm at your service. Free my hands and we'll settle up right now. I choose pistols."

Elisha Cullen grinned wide, showing rows of small white teeth, and Caine thought the man looked rather like a badger. The bandit chuckled and shook his finger in Caine's face as if he were a naughty child. The chuckle grew into a low laugh, but there was no mirth in it. Cullen stood and turned his back on Caine. He spoke to his men over his shoulder as he walked away.

"You can put the boots to him for a spell, but mind you leave his head alone. I want him awake for what's coming."

The men took to their task with relish, and there was little Caine could do to protect himself. With his hands behind him his belly and ribs were open, and it wasn't long before he felt one crack. He tried to fight by kicking, but the few blows he landed did no real harm. None of the bandits got close enough for him to bite.

One of them stomped on his injured hand and broke another finger. In short order, they had him bruised and battered. They undid his hands and stripped him, picking him over with rapid efficiency.

Then they stretched him and rebound his hands over his head. The line binding his wrists was thrown over a high limb and they hoisted him up. He hung, stripped to the waist, with the toes of his bare feet just grazing the snow.

Caine watched in grim silence as Elisha Cullen gave his orders. Some men were tasked with gathering stones and laying up a cairn for the dead boy. Bill Stevenson apparently would be left for the wolves and the ravens, though not before his fellows went through his pockets and stripped his weapons.

Two men arrived with the gang's horses, as well as Caine's mount. A short while later, the mule was led in and Caine cursed silently. He had hoped the mule at least would escape this wretched trap. Caine had formed a small affection for the animal based on admiration for his sensible behavior last night in the cave. The creature had mastered its fear while the horse gave in to histrionics.

Pragmatism it was as well, for Caine thought the creature's proven sense would send it back over the pass to its home stable. Caine had faith that the mule's return without him would have

Roarke up into the pass in a matter of moments, riding to Caine's rescue. Always assuming Cullen didn't tire of his play and kill Caine outright.

That hope was gone now. The road agents rooted through Caine's kit and divvied up the loot. They gloated and ravened with glee over who got his boots, who got his coat, his pistols, and even his hat. Cullen didn't rave. In fact, he remained silent except to issue orders until the bag of mail was discovered.

"Oho," he said and flashed Caine a grin. "That'll be some of Bill Hadley's silver in your purse then. That bastard's cowardice has finally outstripped his greed. These are a bit late."

Caine said nothing, but he chewed on Cullen's remark as the bandit chief poured out the letters and went through them. Clearly the man knew Hadley, but what was so odd about that? Cullen no doubt made his base in Hartsburgh, and Hadley surely traveled there often in his freight business.

Cullen's tone was familiar, though, and a man who made his business on the road would be a strange friend to one whose business was preying on those travelers. Perhaps Hadley paid the road agents for safe passage, an unsavory arrangement, but sensible in its way.

To Caine it felt more sinister. The ambush had been laid on a road little used this time of year, and Caine suspected he had tripped a snare meant for Hadley.

He filed it away for now. He didn't fancy trying to get more information out of his captor and wasn't likely to succeed in the attempt. He had more pressing matters at any rate, for his shoulders were already starting to ache and the cracked rib pained him.

Cullen chose one envelope from the mail bag and read the address carefully. Leaving the rest on the ground, he tucked it under his woolen coat and gave it a pat to assure it was secure. He faced Caine, and the man's eyes flashed hatred across the clearing.

"Our business is near finished, Caine," Cullen said. "I'll be taking the Henry, I think. Tell me. Where did you get this bit of steel?"

He drew Caine's knife, which now hung on Cullen's belt.

"A black witch doctor gave it to me."

"The hell you say!"

Cullen spat in the snow.

"I say true. I lost my own blade and he gave me one of his."

Caine nodded to the cairn, a movement that caused him pain in several places.

"He also taught me the underhand throw I used to put yonder brat in his little stone house."

"Ah, Caine."

Cullen shook the knife as he had earlier shaken his finger. He gave the same laugh as well, but as before there was no humor in the laugh or the eyes.

"You want me to be afeard to take this knife. Or provoke me into using it and making your end a quick one. No such luck. You'd have let Pete die a slow death from a gut wound, and so your end should be slow."

Caine had in fact been about to administer the coup de grace when he was taken, but he decided not to point that out. He had been provoking Cullen out of anger and wounded pride, but he ceased now. He was in a tight spot, but still alive and might make it out yet. He was damned if he could see how, but in the absence of hope or a plan, he would rely on Yankee stubbornness.

"No," Cullen said and put the knife in its sheath. "Much as I'd like to try out this steel on your twice damned hide, I can't have you bleeding out before the Grinder gets you. The Grinder will do the dirty work tonight."

Caine had no idea what the man was talking about. He stopped himself from asking, but noted several of Cullen's bandits looked scared. One even flinched at the word Grinder.

"Still," Cullen went on, "I have to have a little fun. I'll set my mark on you, so the Grinder knows who left him a present."

Cullen held his hand out and Caine again bit back a curse.

"Here's a pretty little thing I found in your coat pocket."

Cullen held up Caine's own whip. He made a show of inspecting it and gave a few lazy swings.

"I know a bit about braids myself, you see. This one would be handy enough in a coat, but I don't think it's much use for stock. That makes me think you carry it for men. Makes me wonder if you've ever felt the lash yourself. Do you know what it'll feel like if this little snake bites you?"

Caine did know.

Though the fashion of dueling was already starting to wane in Caine's youth, fencing was still considered part of a gentleman's education. Most studied in a salon in the French fashion, though some wealthy families hired private teachers. Caine's father had hired a private tutor, but he wasn't French.

Don Octavio was an ancient Spaniard with jet black eyes and snow white hair. The maestro despised the French foil as little more than a toy. Caine learned the small sword and rapier, alone and with a dagger, and the whip. Don Octavio was a font of sayings, and one of his favorites was 'that which causes pain also instructs.' He, of course, had no intention of sharing any of this with Elisha Cullen and just glared.

The silence stretched out and finally Cullen shrugged. The bandit hauled back and swung the whip. The lash bit and Caine flinched. He clenched his teeth and managed not to cry out, but there was no way to avoid jerking at the wounds or hiding the grimace of pain. Cullen moved forehand and back in measured strokes, and put six long stripes on Caine's already battered torso.

"Yup, very pretty. I think I'll keep this, too."

Cullen coiled the whip and put it in his coat pocket. He gave a sign to his men who hauled on the rope and hoisted Caine higher.

"The blood'll bring wolves, maybe cougars as well. Can't have them chewing on Grinder's dinner. You'll be safe up there. 'Course the ravens might peck at you a bit, but that won't kill you. Come nightfall, the Grinder will. I'll see you in Hell, Nathaniel Caine."

And that was that.

The men loaded up their loot and left. Cullen spared not a glance for the hanging man, but several of his men shot fearful looks his way. Fear and shame as well, and none of the blackguards would meet Caine's eye.

There was no dramatic mounting up and riding off. The slope was too steep for riding, they just gathered up the reins and walked away. They went down slope, so there must indeed be a switchback trail that way. Caine noted this for escape, though he had to admit that might be optimistic. Or at least putting the cart before the horse.

The first order of business was to simply take stock. So when Caine thought the gang was safely out of earshot he gave voice to a string of curses. Then he took stock. He started with his injuries.

His broken fingers were the least of it. The most painful were the whip lashes. The stripes hurt like hell when they were opened, but the pain didn't fade. It was a burning sting, hard to bear and every one of them was bleeding.

His position made it hard to properly inspect the gunshot wound. He believed the ball had gone clean through without hitting any bone or major blood vessels—a miracle, and not a small one. It ached abominably. He recalled smacking it into a tree when he was unhorsed, but if he wasn't dead from it yet, he probably wouldn't die from it.

Of course, the way he was hanging would have hurt an uninjured man. It wouldn't be long before pain became agony. Doubtless Cullen knew it well when he gave his orders. The rib was also a concern. Caine didn't think it was broken, just cracked, but like the shoulder, it was still serious and made worse by his stretched position. It already hurt to breathe properly.

Caine looked, as best he could, at the sky, trying to gage the time of day. He was amused to find it was quite early still. Amused though not surprised, for Caine had noticed before how time became distorted in battle. His skirmish with Cullen's damnable bandits had surely taken less than a half hour.

That was mixed news at best. The animals most likely to harry him were more active at night, but that left a long time hung up like a side of beef. Despite the pleasant sunshine, Caine was already chilled, and night would bring cold he wasn't likely to survive.

If he got down, his position would still be dire. He must go downslope and try for the river, then follow the river to town—all barefoot, shirtless, and unarmed. Caine sighed and pushed away panic and despair.

First thing was to get his feet on the ground. He looked up at his bonds and moved his hands to test them. These movements started him swaying and twisting, and his shoulder protested.

The cords were beyond Caine's knowledge of knots. Both wrists had been wrapped in several loops of rope which were gathered into a thick and clever looking knot in the middle. It held him securely and painfully, but left him free to twist and struggle. It also left the whole weight of his body to pull at wrists and shoulders. Caine dreaded the gyrations it might require to get down.

He moved his hands, flexing the fingers and rotating the wrists. Trying to rotate them at any rate, for there was almost no give in the loops and Caine succeeded only in abrading the skin. He ceased for a moment and found he was breathing heavily from just that little test. He didn't care for this sign of approaching fatigue, so he remained still for a bit to calm himself.

He pondered his chances of rescue, but they didn't look promising. Roarke wouldn't start to worry for several more days at least. Even if Roarke did come, he would take the pass, and Caine was well off the road now. Roarke could take an entire posse over the road, and likely Caine would never even know they were there. He would never survive that long without water, assuming he didn't succumb to the cold or beasts.

The thought of beasts turned Caine's mind to the Grinder. Cullen had spoken the word as a name, some fearsome totem, and Cullen's men *had* been afraid. But what was the Grinder? When Roarke spun his tale of townsfolk being taken in Hartsburgh, he had spoken of a beast in the night. This, then, must be the Grinder, though that didn't bring Caine closer to knowing what it was.

The road agents were convinced that it haunted these hills as well as the town. Caine's tired brain finally thought of the creature he had spied in the pass. It had walked on two legs, and Caine recalled the labored sounds of its breath and the ponderous gait, growling like a great millstone.

Grinder.

The name was apt.

Caine had to get down and away before nightfall. He looked again at the knot and examined his options. They were few, but he tried to exercise the first one. Stripped of arms he was, but

Cullen's men had followed orders when beating him. With no blows to the head, Caine still had his teeth.

He pulled himself up and tried to worry the knot with his teeth. The rough hemp scraped at his lips as Caine tried to find a strand to pull. Any cord he could bite on, though, had no perceivable play.

It was only a few moments before the strain of holding himself up grew too great and he had to lower himself. He tried this several times, trying to get a different angle on the knot and soon Caine found himself panting and sweating from the effort. It wouldn't do to sweat in this cold, but he knew if he remained bound he was surely dead.

Caine gathered himself and pulled up again, determined to at least make progress on the knot. He bit and pulled while his muscles strained. He grunted and growled like a beast himself, and the stinging sweat poured into the already burning whip stripes. Caine's whole body was shaking as he forced himself to stay up.

Eventually, it was too much and Caine's strength gave out. He didn't lower himself, just dropped. When the rope brought him up, the bullet wound seemed to explode and white light flashed in Caine's eyes. He gasped, drawing breath that doubtless would have winded a cry of pain if Caine hadn't passed out.

When he came to, the first thing Caine noticed was that he could no longer feel his hands. He had a vague notion they were still there because his wrists hurt, but the hands themselves were totally numb. The second thing he noticed was he was being watched.

His head hung, chin on his breast, and he tried to look around without indicating he was awake. He could see no one on the ground, but presently he heard a soft, throaty sound to his left. To his left and on a level with his head. Caine turned his eyes that way and saw a large raven perched at the clearing's edge.

Caine cared not at all for the speculative look in those shiny black eyes, and raised his head to glare at the bird. The raven made a few more noises in its throat and bobbed its head. Caine stared at it, and then noticed that the line he hung from was lashed to the same tree where the raven perched.

"Why don't you make yourself useful, Corbie," Caine said, "and untie yonder knot?"

The raven took off in a thunder of black wings and cawed at the hanged man. Caine fancied the caws sounded angry, and he hoped the bird would not come back and bring more of its kind.

He tried again to find the sun through the pine boughs, and was distressed at how much time had passed. He stopped himself from simply attacking the knot again, for he doubted he would have any more success. Still, he couldn't escape the fact that the only tool left him was his teeth. He devised a new plan.

Caine took a breath and pulled himself up again with an agonized groan. He didn't try undoing the knot, but instead picked one strand of rope and began to chew. He worked slowly, careful to lower himself for a break before his muscles gave out.

Caine bit and gnawed at the stiff and foul tasting rope until his lips and gums were bleeding. His jaw and teeth were added to the list of hurts, but he kept at it. He bit and sawed his teeth back and forth and was actually making progress. He lost track of time, concentrating on the slow work. He did notice the raven circling and cawing a few times, but he ignored it. In time, he was almost through and Caine forced himself not to hurry.

He lowered himself carefully when his arms were tired and made himself rest. Then he gathered himself for what he was sure would be the last stretch. He gnashed his aching teeth in the frayed rope and shook his head like a terrier.

Finally he was through!

Caine spat strands of hemp and grasped an end of line in his mouth. He twisted and unwound the line as far as he could, then lowered himself. He hung there for a moment, staring at the knot, but nothing happened.

The chewed ends hung free, but it didn't appear to affect the knot itself. Caine shook his arms and then started to bounce, hoping the knot or the rope itself was weakened. But still nothing happened. Caine steeled himself and pulled up to let his whole weight drop, but the infernal bounds held fast.

"Damn it to hell," Caine muttered and hung his head.

* * *

Caine came to again with that sense of being watched. He hadn't passed out this time, merely fallen asleep. It was raven eyes on him this time as well, but now old Corbie had brought friends. Caine could see ten or more perched here and there in the surrounding trees and hear more behind him.

By twisting his head around, Caine could make out where the body of Bill Stevenson lay. There were more ravens at work there. There was some wing flapping as they fidgeted and moved on their perches, as well as the soft cawing amongst themselves. The calls were damnably near speech, and Caine was sure they discussed him. He didn't know how long he had slept, or how much longer it would take the growing murder to build up their courage.

Caine thought of shouting to scare them off, but decided against it. Even if it startled them, they would be back and it would take more to scare them the next time. Instead, he just glared. As he twisted in the wind, Caine wondered what a gruesome scarecrow he must make: covered in bruises and bloodied by his own whip, with a half feral grimace of hate and challenge for the gore-crows and their patient cawing.

Finally, one of them took off and made an investigative flight around Caine. It kept well out of reach and Caine remained still. It landed but made several more quick trips around Caine. He knew this one would make a pass. Of course, they all looked the same, but Caine hoped this one was old Corbie himself.

It took off and started flying right for Caine's face, no doubt already savoring the dainty morsels Caine's eyes would make. Caine had other ideas and timed his strike perfectly. He pulled on the ropes and twisted his whole body. Screaming with pain and anger, Caine lashed out and kicked the black bird out of the air.

A Nathaniel Caine Adventure

The clearing exploded in a riot of flapping black wings, and the ravens' calls thundered in the air. Caine's throat burned from where the whip had choked him, but he still managed to shout over the cacophony.

"Not yet, you shiny black bastards!"

He looked to the ground, hoping he had killed, or at least injured, old Corbie. He saw no body, just a single black feather drifting to the forest floor. He swung as he watched it float down, and the motion gave him a new idea.

The violence of the kick had set him swinging like a pendulum. Caine was hung near the center of the clearing far from the tree trunks. They had chosen a high bow and used a long rope, so he couldn't climb up. But perhaps he could swing to the edge and gain a branch. The closest tree was the one the rope was anchored to, so he aimed for that one and started pumping his legs. There wasn't much movement at first and it took a few tries to get any momentum.

He had seen a trapeze act in Boston years ago, and tried to mimic the graceful movements. He knew there was little of grace in his exertions, being barely more than hanging meat, but swing he did. The numbness of hanging and cold wore off as his shoulders renewed their protest. He ignored them, even when the bullet wound broke open and started bleeding again. His breath came ragged in time with the desperate rhythm of his pumping legs.

If he could get his legs on a branch, he could get his weight off his shoulders. He could rest and work on the knot, or gnaw through the anchor line. Caine reached the apparent limit of his ropes arc, and his bare feet were still several feet shy of any tree limbs.

His tired brain refused to accept it. He told himself it was just a matter of a little more effort and swung again. The gashes on his torso were bleeding freely again as well, but still he swung. As he flew through the chill air, he gathered all the strength he had and swung, reached, grasped for the limb. Something in Caine's side seemed to stretch, strain, and then come loose with a sickening tear. The constant state of agony he had spent the whole day in was not enough to inure him to the fresh hell of this new hurt. A small part of his mind remained calm and cursed inwardly, *damn, the rib.* But the greater part by far gave itself over to a long and wordless scream.

Caine went limp.

* * *

Later, when he thought about it, Caine would try and tell himself that when he went limp he had passed out again. Certainly, his consciousness was compromised. He spun at the end of the rope, but there was no sense of vertigo. It seemed as if it was the world that spun around him.

The pain that scourged his whole body was by far the worst he had ever experienced. It was the all encompassing nature of it, the inescapability and constant state of it. However, that same constancy meant he must pass beyond the point where simple

A Nathaniel Caine Adventure

endurance would normally quit. Caine reached that point now, and the pain seemed to take place outside of himself. It was a curious sensation he was unfamiliar with.

He knew the broken ends of his rib were grinding against each other as his lungs drew deep and even breaths. But even though he felt the pain, he didn't react, merely observed. Caine's movement slowed and eventually stilled, and he hung totally limp. Head low and arms stretched, he dangled, motionless but for the slight sway the wind lent him, a sway that increased as the wind picked up.

Caine felt a deep relaxation, but it wasn't sleep. His eyes were open and stared at the ground, contemplating the patterns his dripping blood made in the snow below. He wondered idly if he was dying and this feeling was his soul loosing it's bonds to his body. Eventually, thoughts ceased and he knew not how long he hung on the windswept tree.

After a time, a feeling grew on Caine. He was being watched. The feeling crept up gradually so that by the time Caine realized he was being watched, he had no idea how long it had been happening. It didn't bother him, and at first he reckoned that it was old Corbie back for revenge. This didn't bother him overmuch either. To the victor go the spoils, and Caine didn't think he could summon the strength to fight off the ravens again.

He decided to try, more out of a sense of New Englander stubbornness than a belief in survival. More time passed, though, and nothing happened, nor did he hear the sly and raspy talk of the ravens. The feeling persisted, neither growing nor abating. Eventually curiosity got the better of Caine, and he raised his head.

Grinder's Keeper

He wasn't expecting anything really, a wolf or some other predator perhaps. Caine stared for a few long moments while he worked out that he had, in fact, been expecting *something*, because what he saw was something he never expected.

He saw an Indian. Caine had been traveling on the frontier for some time, but had never had any personal dealings with the Red Men. And now here one was right before his eyes.

He sat, still as a statue atop the stone cairn that served as a grave for the lad who fell to Caine's knife. He sat so still and unmoving that Caine considered he might not be real. Perhaps just a mirage or phantasm his mind had conjured to distract itself from the agony of his wracked body.

Certainly, the man had made no noise when he approached and sat on the stony grave—just appeared. But Caine had heard the Indians had unsurpassed woodcraft that let them appear and disappear undetected.

The preternatural stillness kept on, and Caine and the Indian stared at each other. It was the clear regard from those black eyes that convinced Caine the man was really there. The silence spun out, and Caine found himself at a complete loss of how to engage the man. It was as if not only were his vocal chords paralyzed, but the thoughts that should form speech weren't even there.

Finally, the statue moved. A simple blink of the large eyes and then the head moved slowly from one side to the other before settling on Caine again. The man produced a pipe. It had a bowl of reddish stone and the stem was wood, long and flat and wrapped with leather. He continued to regard Caine while he packed the pipe from a beaded pouch.

The man began to puff at the pipe, although Caine hadn't seen him strike a flame. The smoke was thick and silvery, and made strange patterns in the air. Caine breathed deep to smell the tobacco, it was a strong scent like fresh cut hay, but richer and earthier.

Anger stirred in Caine's breast. One of the bandits no doubt had his own pipe, and the thought of his cherished meerschaum in one of their foul mouths was an affront that must be answered. Somehow, Caine must escape and call them to account.

The Indian smiled at Caine, flashing straight teeth that gleamed white in the dark face. They were called Red Men, but of course his skin wasn't red as barn paint, just a deep brown as if permanently tanned. There *was* an unusual coppery tint, but the man's face, stern and fierce while he stared, was rendered quite handsome by the smile.

Caine's lips twitched in a weak grin. That was all the answer he could give. It occurred to him that the man might not even speak English.

"I say, these hills aren't entirely safe just lately. There's a dangerous creature hereabouts, and one shouldn't just be hanging about."

Caine gaped. Not only did the Indian speak English, he spoke perfect English with an accent that would have been at home in any Oxfordshire study. Curious.

"I suppose not," Caine said.

Grinder's Keeper

"There are brigands about as well, you know," said the Indian.

"Well, I didn't truss myself up here," Caine said.

"Quite," said the Indian. "Taken unawares, were you?"

"Yes," Caine said. "Quite."

"Hmm."

The Indian stood and puffed his pipe as he studied Caine. The man's clothes were all a buff colored leather. A belted shirt that almost reached the knees hung over fringed leggings. He wore no other garments against the mountain cold. He bore no firearms, no weapons at all save a bone hilted knife sheathed at the belt. His hair was long as a woman's and blue black like the feathers of the ravens that had recently plagued Caine.

He looked Caine up and down, and inspected the clearing as well as the cairn he stood upon. He continued to make thoughtful hums from one side of his mouth, the other side being occupied with the pipe. Caine just swayed in the wind.

"I say," the Indian said after a time, "it appears as if they've taken something."

"Ayuh," Caine said, "they took everything but my pants."

"No, no, something rather more special. Something meant to aid you on your quest to save the townspeople from the terrible monster. That was your intent, I gather?"

"It was," Caine said.

"Well, I hope you'll pardon me for saying so," said the Indian, "but you'll not do it hanging up there."

"Yes, I realize that," Caine said. "Maybe you could get me down."

"Ah, yes. I would but…" the strange Indian man paused for a few puffs on his pipe, "…but it's quite against the rules you see. You'll have to get down yourself."

"I can't get down myself," Caine said. "I can't even feel my arms anymore. Please, just cut me down. I beg of you."

"Terribly sorry, old chap."

His tone was polite but implacable.

"It has to be your own doing. You're quite capable I'm sure."

"Capable?" Caine said. "Capable of what? I'm completely bound."

"You're body is bound, yes," said the Indian, "Bound by your enemies. However, your *mind* is bound by your own hand as it were. Loose those cords and the rest should be frightfully easy."

"I don't have time for riddles."

Caine was growing desperate.

"I've been hanging here since morning. I won't survive the night."

"Certainly not up there, wot?"

"Listen…"

"Sorry, old boy," the Indian cut Caine off. "I must be off. As I said these hills are dangerous just now. Even for me." The Indian jumped off the cairn and started to cross the clearing.

"Wait, you can't just leave me to die," Caine said. "You must help me."

"Well, of course I'll help you," said the Indian who now stood almost directly below the hanged man. "When you get down, follow me and I'll have a warm fire waiting."

"But…"

"Don't worry."

Again the broad white teeth flashed.

"I shall leave a trail that even a white man can follow."

"Hey, you can't just…"

"What's more, I'll give you just a bit to think about."

And now the Indian puffed at his pipe, and the bowl glowed reddish orange to throw sharp shadows on the red man's angular face. He pursed his lips and exhaled and the smoke streamed out, an impossibly long white ribbon.

The smoke turned and writhed as if a living thing, weaving back and forth on itself. It rose and floated before Caine's eyes and he stared, mesmerized by the ball of smoke. He felt he almost recognized the pattern it made. It hovered and seemed to shimmer like quicksilver, and he nearly had the meaning of the pattern.

Just then, the air was rent with the sharp keen of a howling pack of wolves. The smoky will o' wisp was torn by the wind, and Caine swung wildly in that wind. He looked around in panicked confusion.

A moment ago, he hung calmly in a still twilight. Now it was full dark, and the wind was a savage scream. His whole body shivered from the cold, and the Indian was gone—a phantasm of the mind after all, it seemed.

The moon was rising over the mountain tops, and the wolves bayed again. Caine couldn't judge their distance with any accuracy, but they seemed close. Chilling as the sound was, Caine felt he had little to fear from them as long as he was tied by this thrice damned knot. He had to get down, and the knot was the thing.

He tipped his head back on aching neck muscles to gaze again at it. He wondered who had tied it. Cullen or one of his highwaymen? It was infernal in its complicated and Gordian weaves.

Gordian indeed!

Caine knew well the story of Alexander, of course. Rather than struggle with a knot that couldn't be untied, the conqueror had used a swift sword-stroke. A parable Caine had always enjoyed for it's boldness and directness.

He had tried that here with his teeth with no success, but something else stirred at the edge of Caine's mind. He thought again of Shaw and thought of the strange smoke ring the Indian had blown. Caine grasped for it and thought he almost had it, but his concentration was broken by wolf howls.

The howling had been more or less constant for some time, but now the tenor changed. The howling of wolf to wolf was challenge and declaration that *this* pack hunted and ruled *this* territory. Those howls now took on a note of fear and despair that was terrible to hear.

Caine could still not guess at the distance, but he fancied he could make out several different voices. Those voices gave way to vicious snarls and then came a new challenge. A fierce and unholy cry split the night, like the bellow of a mad bullock, but grown huge beyond reckoning.

That fell call grew to cover the whole mountain, and Caine thought he felt a shudder run through the bones of the land, a powerful abrupt earthquake. He felt it in his own bones as well, and it was like being pressed between great stones. It could only be the Grinder, and Caine felt fresh terror shake his whole body.

He strained against the bonds as the howls and growls of the proud wolves turned to yelps and shrieks like so many back alley curs. He had to get down, could think of nothing else. He growled wordless curses at the knot and at his hands and arms, which would no longer obey him. Knowing it was useless didn't make him stop.

Caine saw swift grey shadows pass under him as the pack fled. The Grinder was coming this way.

Finally, Caine mastered his panic, knowing he would surely die if he let it rule him. Caine had survived battlefields, like soldiers before him, by recognizing the terror, acknowledging it, and putting it aside. Only a fool thought that it could be wholly banished, but it could be set aside and Caine did that now. He went so far as to close his eyes and make himself breathe deeply.

The knot was the thing still, and he thought of Alexander. And he thought of Shaw. Shaw had never liked the story of the sword. He sited an older story, where the Phrygian king had tied the knot around the linchpin of the ox cart's yoke. Shaw's preferred version still had Alexander striking at the heart of the problem, but not with a sword stroke. He simply pulled the linchpin to find the ends of the knot.

Caine opened his eyes and looked up at the knot. He stared at it, and his mind's eye saw the Indian's smoke curl and writhe around the knot. Caine even managed a smile, though he could hear slow and heavy footfalls coming down the mountain. The ground shuddered at those fell steps and Caine gathered himself, for he would have only one chance.

Caine heaved and swung his whole body up until his feet were higher than his head. He caught the rope between his legs, grasping with his bare feet, and twining the line between his knees. In this manner, he was able to get his weight off the knot. With slack in the line he could see the strand he needed, and grasped one more time with his teeth.

Caine started to pull. The loops of the knot had been cinched very tight from his weight hanging on them, and they didn't want to give. Caine kept pulling, keeping steady pressure. The measured tread of foot falls from the forest grew. Caine ignored them. He kept pulling, neck muscles straining, and was finally rewarded with movement.

It was just a bit, but it was enough to get a better grip on the knot's linchpin, and Caine bit deep for one last pull. Once started, the hemp slid easier and Caine worked his hands back and forth.

His earlier bite through the outside line proved useful after all. The loops started to loosen and the bitten ends started to unwind. Caine forced his numb hands and wrists to move and twist. It was like shaking pieces of firewood at the ends of his arm, but the strands were coming completely undone now.

Finally, his hands were free and he grabbed for the rope. His brutalized and freezing limbs were not up for the task, and Caine dropped like a stone down a deep well. He hit the ground in a heap of blood and pain. Caine let out a croaking scream. Pain yes, but also a cry of release to be free from the torturous bonds.

An expectant stillness seized the night. No birds cried, and no footsteps sounded, and Caine himself held his breath. The mountain was frozen, but Caine could feel another intelligence— still and waiting like Caine himself, stretching out senses to determine what was out there.

The silence spun out for a long moment, and then Caine heard a sound. It wasn't as loud as the bellow that scattered the pack, but again Caine thought of a bull, massive and menacing.

Caine was up before the lowing moan ended. He started downslope, but he was asking too much of his wracked body. A few lurching spasms that could barely be called steps got him to the edge of the clearing, but he careened into a tree and fell face first into the ground. In the forest up the mountain side, the monster's voice ceased abruptly and the footfalls started back up.

Giving up was not in Caine's nature, but he came close that night. Alone and naked in the wilderness, he felt little better than a beast finally run to ground by a pack of determined hounds. All that was left now was to admit defeat, trade in the pain and despair of going on for the relief of letting it end. Still, if the end it was, it would be more seemly to meet it on one's feet.

So Caine managed to at least raise his head. Right before him and stretching out through the snow was a single set of footprints.

A Nathaniel Caine Adventure

The Indian! He had been real after all, for there were his tracks as promised, headed downslope, but away from the churned mess the bandits had made of the snow.

Caine struggled to his feet, barely aware he was doing so. He took a few steps, and the notion of giving up was driven out. Caine started to run. A shambling and herky-jerky run to be sure, but on he ran, following the trail by moonlight.

He fell often, sometimes scrambling on all fours before he could regain his feet. When the slope was steep he fell and tumbled wildly (he was past feeling the pain this caused with anything more than detached observation). This happened twice and he felt the pain was worth it because he seemed to gain distance on the implacable footsteps behind him.

Always they caught up, though, and Caine started to hear the beast's forge-bellows breathing. He didn't look back, just kept his head to the trail like a hound. The tracks were easy to follow when the moon was out, but clouds began rolling in and the light grew unreliable. Soon the clouds blocked the moon altogether and the wind picked up. Caine kept on, and still the footsteps grew closer.

The already cold wind grew colder and raked Caine like icy knives. Snow started to fall. By the sound, the Grinder must be almost on top of him, but still Caine didn't look back. He kept his eyes on the trail which was rapidly disappearing in the storm and the murk.

He ran and the ground shook, the monster was only a few yards behind. He could think of no way to escape. The only thing he had was the Indian's trail, and he was bent almost double to follow it. So it was an abrupt shock when it ended. Caine froze and stared at the last footprint.

He straightened and took a step, perhaps to cast about for the trail or to face his death. His foot met empty air, and Caine pitched out into the falling snow. The poor visibility took away any sense of falling, and Caine had just enough time to think it felt peaceful before he slammed into the ground. He landed on his back and what little wind was left to him was knocked out.

He looked up and saw he had walked right off a cliff. It rose, sheer faced, to a sort of promontory. Out of the driving snow, the Grinder stepped to the very edge of that promontory. It was impossibly huge and aggressively solid, as if quarry stones had come to life to stalk the mountain. The great block of a head turned on a nonexistent neck as the hateful glowing eyes searched for their prey.

Caine thought the thing had lost him in the driving snow; falling off the cliff must have looked like he just disappeared. It began a slow and ponderous movement that Caine realized was it bending at the waist—or what passed for a waist. There was the sound again of a great millstone, and Caine knew why they called it Grinder.

Caine began to gather his strength to get up and run. His ankles were seized and he was pulled into blackness. He struggled and tried to strike out, but he was fighting blind and hit nothing. Then there was a low voice that spoke with a well cultured English accent

"Hush, now Nathaniel Caine. There's a good lad."

A Nathaniel Caine Adventure

He had hoped to have it out with the Indian for leaving him to hang, but he found now he had no anger. He had no fear or pain either, and reckoned he was just too tired to feel. Blackness took Caine.

Sanctuary

For a time, Caine's consciousness was a patchwork quilt.
Later, he would try to put it all together, but it would never fit in a
pattern that made any real sense. Some of the flashes were brief: a
view of the Indian puffing his pipe near the fire, the sheen of that
firelight on a green paste smeared over the whiplashes on his belly.

Other flashes were longer but made less sense. He worked out
that he was in a cave and, like the cave in the pass, the walls
seemed to dance with moving paintings. But now the Indian
danced, naked save for a leather breech clout, and the paintings
moved with him. Caine couldn't say if the man was mirroring the
paintings or it was the other way around.

At one point, he came to and opened his eyes, but he could see
nothing except a soft green light. He tried to move but he was
wrapped, head to toe it seemed, in a cocoon. There was more, but
none of it made any real sense to Caine. It all felt like a fever
dream. The heat of the fire seemed to roast him and always there
was the sound of drums, though he never saw the Red Man playing
on one.

Finally, Caine opened his eyes and felt, calmly and certainly,
that he was really awake. There was no sound of drums, only the
soft crackle of a small fire. The light from that fire did indeed light
the walls of a cave, but all that danced there were shadows. Caine
turned his head and saw the Indian looking at him. The Red Man

sat tailor fashion and seemed to be waiting for Caine. He flashed the broad and toothy grin.

Caine sat up. He had lain covered in a piece of fur which now slid off his torso. His chest was wrapped in wide strips of buckskin and likewise his shoulder. His belly was covered in some dried paste and bits of moss which fell off when he sat up. The weals were still angry looking, but they were closed. Caine looked at the Indian and opened his mouth, but the Red Man held up a hand.

"Questions, of course, I understand," he said. "But first you should take some nourishment. You've been through an ordeal."

He waved his hand at a gourd and bowl on the ground before the fire. Caine took the gourd first. It held water, cold and fresh, and Caine poured it down his savaged throat. He reached for the bowl, which held a stew and some sort of cakes. The stew was little more than broth really, but it was hot and Caine felt strength returning as he sipped it. The cakes were rather bland and greasy, but they filled Caine's belly.

He made himself go slowly, knowing a man could sicken himself by gorging after a long time with no water. The Indian waited patiently and silently, nodding approval when Caine held the bowl out for more. Caine finished and wiped his mouth with the back of a hand. The Indian again held up a hand. He took up his pipe which lay ready and lit it with a brand from the fire. He held it out to Caine with both hands.

"Smoke first," he said, "then questions."

Caine reached for the pipe. There was a twinge from his ribs, but for the most part Caine felt little pain. He moved the shoulder and it was the same. He was stiff and weak, but it was more like a long night on hard ground than a day's worth of combat and torture.

Caine puffed at the pipe. The tobacco was strong and raw tasting, but not unpleasant. Caine had plenty of questions but didn't know which were the most pertinent. He just asked the one at the top of his mind.

"How long have I been here?"

"It's still night," the Indian said and nodded his head.

Caine looked where he indicated and it was dark beyond the cave mouth. There was no sound of wind or animals from without.

"Night yes," Caine said, "but my wounds feel near healed."

"Certainly," the Indian smiled. "The healing skills of my people are quite extraordinary. They're rather famous hereabouts."

"Your people," Caine said. "This is Indian land then?"

"Well, not quite in the way you mean, and they of course don't call *themselves* Indians. Still, it's near enough."

"I saw no sign of them as I traveled."

"I'm not surprised."

A grim look crossed the Red Man's face.

"They have been killed and scattered by those bloody soldiers. And they shun these lands for fear of the Stone That Walks."

"Stone That Walks?" Caine said. "You mean the Grinder?"

"Is that what the white men call it? He's certainly been grinding up a few of them!"

A Nathaniel Caine Adventure

He seemed more than a little pleased at this and Caine bristled.

"This monstrous beast is killing innocent people," he said. "I mean to stop it."

"Innocent, you say?"

The Indian was unperturbed by Caine's anger. "Some of them undoubtedly, but make no mistake, Nathaniel Caine. It was the white men that unleashed this beast."

"What is it?"

The Indian took the pipe back from Caine and puffed, apparently composing his thoughts. He handed the pipe back, and Caine smoked while the Red Man continued.

"It is both more than it seems, and less so," he said. "My people love the earth. Worship it you would say. The whole land is sacred, but there are places of power that are held especially holy. These mountains are one such. They are old and very powerful. The power of the Earth must be respected, though. The same river a man drinks from may drown him as well, you see?"

"I'm not sure I do," Caine said. "How did they provoke the monster, and why don't they run or fight?"

"Can a man fight a river in flood?" the Indian said. "The white people are all mad. They have fouled the river. They have abandoned their crops and hunting to dig in the ground like badgers."

"Dig? For what?"

"For nothing," said the Indian.

He reached into a pouch at his belt and threw something on the ground. He made a guttural sound that was certainly not English.

Grinder's Keeper

"They dig night and day for a piece like that." Caine picked up the lump of metal, no bigger than his thumb but heavy, and turned it in his fingers. Raw and unpolished as it was, there was no mistaking the yellow gleam in the firelight.

"Damn," was all he said, but the Indian caught something in his tone.

"What is it, man?" he said. "Do you know something I don't?"

"You truly don't know what this is?"

"Of course I do, it's..." the Indian again said the guttural word.

"Well, we call it gold," Caine said, "and you're right to think them mad. People will commit all manner of mad acts for this metal."

"*White* people," said the Indian.

It was part rebuke and part question, and Caine had no answer for either. He handed the gold nugget back.

"This explains much," he said. "Shaw said there was power deep in the ground here. The miners must have hit a vein they weren't expecting."

"There's more to it than that, Caine," the Indian said. "The white people have dug deep holes to be sure, but that's not what loosed the Stone Walker. Some one called on the powers."

"Who? And to what purpose?"

"That I can't say. However, if you truly mean to rid these lands of the Stone That Walks, you will have to see the truth of who's behind it. It is not enough to defeat the beast without confronting the one who called it."

"That's putting the cart well before the horse, I fear," Caine moved his shoulder, working at the stiffness. "I've nearly died half a dozen times today, and I have no weapons."

"Nearly died is not died," the Indian pointed out, "and as for your weapons…I have seen the white man's weapons. They are just more metal and won't help you against stone."

"Well, how am I to defeat the Grinder then?"

"You will have to see the truth of him before you beat him," the Indian said. "You are a man of much knowledge Nathaniel Caine. I can sense a deep wisdom within you, but it is clouded by the veil white men draw over their eyes. I think you'll not win if you don't see the truth. You were given a talisman to help you and you've lost it. That is not good."

"I know nothing of any talisman," Caine said.

"Come now, old boy," the Indian said. "We've shared a pipe and it's unseemly to lie among smoke mates."

"It's not my habit to lie," Caine said. "Where would I get such a talisman?"

"You have recently spoken to the spirits, have you not?"

"No, I…"

Caine broke off. He thought of Shaw's eyes in the firelight, gleaming white like polished ivory. The Indian nodded.

"It's as I thought," he said. "No doubt the thieves have it. You should endeavor to get it back."

"I intend to," said Caine, "but it won't be easy without…"

"Your weapons, yes."

The Indian waved a dismissive hand.

"Braves hold their weapons as dear as their ballocks."

Caine started to bristle again at the characterization. Instead, he shook his head and a rueful grin stole over his grim face. Caine had gotten used to going about heavily armed, a wise course in the wilds of the frontier, and without his revolvers he felt naked. He wondered what the old Patricians back home would make of him. He certainly wouldn't get many repeat invitations to soirees if he showed up bristling iron and laden with cartridges.

"Perhaps you have a point, sir," Caine said, "but it's a fight I'm headed for and weapons will be needed."

"You hung weaponless on that wind swept tree," said the Red Man. "Yet still you escaped. That's the power you will need in the fight ahead. The white man's weapons will not bite on the Stone That Walks. He was made before they, and he won't be unmade by them. See the truth, the essence. Think on this, Nathaniel Caine. Think and sleep."

"I'm not…"

Sleepy was what Caine was going to say, but his tongue failed him. His eyes were next and the cave went dark.

It was sunlight that woke Caine. He lay still and opened one eye to see a blinding triangle of light. The morning sun was shining through the cave opening, and Caine sat up to watch it. It occurred to him that he was very lucky to be looking on another sunrise after the string of close calls he had just gone through.

He looked around for the Indian but he wasn't there, and Caine knew he wouldn't be back. The Indian was gone, but he had left some things behind. The hide blanket which he had slept under, but also a leather tunic. It had bead work at the collar and fringe at the shoulders like the Red Man's own. For all Caine knew it *was* the Red Man's.

There was also a pair of the tall leather moccasins, and a belt, and a good size bag with a shoulder strap. Caine lifted the flap. Inside were some of the tasteless cakes and some dried strips of meat. There was a gourd of water and a soft leather pouch. Caine sniffed at this and smelled the strong tobacco.

The prize however, was the knife. A man in the wilds without a knife is worse than naked, and the Indian had clothed Caine. The bone hilt gleamed, and Caine was sure this was the Indian's own knife. He pulled it from it's sheath and grunted in surprise.

The blade was not steel. It was black and faceted and slick to the touch. Obsidian, and Caine marveled at the workmanship required to knap such a blade. He set the edge to the back of his arm and marveled again. The hair on his arm fairly leapt before it. The black knife's blade was easily as sharp as any razor.

Caine sat for a few moments. He was upset, for he was certain the Indian would not return, and he wished he could thank the man. He should have been angry at being left on the tree, but he wasn't. There was no question in Caine's mind that he would have perished in the night if the Indian hadn't taken him in, and now the knife.

There could be no doubt that Caine had a debt to pay. He realized he didn't even know the man's name, or how the man knew Caine's name. Or why he spoke with a British accent.

"A poor questioner I turned out to be."

Still, he had enough answers to move forward. The threat against the folk in Hartsburgh was supernatural. Caine saw no more point in seeking 'reasonable' explanations. He had seen the monster twice and almost been killed by it. He had to accept that Shaw's visit, whether it be ghost, spirit, or otherwise, had been real.

Caine made a quick breakfast of some cakes and pondered his course. The prudent course would be to turn back. Make for Elkhorn Pass and come back with Roarke and a posse.

The prudent course perhaps, but Caine didn't give it serious consideration. That would settle the bandits, but Caine didn't think it would do much good against the Grinder. Or the Grinder's master which the Red Man had indicated was the heart of the matter.

Who would call up such a monster? Caine still didn't know anything about the town's layout and situation. He had planned on just riding in and seeing for himself, but now he had another thought.

Unarmed and unhorsed he was, but he was also unexpected. Cullen and his lads thought him dead, and Caine now had the advantage of surprise.

Caine finished his breakfast and donned the clothes left for him. He shook out the fur blanket and discovered it was a bearskin. That was easy enough to determine for the hide had been cured with the head still on.

He wrapped it around his shoulders and, after a few moments, worked out that it could be worn as a cloak. The bear's head went over his own to serve as a hood and Caine thought he would be warm enough outside. Time to crawl out of his den and make for Blackfoot Creek and from there to Hartsburgh. Hibernation was over.

Trouble at the Mines

"Come on, Tor. This has to be worth more than that."

"Twenty dollars," Tor said. "No more."

"Are you crazy?"

Will Parson brandished the pipe as if he might bludgeon the man.

"This thing's ivory! It's worth a hundred dollars easy!"

Tor Nielsen sighed and bit his lip. He bit his lip to keep from screaming insults at this cretinous thief. Tor paid tribute to the Colonel and so was supposed to be under his protection. If Parson hurt Tor, he would have to answer for it. However, that might be after Parson stabbed him, or shot him, or God knew what the highwayman was capable of. So Tor bit his lip until he could keep a reasonable tone.

"It's not ivory," he said. "It's meerschaum and it's worth twenty dollars. That'll let you drink and sit at the card tables, and if you're careful you'll still have enough for a whore. Take it or leave it."

Tor laid the twenty next to the pipe and crossed his arms. Parson grimaced and growled and made a great show of thinking it over, stroking his stubbly jaw and drumming his dirty fingers on the counter. Tor remained still, knowing that Will Parson would take the money. After a few moments he did.

"Fine. I'll take it."

Parson scraped up the money; it was in chips not coin.

"All you Swede's are a buncha skinflints."

Tor's expression showed neither triumph at closing the deal, nor offense at the insult. He waited until Parson turned and walked to the bar before taking up the pipe with a sigh.

Not long ago, though it seemed longer, Tor had been an honest merchant. Now he was…well, he didn't know what to call himself. Not a merchant certainly, more of a pawn broker. That was in addition to his newly acquired interests in saloon keeping and prostitution.

Tor should have gotten his family out last summer when the trouble was just starting, before Cullen and the Colonel had control of the roads. The lure of riches had been too tempting, though, and now he was caught like everyone else.

Well, not as bad as those in the mines. Tor had seen early enough that sides must be chosen, and he had bet on Colonel Hayes. The outcome of that wager was still in doubt, although it wasn't wise to express such doubts. In the meantime he had made himself useful with his freight connections and was even turning a profit of sorts. He kept as much gold and hard coin as he could, and he used gambling chips or credit for his customers' currency.

The problem was getting it away from Hartsburgh. If it was just himself, he could steal a horse and take his chances on the road. But Tor had a wife and a small boy. He would need a wagon to get them and their fortune out of town safely.

Tor hoped to see wagons again soon. With the Spring thaw, the passes would be opening up, and he expected Hadley any day.

One way or another, Tor meant to leave on one of Hadley's wagons. Until then, he was a prisoner like everyone else.

At the bar, Parson bought a bottle of cheap whiskey and had a few shots as he scowled about the sorry excuse for a saloon. The pipe was the last of his share of the loot from their recent score in the mountain. Cullen's gang drew pay for their work from Hayes, but that preening Colonel only paid them once a month like his soldiers.

"Irregulars, he calls us."

Parson spat on the floor, even though there was a spittoon nearby. He didn't know how far off pay day was. He didn't even know what day of the week it was, let alone the date. Parson had another shot, and wiped his mustache with the back of his hand while pondering his next move.

He eyed the girls, such as they were. There were only three out front, and the lazy slatterns didn't even bother to look at him. He knew they were well used by Hayes' men.

He turned to the so called gaming tables, which were all but empty. One of the mine overseers was there, Kemp his name was, and one of the soldiers, just a kid whose name escaped Parson. They looked as bored and listless as the whores. You couldn't have a decent game of poker with only two people, and there was no faro.

Parson looked again at the girls and decided he needed to be more desperate or more drunk. Some time at cards would give him a chance to make some more money and failing that, finish his bottle. Maybe then he would be drunk enough to hire a girl. Assuming of course he had enough left if he didn't win at cards.

With that decision made, Parson stumped over to the table and took a seat. He didn't ask to join and the men didn't greet him, just started dealing. Parson only had time to lose one hand before the game was over. One of the goons from the mining outfit ran through the door and whipped his head around with wild eyes. When he saw the soldier, he ran over to the table.

"Where's Murphy?"

"Sarge?" the kid said. "He's back in the cribs having a go at them whores."

"Well, go get him."

"Hell no."

The kid shook his head. Collins. Parson remembered his name was Collins.

"He don't like being interrupted, and I don't fancy a lashing."

"Interrupt him anyway," the goon said. "There's trouble at the mine."

That did the trick, for Collins didn't even waste time on cursing. He disappeared out the back, and in a moment reappeared, followed by a slight man who finished dressing as he walked. The goon made a move to rush over, but Murphy froze him with a look.

"Save it," Murphy said as he buttoned his coat. "The Colonel will have to hear it, so let's get to the fort and you can tell the tale once."

The man's voice was gravelly and deeper than his frame might suggest, and it was not softened by the Irish brogue. Parson spat on the floor. The army was full of these Irish pissants, and he resented the fact that they were the authority in this town.

Murphy's gun belt was slung over his shoulder. He swung it around his hips and buckled it in one quick move. He settled his weapons and settled his hat. It was a cavalryman's hat, but bore neither cord nor insignia. Just a single raven feather that gleamed in the lamplight.

"You and you."

Murphy pointed at Parson and Kemp.

"Both of you come as well."

Parson's resentment made his lips curl under his mustache, but it didn't stop him from obeying. The soldiers and townsfolk alike were afraid of Murphy. The troopers told tales of his savagery fighting the Injuns, but Parson had never seen him do much. Of course, Parson kept the expressions of his resentment and his bravadoes among friends.

The truth was Parson couldn't even meet Murphy's eye. There was a coldness there that bordered on madness, much like his boss Elisha Cullen. Parson had seen plenty of what Cullen could do, and had no desire to test Murphy against that standard.

The men stomped out, and Murphy was off at a gallop as soon as his boots were in the stirrups. The others were left to follow as best as they could, and Parson ended up on drogue. The fort wasn't far, you could see it from town, and their course took them past the Colonel's abandoned house. Parson's sneer now was one of satisfaction. High and mighty Colonel Hayes might be, but he was still a man driven from his own house.

There was no challenge as they approached the fort. Murphy's men recognized him at a distance, and hurried to open the gate. Murphy didn't slow, but galloped through and hauled up on the reins. His mount stopped and reared, and Murphy leapt from the saddle before the beast was settled.

"Where's the Colonel?"

"In his office, Sarge," the trooper answered while grabbing at the horses reins. "Cullen's in there with him."

"Good."

Murphy set off at his customary pace. Parson and the others fell in line behind him, and in a moment Murphy was rapping on the Colonel's door. He waited with his hand on the latch, and as soon as the call to enter came, he threw open the door and strode in. He gave neither greeting nor salute as he walked to stand in front of Hayes' desk. Hayes and Cullen looked to be in the middle of a conversation, but Murphy made no apology for the interruption.

"Trouble at the mines, Colonel," he said.

Hayes and Cullen both sat up in their chairs, and Murphy jerked a thumb at the goon.

"Let's have it, then."

"Well, Colonel."

The overseer looked nervous and cleared his throat a few times before he could get going.

"It looks like Indian trouble."

"I thought we had them sorted out," Hayes said.

If the news upset him, he gave no sign. He had been about to light a cigar when Murphy strode in and he struck the match now. Parson had taken to the West as the war was heating up, so he had never seen a Colonel before. He didn't know if they all wore such fancy and fine tailored uniforms as Hayes.

Hayes might have been rather unassuming, but for all the trappings of rank. Polished brass buttons and gold braid at the shoulder. High leather boots that were always clean and polished. In fact everything about Hayes was clean and polished, and that set him apart a bit on the frontier.

"How many Indians are there?"

"Well…as far as I…that is to say we…can tell," the overseer said, "one."

Hayes looked up, but didn't stop lighting his cigar. He puffed and turned it in the flame until it was evenly lit. He shook out the match and tossed it in a silver ashtray.

He leaned back in his chair, the leather upholstery creaked, and exchanged a glance with Elisha Cullen. Cullen looked tattered and shabby in the well appointed office—a black buzzard in a turtledove's cage—but he sat comfortably enough. He merely shrugged at Hayes, and the Colonel turned back to the overseer.

"One?"

"Well, that's all we saw, sir."

The man turned his hat over in his hands and mostly looked at the floor.

"Swenson said it was only one, but it had to be more."

A Nathaniel Caine Adventure

"Christ's blood, you idiot," Murphy said. "Start from the beginning and let's have it straight. Straight mind. Stick to the facts."

"Okay, then."

The overseer continued to worry his hat and seemed more than happy to address his tale to the floorboards. "I guess it started an hour or so after shift change. We was in the bunkhouse playing cards. John Patterson said he had to go to the shitter."

"Patterson," Hayes said and looked at Cullen. "One of yours?"

Cullen nodded and Hayes indicated the overseer should continue.

"Well, he went out and that ain't nothing peculiar," the man went on. "But he was taking an awful long time. We started to joke about it. Maybe he fell in, that sort of thing, but more and more time went and he didn't come back. Finally, Briggs went out to check, and he hollered for us right quick. We all hurried out, and the outhouse was standing empty with the door open. Patterson wasn't around, but his hat was laying there on the ground."

"Was Gallagher there?" Murphy asked, and the overseer nodded. "What did he do?"

"He hollered up a couple of his boys and had us all get rifles. He sent two of the soldiers down to the miners camp and had the rest of us follow the tracks with Swenson."

Murphy nodded, more to himself than anything, but the man took it to mean keep talking.

"Anyway, the track from the outhouse wasn't hard to follow," he said. "There's still a lot of snow on the ground, and it looked like someone was being dragged. We followed the drag marks into the woods and found John Patterson hanging from a tree."

"Hanging?" Hayes said. "From a limb?"

"No, sir. From a rope."

Cullen's eyes sharpened at that and flashed to Parson. Parson merely looked bored and churlish as usual. It had been more than two weeks since they left the dark haired rider to swing in the wind. He was long dead and this merely coincidence. Still, Cullen was a man who lived largely by instinct, and his thin dirty fingers played at the hilt of the strange knife he had taken as a trophy.

"There was blood everywhere," the overseer went on. "They hung him up and slit his throat like a hog. We cut him down, and his pistols was missing. And his finger."

"What about his finger?" Murphy said.

"It was missing, too," said the overseer. "It was lopped off."

"Does that mean something?" Hayes asked Murphy.

"Sure and it might. The savages are big on mutilating the dead, and one of the local tribes like to cut off fingers," Murphy said and turned back to the overseer. "What did Swenson say?"

"Pretty much the same thing. There were tracks going away. Swenson said one man in moccasins. He lost them in a ravine."

"Swenson lost a trail?" Murphy said and the man nodded.

"He took a couple men to try and pick it up, and Gallagher sent me back to find you and make my report."

"Well, Sergeant Murphy?"

Hayes knocked cigar ash into the silver ashtray and leaned back in his chair.

"What do you make of it?"

"Well, it's trouble sure enough. I just don't know how big. One man isn't much to worry about, but one savage…that sounds like a scout. And if Swenson lost his trail he's a damned good one, too."

He went to the window and stared out, drumming his fingers on the sill. After a moment he spoke but continued to look out the window.

"Gallagher's a stout man. He'll make sure the mines are buttoned up and then head back to the camp. He'll hole up there and be ready for an attack. It's almost sundown now, so even if we ride hard we couldn't get there before dark."

There were nervous looks and shuffling at this. Even Hayes' composure gave way to a spooked look, which he tried to hide with a cough. Murphy continued to look out the window, but he still caught the mood and gave a short laugh without mirth.

"That's right. Sure and the Grinder'll be out and about."

He finally turned and faced the room.

"I don't think there's much we can do tonight. I say we close up the fort and ride out at first light—in force. With luck, Swenson'll have more information. If it is those red devils, I'll sort it out before they can make their move."

"I'll go with you," Cullen said, "and bring some of my boys."

"Well then, it's settled," Colonel Hayes said.

The room started to clear out, but Hayes kept Murphy back. He waved his cigar at the whiskey decanter, and Murphy needed no more invitation. Hayes kept Scotch rather than Irish whiskey, but it was a damn sight better than the rotgut bourbon at Tor's place. Murphy poured for the other men and started knocking back shots for himself. Hayes placed a folded piece of paper before him on the desk.

"What's that, then?" Murphy said.

He could read, but he was slow at it. Murphy preferred to get right to the point, and anyway the reading of it would get in the way of drinking.

"It's a letter," said the Colonel.

"Is it now?"

Sergeant Murphy ignored the Colonel's sarcastic tone.

"I haven't seen Hadley or any of his riders."

A brief glance passed between Hayes and Cullen, and Murphy chuckled.

"It's like that is it?" Murphy said. "So it wasn't one of Hadley's regulars, or you wouldn't have waylaid him. Hadley's cowardice is finally getting stronger than his greed."

"Just so," said Colonel Hayes, "but it's still a near thing. Hadley was planning on making one more trip as soon as the passes were clear enough for wagons. Apparently he had an arrangement with Mr. Nielsen. They were planning on taking all the loot from Nielsen's profiteering, as well as all the gold they could lay their hands on, and abandon our little enterprise."

"Old Tor?" Murphy said and shrugged. "He's got more sand than I thought. I'll give him that. And he's a shrewd businessman, sure. I guess he decided it was time to cash out. But here now. Why would Hadley put all that in a letter and send it with a rider he didn't know? That's chancy."

"Indeed," said Hayes. "It appears they had another conspirator. The letter isn't addressed to Hadley. It's addressed to the quartermaster."

Murphy was in the act of raising another glass, but now he froze and his eyes started to smolder.

"The hell you say. Riley?"

"It's all right there."

Hayes indicated the letter. Murphy didn't look at the letter, but after a long moment he tossed back his drink and slammed the glass on the desk.

"The mines are the main thing," he said.

His voice hadn't changed tone, and he appeared calm, or as calm as he ever appeared. But still those dark eyes smoldered.

"We'll have to see to them before I explain to Tor that he can't get out of the arrangement. Hadley can wait. He'll come to us, and I'll sort him out then. But Riley now. That'll have to be seen to right away."

Murphy again offered no salute, just turned on his heel and started stalking away. He was almost out the door when Hayes stopped him.

"One more thing, Sergeant," he said and Murphy turned. "I'm sick and goddamn tired of sleeping in this fort. I want to sleep in my bed, in my house. When you take the men out tomorrow, tell them I've doubled the bounty. Two thousand dollars in gold to the man that brings me the bitch's head."

Just One Man

"A quick bit of business, Cullen." Sergeant Murphy's breath steamed in the gray dawn air. "Then we'll ride hard for the camp."

"Fine by me," said Cullen.

Ride hard Murphy said. That's the only way Murphy ever rode. Even now, he leaned forward in his saddle, and the horse stamped at the rider's nerves. Cullen thought of a fighting dog straining at the leash, and he readied himself to follow the crazed Irishman. Two troopers were swinging open the heavy gate, and sure enough, as soon as there was room for a horse to pass, Murphy was off.

He gave no order for his men to follow, and they weren't as ready as Cullen. Off they galloped with the others following, trying to catch up. Murphy rode down the hill and made straight for Colonel Hayes' fine house. Cullen had to allow a measure of grudging respect for Murphy's cruelty. The man knew how to lead a pack of vicious curs.

Murphy rode right up to the porch and reined in, jumping out of the saddle. A hard grin split his face when he saw the front doors hanging wide open. He had been sure to leave them closed last night.

He made a quick loop over the porch rail with the rein and turned to make sure the men were catching up. They needed to see him walk in with no fear or hesitation. The troop rode up and jostled about in a loose semicircle. Nobody wanted to get too close to the cursed house, but morbid curiosity kept them edging nearer the porch. Murphy was satisfied and mounted the steps.

The sun was barely up so the house's interior was still quite dim, but Murphy strode through the open doors. He spared no glance for the once fine parlor, but instead made for the staircase. The staircase was also fine once, with a banister and a carpet runner down the middle.

All of that was a shambles now, smeared with blood and bits of offal. With the poor light, it was hard to tell if any of the smears were fresh, but Murphy was confident.

He went to the master bedroom, and again the door which he had shut last night stood open. Inside was a large bed with a feather mattress and four stout posts. Fastened to one of those posts was a set of manacles.

After stalking out of Colonel Hayes' office last night, Murphy had pointed at the first man he saw and told him to fetch these very irons. He pointed at the next man and ordered him to tell the quartermaster that Murphy wanted to talk to him. Then Murphy had simply started pacing around the courtyard, wondering who would get there first. As it turned out, Riley arrived first.

"You wanted to see me, Sarge?" Riley said.

"I did, buck," Murphy said. "I did at that. I was wondering if you'd had any word from Bill Hadley?"

There was the briefest flash of apprehension on Riley's face. Gone in an instant, Murphy wasn't sure he would have seen it if he wasn't looking for it. Riley was a fine liar and schooled his

A Nathaniel Caine Adventure

features to friendly boredom. As if he had better things to do, but he would be happy to pass a few words with his old pal Murphy.

"Nah, Sarge," Riley shook his head as he spoke, "the passes are probably still chancy for wagons, and I ain't seen no rider. Why do you ask?"

"Just concerned about supplies is all," Murphy said, "and that's your job."

Murphy's tone was casual, but Riley's smile began to slip under the sergeant's glare. Those black eyes were hard at the best of times. Now they were starting to shine with a bale-fire.

"My job, now," Murphy went on still casual, "is to make sure everyone is doing *their* job."

"Are you mad at me, Murphy?" Riley said. "If I didn't do something, Sarge, let me know and I'll take care of it."

"Not just that they're doing their jobs," Murphy continued as if Riley hadn't spoken, "but that they're all pulling for the same team. We're like a family, Riley. You can't quit yer family."

The yard had gone still and quiet except for a soft clink of metal. Riley turned at the sound and saw the trooper approaching them with the manacles. Soldiers stood all around, curious about the irons or just sensitive to Murphy's mood. Riley turned back to Murphy, and if he thought to ask what was amiss or talk his way out of things, he gave that idea up immediately.

Murphy was smiling.

Riley went for his saber.

Murphy didn't wear a saber and he had good reason. For one, the metal scabbard was far too noisy for the work required of an

Indian fighter. He considered it next to useless for close quarters on the ground and little better ahorse. Instead of a sword he simply wore extra guns. If he fired those dry, he carried a short wooden club not much different from some the Indians themselves used, though his was bound in strips of iron.

Then there was the matter of training. He was a city boy, born and bred in the slums of Dublin. He had no training at all with the curved blade, and the army hadn't given him any, either. A man was a fool to bet his life on a weapon he didn't know how to use.

But for Murphy, the biggest reason was he felt the saber was more suited to a strutting English pederast who'd never done an honest day's work in his life. The kind of man who thought it was his God given right to use that saber to point the way for the lowborn to charge while he sat his horse in the rear of the fight.

Riley had no more training with the weapon than Murphy himself. So when he snatched at the blade Murphy let him. He even let Riley go so far as to get his hand in the basket and close around the hilt.

Then Murphy lashed out with a straight left. Riley's nose shattered in a splatter of blood. Fists were something Murphy had plenty of training in, and he went to work now. The first blow to the nose was just to blind Riley so he could work. After that he stuck mostly to the body, for he wanted Riley awake and alert for the coming night. It was only a matter of moments before Riley lay in a groaning heap at Murphy's feet. Murphy finally stopped smiling.

"Get him in irons, and get him on a horse."

A Nathaniel Caine Adventure

The men obeyed without question, indeed with no sound at all. This too, was part of Murphy's plan. He wanted to see if there would be any mutinous grumbling, or if Riley had any co-conspirators who might defend him. There was none of that in the yard, and none when Murphy mounted and took half a dozen men down to Hayes' fine house. He gave no explanation of Riley's offense or of his own actions.

Riley had tried to bear it like a man at first. But as the house loomed, he began begging for his life. Murphy's hard black eyes were all the answer Riley got, and he started begging at least for a bullet or the knife. Even a dance at the end of a rope would be preferable to the Grinder.

Murphy said not a word as they rode. Nor yet as he and the white-faced troopers dragged the whimpering quartermaster to the bloody bed. When Riley was laid out and chained, Murphy finally spoke.

"You should try and get some sleep, buck."

He patted Riley on the cheek.

"For when you wake, you'll be in Hell. Don't worry, though. You won't be alone for long. I'm going to find you're bosom pal, Bill Hadley, and send him to you straight."

Murphy had turned and left Riley to wail and gibber and rattle against his chains. Those chains were pretty much all that was left this morning. You could never be sure what the Grinder was going to do to his victims.

Sometimes he would just rip off a leg or an arm and leave a man screaming in agony for the last few moments of his life.

Other times he would tear and gnash and strew the bits and pieces about. That's how the Colonel's house had become a stinking abattoir.

Other times the Grinder would carry people off whole, and God alone knew what became of them. They were never found and Murphy thought it was likely the Grinder devoured them in his lair, wherever that was. Murphy allowed himself to brood for a moment on that problem.

He had seen the Grinder, when he tried to fight it early on. Once in an ambush set in this very house. May as well try to fight a mountain for all the good it did him. The beast's own roars drowned the gunfire. Then it was only grinding and shrieking as he killed at will.

Murphy had rushed the creature to club it with a rifle butt. Pure battle madness, for the rifle's bullets had done nothing. The Grinder swatted him like a fly, and Murphy had crashed into the stone hearth to fall senseless. When he came to, he could still hear the screams of one of the troopers dragged off into the forest.

Murphy followed with a few of the men left whole, but the screams ended abruptly. No one had been able to follow any of the beast's tracks to its lair, despite offers of money from Hayes and offers of violence from Murphy himself. He knew if they found the beast's lair, they would find that damned witch who had called it and they could end this. Murphy gnashed his teeth together until he sounded like a little grinder himself.

He shook himself and removed the manacles, sticky with congealed blood. He went back downstairs, and when he strode out on the porch, all eyes turned toward him and the bloody irons. He held them aloft and they clanked as he shook them at the mob.

"We all need to be clear about what's expected of us," Murphy said.

He didn't raise his voice. He didn't have to. Every man in the troop was deadly silent. There wasn't so much as the creak of harness.

"This isn't shift work at the local mill, bucks. This is a grand venture with grand fortunes at stake. Every man here had their chance to strike off, but every man here decided to be a part of this grand venture. That carries risk as well as reward.

"We're bound together sure as these irons bind. But the dear departed Riley thought he could slip those bonds. He thought he could steal what we've worked for and just slip away.

"It don't work that way, my fine young bucks. We're all in this together, and we're all in it to the end."

The gore streaked manacles chimed again as Murphy cast them into the churned snow.

"Thus for traitors like Riley, and thus for Bill Hadley. Sure and Riley wasn't alone in this. You see that mule skinning son of a bitch, and you bring him to me alive.

"But the Colonel has more business for us. No doubt you've heard of Cullen's man being killed out at the mines. Some red savage sending a message perhaps. So we'll send one of our own."

This met with nods of approval and hard grins. Soldiering was boring work for the most part. The prospect of some action was well received.

"The Indian is not what concerns me most, though. What concerns me is the Grinder, and more, the white-haired witch that set him upon us."

Some men spat, some crossed themselves or made the old sign to avert evil. Some did all three, but they were all afraid and that didn't please Murphy.

"Hear me well, boys. I want that woman dead. She's the Grinder's keeper. As long as she's out there, he'll keep coming. Even worse, as long as she lives, those clod-hopping Swedes have a hero and hope. Colonel Hayes is of a like mind and has doubled the bounty on her head. Two thousand in gold! What say you to that, my fine hounds?"

The men, so still and somber before, actually broke out in cheers. Fists were raised and the horses stamped. Cullen glanced at his own men and nodded. The bounty wasn't just for soldiers but for any man who brought Hayes the witch's head.

Murphy leapt to horse and set the spurs. He rode off with a yell, and his troopers followed with matching whoops and cries. Cullen was not as ready this time, and he and his men fell in behind the wild soldiers.

They tore straight through the center of town, and the hooves threw the night-frozen mud high into the air. The buildings were still empty this early, but Cullen saw some heads poke through the flaps of tents set up in the alleys. Not strictly necessary of course, but Cullen approved. Murphy put the fear in his troopers and was now putting the fear in the sheep-headed townsfolk.

The sergeant kept his usual breakneck pace going until they were well out of earshot of town. After that, he slowed enough to spare the horses but still pushed for speed. Cullen wondered just what was going on out at the mines.

He had no good reason to doubt Murphy's assessment of a lone scout. Murphy had shown himself to be an effective Indian fighter, and Cullen's strong talent lay as a highwayman. So Cullen didn't know enough to explain his misgivings.

The red men liked to mutilate their kills, it was true, but he had never heard of them being hung up like Patterson. For that matter, why Patterson?

Surely a scout after revenge or information would have taken one of the hated blue coats. None of Cullen's men had taken part in the raids and massacres, yet Cullen's gut told him the attack was purposely on his man. With an effort, he put it aside. They would know more when they got to the camp.

The sun climbed into a clear sky but did little to lessen the chill. The woods seemed quiet this morning, which made Cullen uneasy. The troop stretched into single file as the trail narrowed to a rocky defile, and Cullen held his men back to the rear.

Bushwhacker that he was, he was chary of good ambush spots like this one, and he wanted room to break loose if they were attacked. It was done almost unconsciously, but the column came to a sudden stop, and Cullen's hand went to his gun butt. His eyes scanned the trail sides for enemies, but there were no shots, and from here he couldn't see Murphy in the lead.

Then he heard the sergeant call out, and the column shot forward at the gallop. Cullen paused for only a moment and then waved on his own men with his pistol, unaware that he had drawn it. There were still no shots and no sign of attack, but after a moment, Cullen knew what had gotten Murphy moving. The morning breeze was in their faces and carried the smell of smoke.

The narrow trail gave out on a wider vale where the camp itself lay in sight of the miner's quarters. The horsemen poured out, drew weapons, and came abreast as they rode up on the camp. Or what was left of the camp, for even from here, they could see it was nothing but a pile of smoking embers.

They galloped up and drew rein. Murphy's horse danced in tight circles as the Irishman's eyes and pistol cast about, looking for someone to kill. There were no enemies in evidence, and the few soldiers standing about barely glanced at the troopers.

There were dead men laid out in a row. Cullen saw mostly the blue uniforms of Hayes' troopers and a few of the thugs that worked as overseers, but none of his own men. There were charred corpses in the ruins of the barracks, but they were burnt beyond recognition. Murphy yanked at the reins to bring his horse in front of a dazed-looking soldier.

"What happened?" Murphy said.

The soldier shrugged and looked around.

"We got hit, Sarge."

"I can see that, ye feck ye."

Murphy's fury was thickening his brogue.

"Was it Injuns? How many were there?"

A Nathaniel Caine Adventure

Again the soldier shrugged and looked around.

"I don't know, Sarge. I never really saw 'em. I never heard no war cries. There was just a lot of fire and shootin'."

"What do ye mean ye never saw 'em?"

Murphy dismounted and Cullen thought he might kill the trooper. The man must have had the same thought, for he started to back away and seemed to wake up a bit.

"I'm sorry, Sarge"

The man was a foot taller than Murphy, but fell back as if he were being charged by a bull.

"It happened fast. We were holed up in the barracks and it caught fire. We were busy with the fire when the shooting started. I didn't see how many there were."

"There was only one."

Everyone whirled at the voice. More than a few pointed weapons. That didn't seem to bother the tall man, who continued to stride forward.

"Swenson! Thank Christ," Murphy said and whirled away from the hapless trooper. "What the hell happened here? How could this be just one man?"

Swenson didn't answer right away. He had been carrying a rifle in his right hand. He moved it to the crook of his left elbow, and tugged on the ends of his long mustaches with his right.

Even in this motley crew, Swenson looked out of place. He towered over Murphy and the other Irishmen, and where they were dark he was fair: bone-white hair in two long braids and icy blue eyes. They all wore wool against the cold, but Swenson wore buckskins like the Indians, and if he felt the cold, he gave no sign of it.

Now he looked at the pile of dead men, then to the charred barracks. He threw a long look over his shoulder at the woods he had just left before bowing his head. After another moment he raised it and spoke.

"My people are great feudists, Murphy," he said. "From long before the days of Kings and long after."

The Irish were certainly no strangers to the blood feud, so Murphy nodded, though not patiently, and Swenson went on.

"Of course, when you're feuding you get in the habit of traveling in groups, but sometimes you find yourself short on men. I suppose the smart thing to do would be wait to attack, but my people had a trick for when you were alone. This was a hall burning."

Murphy looked at the smoky remains of his outpost. Not just the burnt barracks but the corrals, empty of horses. He didn't have the trail craft that Swenson did, but he could read a battlefield. He had never heard the phrase 'hall burning', yet he instantly grasped Swenson's meaning.

"So, you're one against many in a strong position. You wait 'til black of night. Sure and there were sentries, but they can be killed or even slipped past. And then you use what every man fears. Fire. Drive off the horses and light the roof. While the place blazes, you kill them as they run out or in the panic of fighting the fire."

"That's about it," Swenson said. "Once the shooting started, most of the men were still panicked and just shot into the woods whether they could see anything or not. I never got a shot off myself."

"Gallagher?"

Murphy knew the answer

"Dead."

"The miners?"

Murphy thought he knew the answer to this one as well. Even from up here, the little tent town that was the miners quarters had a curious empty look.

"Gone," Swenson said. "Probably back to their farms for now. I didn't follow their tracks. I figured the attacker was more important."

Murphy nodded again, but he had the same decision. Round up the sod busters or deal with the attack. The Swedes would surely run to their farms as Swenson thought, but would just as surely try to escape the valley. They needed them to work the mines, but they were slow moving and could be gathered up later.

And none too gentle my wayward lambs, he thought.

"So the Indian then," he said aloud. "I suppose it's too much to hope for one bit of good news this morning. Did you find him?"

"No. I lost the trail," Swenson said. "I don't think it's an Indian, either."

"The report yesterday said Indian."

Murphy's mind raced even faster. The whole enterprise depended on keeping the mine a secret. If this hall burner got the word out that there was gold in the ground here, the whole thing was finished.

"He wears moccasins like an Indian, but he walks heel-to-toe. And…"

Swenson looked behind him again.

"There's something you should see."

"I'm in a hurry, Swenson," Murphy said.

"You should still see it for yourself," Swenson said and jerked his chin at Cullen. "You should see this too."

Murphy left orders to check on the gold and water the horses before following Swenson. It was just the three of them and they went on foot at Swenson's insistence. It didn't take long to see why, for after a hundred yards or so the trees started to close up. Another hundred yards and it was almost impassable for a mounted man, and soon even the men were limited to single file.

"Don't worry," Swenson said over his shoulder, "it opens up a ways ahead."

It 'opened up' abruptly into a good sized clearing, more or less circular, that the men filed into. Swenson stopped, and Murphy and Cullen looked around. The tracker nodded upwards and both looked.

"Damn, Cullen," Murphy said. "That's most of you're gang gone, eh?"

Cullen said nothing, just stared at the five men in the trees. His men.

"This wasn't Indians," Swenson said. "They'll mutilate a corpse and torture prisoners, but these men were killed quickly, if roughly. And why hang them?"

For each man was trussed, tied by his wrists and hauled up to swing from the limbs overhead. It was difficult to tell if they were killed first and then hung, or the the other way around. Cullen supposed it didn't matter. What mattered was the way they were hung.

It wasn't possible. Even if the Grinder hadn't done his work, the night on the mountain would have finished the dark haired stranger. Others had died true, but only *his* men were being displayed.

It was a message. First your men, then you. He only had six men left. Four he had brought with him today and two left in town.

It wasn't possible, but it could only be one man.

"We need to get back to town, quick," Cullen said. "I know who did this."

A Stranger in Hartsburgh

Tor went through the motions of opening the saloon with no real hope of business. Everyone had seen or heard that the madman Murphy was up at the Colonel's house last night. That meant the Grinder would be coming and folks would make themselves scarce.

When the curse had first been laid on the town, most folk weren't worried. Most took it for the mad ranting of a grief-stricken woman. Tor himself had thought that very thing until the Grinder started coming.

At first it was just the Colonel's house. Who could blame her for her grief and her rage? *No one shall sleep beneath his roof without bloodshed by sunrise.*

Tor's grandmother had told him stories of the old days, of trolls and witches. Tor shuddered to remember the woman in the street with the blood running down her white arms. It was a witch right out of Grandma's tales of wicked revenge.

He looked up the main street to the Colonel's empty house and shuddered again to remember that first night. The screams, and the gunfire, and over it all that horrible roar. The roar like a landslide and then the silence.

And now the beast had been out again, and that usually kept folks away from town. Tor wouldn't have bothered opening, but Murphy and his wild troop had woken him anyway. The clop of hooves sounded from up the way, and Tor saw two riders approaching. Maybe he would get some customers after all.

They were Elisha Cullen's men, a pair that stuck together. They only gave their names as Smith and Jones as if it was a joke. It was a joke Tor didn't get.

"Morning, Tor," said Smith.

Or maybe it was Jones. Tor hated them both.

"Good morning, gentlemen," Tor said and plastered a smile on his face. "I have just opened."

"Good," said Jones. "We're hungry."

"Ah. Yes. Well, as I said I just opened the doors," Tor said. "There is no food yet. The coffee isn't even ready."

"That's alright," said Smith.

The men shouldered past Tor and sauntered into the saloon.

"We'll just spend a little time with the girls while the grub's cooking."

"The girls, yes."

Tor tried to hover and keep his distance at the same time. He didn't like their attitude this morning (not that he ever did) and was keenly aware of Murphy's absence. Murphy was the only one who could keep these scum in line. "They are still abed in the tents."

"Well, go wake 'em up ya tow-headed idiot," said Jones.

He leaned over the bar and snagged a bottle of whiskey.

"Ah, I should really stay near the bar in case someone wants to buy a drink."

Tor still kept his distance, but he put a slight emphasis on the word buy. Jones had pulled the cork with his teeth and now gave Tor a sharp look. He spit the cork on the floor.

"You gittin uppity with me?" he asked and took a long pull.

"You know how these fish-eatin bastards are, Jonesy," said Smith and reached into his pocket. "All they care about's money."

He threw a few nuggets on the floor and the gold rang heavily on the planks.

"The cards were good to us last night, Tor," Smith said. "We'll wake up the whores ourselves. You just see to that breakfast."

He spit a long stream of tobacco juice over the gold and walked out the back with Jones. Tor stood in the spot as if rooted. He stared at the gold, which had made little craters in the sawdust on the floor.

The tents where the girls slept were directly in back of the saloon, and Tor could hear their groans of protest as Smith and Jones rousted them. They returned presently and the soiled doves were rubbing sleep from their eyes. They were still in their nightclothes and looked like a small flock of sheep. Tor watched as Smith and Jones herded the little lambs upstairs to the rooms.

He continued to stare at the doors for long moments after they closed, but soon enough his eyes dropped back to the gleaming gold. Tor heaved a sigh and knelt down to gather up the heavy nuggets. He stood and turned and nearly dropped the gold in fright.

"Mother of Christ!" Tor cried in his native tongue. He staggered back a step and clutched at his chest, for there was one of the great brown mountain bears. It stood on its hind legs with it's front paws on the counter. Tor shook his head and looked again, for surely it could not be.

It was no bear, just a man with a bear skin cloak, head and all. Tor shook his head again and stared, suspicious. He hadn't just *thought* the man looked like a bear, he had *seen* a bear.

Tor could get no real sense of the man except height. He glanced at the counter, and where a moment ago he had seen great furry paws, he now saw merely long-fingered hands, quite human. Yet his heart still pounded, and he actually looked at the back door which Smith and Jones had left open.

"Good morning, sir. Are you the proprietor here?"

Tor started again, though the voice was quite ordinary, even pleasant. He opened his mouth, but no words came out. One of the long-fingered hands indicated the glass of the display case.

"I'm interested in this pipe," the man said. "Very interested."

The bear head swiveled to regard him. Or rather, the man turned to regard him, but Tor could only stare at the gleaming teeth of the bear head.

"Of course," the voice came from within. "It has a fearsome look does it not? I beg your pardon."

The long-fingered hands came up and took down the hood. The man shrugged out of the great pelt and laid it on the counter. Tor let out a breath he hadn't known he was holding. The man was white despite the savage aspect of his clothes, for under the bearskin he wore a fringed leather shirt and his black hair was rather long. But the face was white and no Indian had grey eyes like this fellow.

"I...that is," Tor stammered for a bit before collecting himself. "I am sorry. I took you for an Indian. I mean no offense."

"I take no offense," the man said with a shrug. "Now then. What can you tell me about this beautiful pipe? I'm especially interested in where you acquired it."

"One of the locals sold it to me," Tor said.

He started to move toward the counter, hesitant at first, skirting around the edge of the room until he could get the counter between him and the stranger. Tor had a .36 under the counter that he had never had occasion to fire. Marshal Rollins, when he was alive, had told Tor he should put a shotgun under there, but Tor had never bothered. He wished now that he had, for the stranger, despite the well spoken and pleasant tone, had a predatory look about him. It could have been his savage dress. The only white man Tor knew who dressed like the Indians was Sven Swenson. No comfort there, for the scout was a wolfish man like this one.

"Possibly one of the gentlemen I just saw go upstairs?" the stranger asked.

"No, sir," Tor said, "it wasn't them."

"Perhaps a friend of theirs, though?"

"Well, yes actually. How did you know that?"

"Lucky guess," said the stranger. "It's a small town after all, and there don't appear to be many people here."

"Yes, I suppose so Mister...?"

"Caine's the name. Nathaniel Caine."

A Nathaniel Caine Adventure

The stranger held out his hand and Tor shook it. Caine shook back, but when Tor tried to take his hand back Caine held on. He didn't grip hard enough to hurt, just hard enough so Tor couldn't let go.

Tor didn't know what to do, so he just stood there while the stranger stared at him with flinty eyes. Caine smiled and Tor thought again of a wolf. With an effort, Tor broke his gaze, but still Caine held his hand and Tor noticed Caine wore a heavy silver ring on his little finger.

"Now then, Mister Nielsen."

Caine finally let Tor's hand go.

"How much for the pipe?"

"It's used, but well cared for," Tor said rubbing his hand. "Very well made, too. Eighty dollars."

"Oh, come now, Mister Nielsen," Caine said. "An honest profit is all well and good, but eighty is a bit dear. Why, it's highway robbery."

"I suppose I could come down a bit," Tor said. "How does fifty sound?"

"I'll give you thirty," Caine said. "A fair price considering what you paid for it...and where you got it."

Caine's voice had turned hard, and Tor thought it best not to argue, so he just nodded.

"And breakfast, Mister Nielsen," Caine said. "I've quite an appetite."

"The kitchen isn't open yet, Mister Caine."

"There's coffee, at least," Caine said. "And surely I smell bacon cooking."

Tor turned and sniffed and he thought he could indeed smell bacon. His wife must have risen and started breakfast.

"Well, sir," Tor said, "I suppose for three dollars you can eat your fill."

"I don't suppose you have cream for the coffee?"

"Yes, sir. We have cream."

"Excellent," Caine said.

He reached down, plucked a pair of saddlebags off the floor and dropped them on the counter. Tor hadn't really noticed them and he looked outside now. The only horses belonged to Smith and Jones. If Caine had ridden, his horse was tethered elsewhere.

Caine undid the buckle on one of the bags and rummaged for a moment. Tor assumed he was looking for money, but Caine brought out a coil of rope. He looped it around his shoulder and walked away.

Tor watched, perplexed as he strode up the stairs and along the narrow balcony to the room Smith, or perhaps Jones, had taken his whores. Caine didn't pause or knock, just turned the knob and walked in.

He couldn't make out the words, but he heard Smith's voice in an angry interrogative cut short. The whores started screaming and, jaded as they were by their work, they still sounded like scared little girls. Close on came the sounds of a scuffle, furniture moving and the crash of breaking glass. Tor hoped it was a basin and not the window, for window's were expensive and hard to get.

A Nathaniel Caine Adventure

The other door opened and Jones came out on the balcony. He had pulled on his trousers and had the hammer back on his Colt. The scuffle ended with a final sounding thud, and the girls ran out.

Jones was a wily scoundrel and didn't run into the room, rather he edged up to the doorway in a semi-crouch. He peered into the room, but there was no sound and apparently no enemy to see, for Jones didn't fire. It was only a moment surely, but to Tor it seemed a long time Jones stood there.

Tor had a wild thought; the stranger had used the rope to climb out the window. Then there was the bark of pistol fire, three shots, and Jones jerked. He fell to his knees and Tor could see the bullet holes in the wall he had been leaning against.

The stranger stepped into the doorway, tall and grim with a smoking pistol in each hand. A long stride took him to Jones, and he pinned the hand with the Colt to the planks. Jones' breath came ragged and his head hung. Caine simply waited. Finally, Jones looked up and the terror that came over his face was plain, even from where Tor stood rooted.

"No," Jones gasped.

"Yes," Caine said and put a bullet through Jones' head.

Caine replaced his pistols and stooped for the Colt. He gave it a quick inspection before lowering the hammer and adding it to the collection on his belt. He made shooing gestures at the terrified prostitutes, and they scampered down the stairs and out the back. The coil of rope was still over Caine's shoulder, and he removed it now before disappearing back into the room.

"What in God's name is going on?" came a harsh whisper to Tor's left.

He hadn't moved during the violence, but now he jumped and turned. His wife was poking her head through the side door.

"Nothing," Tor said and managed to keep his voice steady, "get back in the kitchen, woman."

She gave him a withering look, but she obeyed. Tor looked around at a complete loss. He wasn't sure what had just happened and was less sure what to do. Rough this town was, but he had actually managed to avoid any real violence in the place. Only luck perhaps, and that luck had just run out.

Tor retrieved the .36 from under the counter and almost laughed, for it seemed little more than a toy now. He stuffed it in his pocket anyway and Caine came back out, trailing the rope.

He bent down to Jones and started going through his pockets. He made quick work of that and started binding the corpse's hands at the wrist. This he also did with quick sure movements, and he was humming to himself like a man at an easy chore.

Caine stood and grasped the rail with a hand. He leaned and pulled and gave it a testing glance. He nodded, satisfied, and threw a few turns of the rope about the rail and a quick hitch. With that, Caine stooped again, and there must be considerable strength in the lean frame for he picked up Jones' body and heaved it over the rail.

The dead man reached the end of his rope with a sharp snap of hemp and twisted and turned. Caine ducked back into the room, and in a moment came back dragging Smith, similarly bound at the

A Nathaniel Caine Adventure

end of a rope of his own. Caine made the line fast and heaved Smith over as well.

Smith wore dingy long johns and his head lolled. Caine stood back with fists on hips. Tor thought again of a man at chores, the satisfied air of a job that needed doing being taken care of. But then Caine looked up. The tall man's face was cold and keen as a blade, anger and rage were there trying to break away from a steely control.

Tor didn't understand why this had happened, but he knew now that it wasn't random. Caine had business with these men—some vengeance—and he thought again of his Granddame's tales of feuding. Caine mastered his features and came down the stairway to stand in front of the counter.

"Now then, Nielsen," Caine said, and his voice was still perfectly normal.

Tor didn't want to look Caine in the eye, but he felt he had no choice.

"How…?"

Tor was going to ask him how he knew his name. Caine had been using it, but he was almost sure he hadn't given it.

"If you're going to shoot me, you'd better go for the head," Caine said. "Even assuming you could outdraw me from your pocket, that .36 isn't going to kill me before I put a bullet through your heart."

Tor felt frozen but managed to shake his head the tiniest fraction.

"Very well," Caine said and clapped his hands together. "The pipe."

Whatever spell he was under broke, and Tor took a deep breath. He couldn't have been holding it for the entire episode, but it felt that way. He felt like he could move again, so he took out the meerschaum and Caine began to inspect it.

"The rodent who sold you this," he said. "I don't suppose you know if he smoked it?"

"No, I don't think so," Tor said. "It was Will Parson and he smokes cigarettes."

"Cigarettes?" Caine said. "You know I met a cowboy in Kansas who smoked cigarettes. He rolled them one-handed in the saddle. Never took his other hand off the reins."

"Oh, yeah?"

"Indeed. A neat trick to be sure, but I never cared for them myself. Still, I'm glad this Will Parson hasn't had his filthy mouth on it. I don't suppose you know where this Parson is now?"

"Probably with Cullen," Tor said. "Elisha Cullen that is."

"Yes. I know that name."

"Murphy and a bunch of soldiers rode out about sunup," Tor said. "I believe Cullen and some of his men were with them."

Tor waited for Caine to ask him where they had gone and worried about his answers. From the beginning, Hayes had made it clear that strangers were to be made unwelcome, and obviously the gold mines needed to stay a secret. He also knew that if he tried to lie to Caine, the strange man would know it instantly. Caine, though, just nodded and laid some coins on the counter.

A Nathaniel Caine Adventure

"I think those fellows overstated their take at the card tables," he said.

He selected two of the many revolvers at his waist and laid them on the counter next to the money.

"There's also the matter of damages and cleanup. You seem a merchant who's open to barter. Does this seem a fair trade?"

Tor looked down at the heavy pistols. One was the Colt that Jones had held just minutes before. Caine had lain them with the butts toward Tor. He stared at the polished wood and thought hard about the bargain being offered. Finally, he nodded.

"More than fair," Tor said. "And I can give you a couple tins of decent tobacco."

Caine nodded himself, clearly satisfied. He gathered his new purchases and took a seat at one of the tables. He sat in the middle of the room with his back to the open front door. It seemed an odd choice for such a chary man, but Tor shrugged and got Caine some coffee.

Tor didn't really want to look at the hanging men, but he couldn't really help himself, either. So he was looking right at Smith when his eyes fluttered and snapped open. He was setting a small pitcher of cream on the table and almost spilled it in fright.

Caine just gazed at Smith while the man tried to work out his predicament. He shook his head to clear the blood from his eyes, and that set him to swinging. He glanced at Tor and Caine, and then side to side. When he saw Jones hanging nearby, he started to struggle at his bonds and grunt, fighting panic.

Caine said nothing while this went on. He just poured cream in his coffee and began to stir it. The rhythmic clink of spoon on cup drew Smith's eye, and he abruptly ceased his struggles.

He stared at Caine, and Tor saw recognition and disbelief at war on Smith's gory face. Caine saw it too, and he chuckled a bit before taking a sip of coffee.

"It can't be," Smith said.

"Can't be what?" Caine said.

"You should be dead."

"Perhaps," said Caine. "But I might say the same of you."

"Come on, mister it wasn't me."

Smith didn't try to hide his fear.

"It was the boss. It was Cullen. Please don't kill me."

"Kill you?" Caine said.

He took a sip of coffee and appeared to be thinking it over. Caine drew a revolver and thumbed the hammer before aiming it at Smith's chest. Smith shook his head and made desperate grunting noises. He swung and jerked his legs in a vain effort to get away, but the bore just followed him. The front of Smith's already dirty long johns darkened in a quick spreading stain. Smith's urine ran down his leg and dripped off his foot to spatter in the sawdust below. Caine turned to Tor, though the pistol stayed on target.

"I suppose you'll add that to my cleaning bill, eh Mr. Nielsen?"

Tor laughed. He couldn't help himself. Caine lowered the hammer on the revolver and laid it on the table. "I'm not going to kill you, dog. Calm down before you fill your back flap as well."

Smith stopped mewling, but his eyes were still wide with terror.

"Are you gonna let me down, mister?" Smith said.

"I said I'm not going to kill you," Caine said. "You'll have the same chance I had. Of course, there is the matter of compensation."

"What's that?" Smith said.

"You owe me, you thieving bastard," Caine said. "I was quite fond of that Smith & Wesson, but I find myself admiring these Remingtons. They seem quite stout, but they balance well."

"Take 'em mister," Smith said. "They're yours."

"I understand they make a repeating rifle that uses the same cartridges," Caine said. "That would be handy for a traveling man."

"Yeah, I got a rifle like that," Smith said. "It's in a scabbard on my horse. You can have it."

"Of course, a man can't travel in these parts without a horse," Caine said, "and mine was stolen."

"You can have mine," Smith said. "The saddle and tack too."

"Well, there you go," Caine said. "Do we need to draw up a bill of sale? I'm sure Mr. Nielsen will witness it."

"No, no," said Smith. "We got a deal."

"Excellent," Caine said. "Mr. Nielsen, I'm starving."

"Oh. Yes, sir."

Tor hurried into the kitchen. He came back with bacon, eggs, and fried potatoes, and Caine set to. Tor brought biscuits with butter and managed to find some preserves as well as a few tins of peaches. Caine devoured all that was set in front of him.

Smith struggled against his bonds and made a few attempts to talk Caine into letting him down. Caine chuckled at these and continued eating. Finally, Caine had his fill and pushed his plate away. He opened one of his new tins of tobacco while Tor filled his coffee cup again.

"Won't you join me, Mr. Nielsen?" he asked. "It's nice to have a smoke after a good meal, and I'd like to hear about your town."

"Hey!"

Smith had been silent for some time, but now his head came up and he glared at Tor.

"You don't say *nothin*, Tor. We all agreed."

"Shut up," Tor said with sudden venom. "I am done with all of you."

He turned to Caine, but the man's face remained impassive while he packed his pipe. Tor nodded, apparently to himself, and went to the bar. He gave the whiskey bottles a hard look before grabbing a beer mug. Tor poured himself a full mug and sat at the table with his back to Smith and Jones. He took a long pull off his mug and sighed. Caine pushed the tobacco across the table.

"Thank you," Tor said and Caine nodded.

Tor started to pack his own pipe, a stout briar that had traveled with him from the old country. Neither man spoke as they got their fires going, and soon a decent cloud of blue-white smoke hung between them. Tor regarded the strange figure before him and broke the silence.

A Nathaniel Caine Adventure

"Who are you, Caine?"

"A traveler, as I said," Caine shrugged. "I was delivering a bag of mail when I was waylaid."

"Mail?" Tor said. "From Bill Hadley?"

"The same."

"So at least he is still alive," Tor said. "I was beginning to wonder. He was..."

Tor broke off and took another long pull of beer. He went back to regarding Caine as he puffed on his pipe. A traveler the man said, but surely there was more. And yet, how could just one man do anything against Murphy and his dragoons? Against the Grinder and his keeper? Tor fought down fear and plunged on.

"It's like this, Caine," he said. "I have been waiting on word from Hadley. He was to bring a load of supplies and I was going to pay to use his wagons to get away from Hartsburgh."

"You son of a bitch," Smith spat from where he hung. "Hayes is gonna have your hide for this."

"Perhaps we should have this conversation elsewhere," Caine said, but Tor just waved his hand.

"I said I'm done with them, and I meant it. I made a deal with the Devil when I sided with Colonel Hayes. I may not be able to make amends for that, but I mean to try. Or am I wrong? You are here to help this town, yes?"

"I am, Mr. Nielsen," Caine said, "if I can. You say you were waiting for Hadley's wagons. Are there no wagons in town?"

"Not in town, nor on the farms," Tor said. "Hayes confiscated every one of them. Most are broken down and stored up at the fort. They have a few out at the mine, but they are always guarded. Only a few of the farms are running. Hayes has most of them working in the mines, and they sleep under guard."

"In a camp in the hills?" said Caine and Tor nodded. "Not any longer."

"You freed them? By yourself?"

"I helped them free themselves," Caine said. "They have gone back to their farms for now, but obviously they're far from safe. They all fear Hayes and his hound, this Murphy fellow, but they all fear the Grinder too.

As you say, there are no wagons to move them out and a journey on foot would be hard. Hard on it's own, but dangerous with the monster about. Besides, a mounted troop would hunt them down with no trouble at all."

"Yah. Even if we had wagons, Murphy would move faster."

"All too true," Caine said. "So. Both Hayes and the Grinder must be dealt with, and so here I am to see what I'm up against. Tell me about the Grinder. What is it and where did it come from."

"Well, sir, that's a tale," Tor said and gave a great sigh. "A tale that needs another beer. Would you like one? Or whiskey if you prefer?"

"A tale, you say? Well, then…I'll have a beer."

Tor's Tale

"My grandmother was a wise woman," Tor began after a deep draught. "She knew many stories and had many sayings. One of them went, 'If a thing seems too good to be, true it probably isn't.' I never knew if that meant it wasn't too good or it wasn't true, but now I know it's the same thing.

"My people are mostly farmers and fishermen, going way back. My father was a merchant, though, and that seemed better than pulling nets. Easier at least. When I came to America, there were plenty of people from the old country, but they were all farmers. There wasn't much room for them or for merchants unless you kept moving west.

"It was Nils Olsen who came to me with the offer of Hayes' venture. Too good to be true, it seemed. They already had a sizable group of farmers who were promised large tracts in the valley. The Army was already securing the area from Indians, and the troopers would even escort the wagon train. Nils himself is a farmer, but he knew the little town would need a merchant, and there was already a store built and waiting."

"Hayes' venture you call it," Caine said, "but what was in it for him?"

"Profit to be sure," Tor said, "but it seemed honest profit he was after. I met him, for he had come personally to gather the settlers. It all seemed like a good plan. He wanted to take an active hand in the settling. He and his troopers would provide protection, and the fort would buy provender from the farms. He offered lots to families with no stake at very reasonable terms of rent. Too reasonable, maybe. Too good to be true."

"How long before they found gold?" Caine asked.

"I came out in early spring. It was late the next spring when they found it. The scout, Swenson, was hunting with some of the men. They found a nugget on the banks of a stream. This wasn't in the valley but up in the mountains, so there was no real claim. Since Colonel Hayes was the only real authority, he was consulted, and showed himself again to be a man of vision.

"He put together a group of workers to pan the stream and make some exploration of the hills thereabout. It was clear soon enough that there were workable veins and there was fortune to be had. But still no claim."

"I suppose the Colonel had a vision for that, too."

"He did," Tor said. "It was his idea to keep it quiet. He told us what happened at Sutter's Mill, and we didn't want our little farm town turning into a boomtown. Keep it to ourselves and we would all get shares. The smallest share would still be a fortune most of us couldn't dream of. So farmers became miners, and soon enough they hit rich veins."

"That's a big secret for so many to keep," said Caine. "No one wrote to relatives back east or bragged to travelers?"

"Well, we didn't have a great number of travelers to begin with. Mostly the wagon drivers with supplies and the like," Tor said.

"The few we did have began to taper off, and soon disappeared altogether."

"Ah," Caine said. "I think I see Cullen's part in this more fully. And I'm thinking any mail went by Hadley, so Hayes had complete control over written messages."

"Most folks didn't have anyone to write to anyway," Tor said. "Any relatives were the family we had here or back in the old country."

"When did it go bad?"

"Well, there were signs pretty quick," said Tor. "There were no more hunting parties, and if you went out riding or some such, you would likely run into one of Murphy's patrols. They said they were keeping us safe from the Indians, but it was pretty clear we were being watched.

The men doing the work at the mine were all farmers, and the men in charge were all Hayes' men. The foremen kept pushing the miners for more and more work, and there was grumbling. Just grumbling, though, for everyone's share would make the poorest of us kings."

"King of what?" Caine said.

"There you have it, Caine. It was only a matter of time before somebody wanted to cash out. Christensen was the first, and Hayes tried to talk him out of it. It got a little heated, but finally he was allowed to take his share and go if he swore to keep the mine a secret. A few more families followed, but not many. It seemed you could leave whenever you wanted, so why not stay and gather yet more wealth?"

Tor fell silent and stared into his beer. Caine supposed the ones who left were not living the high life in New York City with their new-dug gold. Tor's silence continued and finally Caine asked, "How were the murders discovered?"

"It was a couple of young boys. The men weren't supposed to spend any time hunting, as I've said, so these boys decided to bring home some venison.

"They came across a slaughtered family and came running to the mines to report it. The overseers tried to keep the workers there, but they went anyway. The whole family was murdered and left to rot. It was clear it wasn't Indians.

"All the gold they left with was gone and the horses, but the wagon was still there. Everything they owned was still there, rifle and ammunition, cloth and food. Indians would have stripped it.

"The overseers argued still that it was Indians, and there was a scuffle. The goons were outnumbered, so they couldn't make much of it there. It was Willem Jorgensen that rallied the workers, and a group of them marched into town to confront the Colonel.

"Foolish it was," Tor sighed. "They were a small group and not even armed, so I don't know what they thought would happen. Hayes was sitting right here when they showed up. He was waiting for them, him and Murphy.

"Hayes maintained that it was Indians, and that it would be smart for everyone to stay under the Colonel's protection. Jorgenson wouldn't have it, though, and ranted and raved for a bit, but Hayes just laughed at him.

"Jorgenson was a young man and a hot head. He knocked over Hayes' drink and took a swing at him, but it never came close. Murphy was on him like a terrier on a rat. Jorgenson was a big tall fellow, but Murphy used that club of his. It was over in a second. The other workers tried to move in, but Murphy had his soldiers all about. They didn't even have to fire a shot. The mob drew back before the guns, and the soldiers drove them out into the street with rifle butts and kicks."

"And what happened to young Jorgenson?" Caine asked.

The beer mugs were empty, but Tor made no move to refill them, nor did Caine ask. He sensed they were coming to the crux of the matter and didn't want to break Tor's momentum.

"A dark day," Tor said, "and a dark night. Murphy had him brought around and dragged out front. They tied him to a hitching rail and tore off his shirt and lashed him. Murphy himself swung the whip. Hayes sat in a chair smoking a cigar.

"It was awful. I know they use whipping as a punishment in the army, but this wasn't human.

"Jorgenson was a big fellow, as I said, and strong. He tried to stand up and bear it, but Murphy just kept laying on the lash. Jorgenson was screaming at ten lashes and collapsed at twenty. By thirty he was begging. I stopped counting at forty. But Murphy wouldn't stop.

"Jorgenson's blood was pouring over the rail and making a pool in the dirt. It flew in drops from the whip, and still Murphy swung. There was no space on his back that wasn't striped, so Murphy hit his arms. He wouldn't stop even when the skin was gone, and he laid the whip right into the meat of him.

"Jorgenson's screams were terrible. but the sound of the whip was worse. Jorgenson finally passed out, thank Christ, but Murphy kept on and there was the sound of that wet, bloody leather eating Jorgenson alive.

"None of us made a move to stop it. The soldiers had guns on us, but maybe we could have rushed them. No one even yelled to stop. We just stood there terrified. Finally the Colonel held up his hand and Murphy stopped. He dropped the whip in the street and dusted his hands, like he was just a crofter finished chopping some wood.

"Hayes went to inspect Jorgenson. He lifted the boy's head by his hair, and Jorgenson opened his eyes. He still lived, and I'll never forget that moan any more than I'll forget the sound of that whip. Hayes dropped him and faced the crowd. I think we were expecting a speech or an explanation or something, but all he did was nod. 'Sergeant Murphy,' he said. 'Lock it down.'

"Murphy and his men swung into action, and it's obvious they had planned for this. They rounded up all the mine workers. Took them off their farms and drove them into the camp at the mines.

"I heard some folks tried to resist, but they were just shot for their trouble. I heard, too, that some women and children were killed, and that pretty much broke the farmers' will.

"Some of us in town had a choice. Keep on with Hayes in charge, or end up shot. Or like Jorgenson. We all picked Hayes."

"So," Caine said. "Colonel Hayes is in charge of everything. He has the whole town under his control and the mine. He controls the surrounding territory including the roads. Murphy and his guns for the town, goons for the mine, Cullen and his highwaymen for the roads. Everything perfect. Except..."

"Except for Ana," Tor said. "Jorgenson's mother. My grandmother knew many stories, as I said. They were old stories, Caine, of witches and warriors. Makers and singers in the woods, and creatures that dwelt there. Swart elves and trolls who turned to the stone they came from if the sun caught them.

"Many of them scared me and my brothers when we were children. My mother didn't like us to hear them, for she felt they weren't Christian. I never really believed them, although my brother, I think, still worries a night hag will come for him in his bed."

"Now though..." Tor shrugged. "It seems there was wisdom in Granny's stories as well as her sayings.

"It was near sundown when Ana came into town for her boy, that poor woman, walked all the way. She cried out when she saw him, and we all went out as she ran up and dropped in the dirt beside him.

"She lifted his head, and he moaned, and I'm damned if I know how the boy yet lived. He was muttering in Swedish, talking to his Pa, he who died years ago, you understand. Apologizing for not taking care of his Ma.

"She crooned and soothed him, and her face was twisted in pain, but her voice was steady. Maybe he heard her, maybe he was holding on for her. I don't know, but he died at last with his head in her hands.

"She gave out a keen that cut the heart, and we all hung our heads. In shame as much as grief, for none of us had helped him.

"She wrapped her arms around him trying to lift him up or maybe just hugging her son. But she is a slight woman and Willem was a big man, as I've said. Ana stopped her keening abruptly and stood.

"I said she was slight, but she held her head high, and she looked queenly and dangerous. She cast a fell gaze all around, and nobody could meet her eye."

"'Who has done this evil thing to my son?' she demanded. I'm sure everyone wanted to slink away, as I did myself, but we just stood there, abashed.

"'It was Murphy, Ana,' someone said.

"'Murphy's the dog is all,' Anna said, 'and it's Colonel Hayes that's the master. And who here raised a hand or voice to help my dear son? Or even went to him? To cut him down and ease his torment?'

"She raised up her arms and the setting sun shone on the son's blood, glistening on the mother's hands. 'My son's blood. My blood,' she said in her hard voice. 'Blood will be answered with blood. You've all bowed to your king and his piles of gold, but what have you bought with it? Deep your king has delved in the dark mountains. Who knows what he has uncovered in the black of the earth? No one shall sleep beneath his roof without bloodshed by sunrise.'

A Nathaniel Caine Adventure

"Then she began to sing. To chant in a tongue I couldn't understand, for it wasn't Swedish. Willem's father was a Swede, yeah, but not Anna. They say she was a Finn, and I should tell you, in the old days the Finns had a reputation as makers, magic users you understand. In fact there are places where they still have that reputation, and if none of us took it seriously then, we do now."

"Nothing happened at first. Anna chanted and sang all the way up to Hayes' house. I didn't follow her up there, but some did.

"They say she lay her bloody hands on his door and sang until he came out. He opened the door himself, and they say there were no words between them.

"She knelt as if before a king and held out her red hands. Hayes just laughed and turned his back. The door closed on the old woman and she rose, returned down the street and walked into the red sunset.

"Some folk put their heads together and whispered, but most of us got quickly indoors and no one touched the corpse for fear of Murphy and the soldiers. In the morning it was gone and Hayes was angry, but no one would admit to moving him. I don't think anyone did. I think it was Anna, though how she managed it I can't imagine.

"It wasn't long before they had everything to their liking, and Hayes had a night of celebration. It started here in the saloon, and all the soldiers were drunk as lords. Later in the night, the colonel and those close to him retired to his house for a more private party.

"I wasn't there that night, I heard what happened from some of the girls and from talk later, so maybe it's exaggeration. It was a festive night apparently, with food and drink in plenty. Hayes had all the prettiest girls up there for his cronies, and there was boasting of how they were lords of these mountains, and when they had got all the gold they would be lords wherever they went.

"Long into the night they caroused, but finally they slept. It must have been in the deepest dark when the thing did it's work, for no one marked his coming or his going.

"In the morning, Hayes woke to find his fine house a place of slaughter. Men were ripped to shreds and blood painted the walls, and it was a horrible sight.

"More horrible to think that so many slept through it, drunk or no. Six men were lying in shattered bits, ground to paste.

"The gunmen poured out like ants from a kicked hill. They scoured the town and the countryside. Some thought it was a band of men and some thought it was a beast. They weren't scared yet, just angry. But they found nothing.

"So that night, a band of soldiers stayed in the house. This time the beast's coming was marked. Deep in the night the house crackled with gunfire. Something fell on the soldiers, but even with their guns most of them were killed.

"One man was taken off. He could be heard screaming in the woods for a bit. When they found him, it was like the others. Utterly ruined as if he had been put under a millstone.

"The troopers were even angrier, but now they were also terrified. The survivors spoke of a hulking monster, and they swore they hit it with their weapons.

"Again they searched the forest, but if it took hurt from the bullets there was no sign. The same thing happened the next night and they searched the whole town, thinking maybe one of us was harboring the thing.

"Murphy sent the scout, Swenson, a peerless tracker of man and beast. He found tracks, but he couldn't say what made them and the trail disappeared.

"They went out to the Jorgenson's farm, but they found nothing. Ana wasn't there and neither was the body of her son. The soldiers burned it down anyway and slaughtered all the stock. Just killed them and left them to rot.

"The thing came again, and I don't know how Colonel Hayes managed to escape. An ambush was set the next night, but not in the house. Soldiers were all over the town, on the roofs and hiding at windows.

"It was that night that I saw him. I don't know who first named him Grinder, but it was well placed. Surely he must be a troll straight out of my old Gran's stories. It stalked straight up the street, and it's moving was like the grinding of boulders. He grinds when he moves, and he grinds up men when he catches them.

"The soldiers opened fire and there was no way they could have all missed, but it shrugged off the flying bullets. It went after the men hiding in the barber's shop and killed them all. Murphy tried to corner it, but it smashed it's way out and escaped again into the forest.

"The Grinder came again the next night, but he found Hayes not at home. The Colonel had abandoned his house to sleep in the fort.

"The Grinder attacked the fort, but he couldn't get in. The monster raged and all the mountains echoed with his roars. This went on for many nights, but the Grinder never got in.

"That's when he turned to the town. Many people have been taken, Caine. No weapons can harm him and no doors can stop him, no matter how strongly they are barred. "The Grinder comes at will and kills however he wants. Maybe only carrying off one or maybe slaughtering everyone in a house, but every night he comes.

"We worried much for the miners with nothing but tents between them and the terror. But here was a bit of a joke, maybe an accident or maybe the witch knew her business.

"The miners were fine. The overseers had been on watch since the first attack, but the thing left the camp alone. He was sighted once or twice and fired on, but he never went after the tents or any of the farms.

"No one would sleep under his roof, she said, but that's what we were doing in town. All these buildings belong to Hayes. So we who are left live in tents and alleys, and it's been a hard cold winter, I can tell you. Hard and cold as any I had back in Sweden.

"And now Spring is here and you are here, though what you can do against the Grinder I don't know. But if I can help you, I will."

The Hall Burning

Caine finished the last of his beer as Tor finished his tale. Here at least was the why of the monster's coming—revenge for a kinsman wronged and slain. The creature had been called, and Caine had no reason to doubt Tor's story of a mother's curse.

Caine was working on a knot just as surely as when he hung on the tree, and this new strand felt right. Indeed there was only one thing Tor's story had left him to question.

"How is it," Caine said, "that the Grinder ravages the town at will, but can't get at Hayes in the fort?"

"Who can say?" Tor said. "No other wall or door has been proof against him, but the fort stands. It is a nasty stalemate. Ana can't get at Colonel Hayes in his fort, and Hayes can't find the witch in the forest."

"I have been in the forest and seen no sign of her," Caine said. "Of course, I wasn't searching for her, and I was trying to avoid the Grinder. I think I shall have to look at this fort and meet Colonel Hayes, and then I'll face the monster."

"In God's name how, Caine? How can you fight such a devil when no weapon will bite on him?"

"In truth, I'm not sure," Caine said. "But it must be done and done tonight. Time presses, and your folk can't stay at their farms. It's not enough to deal with the Grinder, at any rate. Hayes and his men must also be dealt with."

"They guard the fort well," Tor said. "How will you get in?"

"I'll ride through the gate," Caine said. "I believe my escort will be here shortly. It might be wise if you stand behind the bar. At least for now, they shouldn't know you've helped me."

"I don't understand," Tor said. "What escort?"

Caine said nothing and Tor wondered if he had put his trust in a madman. He was about to question further when he heard a sound, soft but growing louder. It was hoof beats. Murphy was riding back into town.

Tor was scared to face Murphy, but he meant to stay where he was anyway. Caine smiled at him, and Tor was sure the man divined his thoughts. Caine said nothing but shook his head, and Tor got up and went behind the bar.

Caine watched the merchant go and knocked out the dottle of his pipe. He felt Tor's eyes on him and felt the man's worry grow as the sound of horses grew. Caine himself was curious about the men those horses bore, but not very worried. They had shown themselves to be little more than wild dogs: dangerous enough in their packs, but one cunning wolf could lay them at nines.

Caine had used that cunning up at the mines. It was now the sixth day since he had left the Red Man's cave. He only remembered one night in the cave, but when the moon came out it was almost full. He could have sworn it was just at the quarter the night he hung on the tree.

Even if Caine could have reckoned for the lost days, it wouldn't account for his injuries. Stiff he was when he set off from the cave, but whole and not just the marks from the whip. His broken fingers and ribs were fully mended. It was the same with the bullet wound.

He moved off into the valley where he found most of the farms abandoned. Caine had taken a few items, some food here and there, some rope and matches. He had decided against sleeping in any of the houses, and instead stayed in the forest, wrapped in his bearskin.

He had at first felt hampered by his lack of a mount, but that feeling changed when he went back up into the hills. The troopers were all mounted and limited to the trails. Caine himself was free to move anywhere, and it was easy to avoid patrols.

He found the mine and the camps, and he spent his days and nights circling and stalking, looking for weak spots and formulating a plan of attack. The plan, such as it was, was quickly hit upon. He was one and they were many, so it had to be at night, and fire would confuse and distract.

Yet something held Caine back.

He crept about watching and waiting, for what he didn't know. The bandits were among the overseers, and when Caine saw them, anger smoldered in his breast. Here was one wearing his hat, there one wearing his coat, and doubtless they were gambling away his money.

Still Caine waited, creeping to within yards of the building sometimes, and he marveled that none ever saw him.

Then one evening he lay on his belly, motionless and waiting, and he could hear the men inside. Their rough laughter was muted by the timber walls, but suddenly loud and clear the door was thrown open. Only Caine's eyes moved, flicked to the door and the man who slammed it closed to walk out.

It was one of the thieves that had left Caine hanging, and as he walked along the side of the building, his hand flashed and flickered in the lowering sun. No, not his hand, but the silver ring on it. Caine's teeth flashed in an unconscious and mirthless grin. The thief was heading to the outhouse.

No sooner had the door closed on the privy than Caine was in motion. He ran swiftly from tree to tree and uncoiled the rope he had taken from the farms in the valley. He made no noise in his soft soled boots as he crept up behind the. There he crouched, fashioning a sliding loop in one end of his rope, and there he waited. There were guards, but their concerns were more with the tents of the miners than with one man from the forest.

Soon enough the bandit had finished his business and the outhouse door opened. He took a few steps, then Caine again sprang into action. He rose and threw in one motion, and the loop dropped neatly over the thief's head. He jerked back on the line like an angler setting the hook. The bandit only had time for a brief grunt of surprise before the noose tightened and he went flying backward.

Caine set his shoulder to the rope and set off at a run. Caine had surprised people before by the strength he could wring from his lean frame, and he poured it on now. He bent almost double to get his whole body into dragging his catch away from the safety of the pack.

For his part, the bandit (John Patterson was his name, although Caine never learned it) never quite figured out what was happening. The barracks was almost out of sight before he thought to call out for help. By then he couldn't speak for the cruel noose cutting off his air.

His fingers dug at the rough line and he clawed above his head thinking to gain a hold on the line and get some slack. That proved fruitless, and the view of trees passing overhead was starting to go dark and fuzzy at the edges. Finally he remembered his guns and one hand dropped to his belt, but he couldn't seem to make it find the pistol, let alone draw it before everything went black.

Caine kept up his mad pace for quite some time. He wanted plenty of distance between him and the barracks. Not for safety, though, or even privacy, for his business with the bandit wouldn't take long.

Distance now would equal fear. He wanted this blackguard found, but not right away. A nice long walk into the dark forest, a true sense of how isolated they were in these wild mountains, that was what was called for. Let them wonder who had snatched their friend and carried him off. Wonder who walked at will in the Grinder's wood.

Caine finally reached a glen and came to a halt. He was puffing like a dray horse and took some time to catch his breath. After a few moments, he straightened and stretched the muscles in his back. Finally he turned to his catch and knelt down to take off the rope.

Caine was surprised when the man drew a ragged breath. The noose was sunk deep and Caine had dragged him over some rough country, but the murderous bastard yet lived. Caine nodded, pleased. Perhaps he could get some personal satisfaction as well as his ring back.

The bandit wore two guns on a broad belt, which Caine took. He made a quick search and found a clasp knife, but it was of poor quality and Caine just tossed it into the brush. He tied the man's hands at the wrist, and sat him up with his back propped against a tree. His head lolled and his breath came in thin wheezes.

Caine hunkered and waited until his own breath slowed. The bandit was still unconscious, so Caine leaned forward and slapped him. His head continued to flop on a limp neck, but finally the eyelids fluttered and opened. The man was fighting for consciousness, and his eyes went in and out of focus.

They settled on the bear head atop of Caine's own, and his boots began to kick at the ground to get away. He drew breath to scream, but his ravaged throat only allowed raspy grunts of fear. Caine's hand shot out once more in a sharp smack. The bandit started to slip to the ground and Caine jerked him forward by the rope before slamming him back against the tree.

"Calm yourself, fool," Caine said. "I'm no bear and I don't intend to make you my supper."

"What..."

The bandit choked and struggled to force his bruised throat make speech.

"What the hell is going on?"

"I've taken you," Caine said. "We have business, you and I. I'm here to claim my property."

"Property? What in hell are you talking about?"

He peered into the shadow of the bearskin hood, trying to see his captor's face.

"Do you know who I am? Do you know who I work for?"

"Oh, I know who you work for. You're one of Cullen's worthless curs," Caine said, "but I don't give a damn what your name is. You know my name, though."

"I don't know you, you crazy bastard," the bandit said.

Caine stood and drew back his hood. He said nothing, just stood and stared while the bandit studied his face. It took a few moments, but finally the bandit's eyes widened in recognition. Recognition and fear.

"Oh shit," the bandit said. "How did you...You should be...Look mister, don't kill me. I was just doing what the boss said. Please don't kill me."

"I'll tell you what," Caine said. "I won't kill you. I'll give you the same chance you gave me. But first return me my property."

"Your property?"

"That's my ring, you son of a bitch."

"Oh sure, mister!"

The bandit started tugging at the ring, but it was awkward with his hands tied.

"It's Caine, right? I didn't even take it that day. I won it at cards, but sure here you go."

He held out his hand with an eager look on his face. Caine was cautious, but hunkered down and began pulling at the ring. It was too small for the man's fingers and so it wouldn't come off. They both worked on it for several moments, but all the tugging and twisting was having no effect. There was no question that Nathaniel Caine was a dangerous man to have as an enemy. It was also true that he tended toward grim melancholies on occasion. But Caine was not by nature a cruel man. So he was surprised by the impulse that seized him and how quickly he acted on it.

Caine let go the ring and grabbed the bandit's dirty finger with his left hand, drew the obsidian knife with his right. The bandit's eyes widened, but he didn't have time to pull back or protest, for Caine was quick and sure.

He set the knife to flesh and pulled hard. The stone knife, slender and delicate looking as it was, went straight through the bone. It cut so easily that Caine and the bandit fell apart at the suddenness of no longer holding on to each other. The bandit began wailing, but Caine just looked at the surgical cut the primitive knife had made.

He should have been watching his captive, for the man lashed out with a curse and caught Caine with a boot heel. He lurched to his feet and made a run for it, still cursing and screaming for his mutilated hand. The man was in a panic and forgot about the rope. Within a few strides his feet became entangled and he fell down. He tried to get up again, but Caine was on him and opened his throat as easily as he had removed his finger.

Caine stood and glanced at the spreading pool of bandit's blood. The glance was cursory, for a strange feeling was on him. He left the man to die, and went back to search for the ring.

There was snow on the ground here, but it was easy enough to find, for the finger left a bloody mark when it fell in the snow. He scratched about, eager to find the silver ring, the sight of which had set him on the bandit like a wolf on a lamb.

His searching hands found it and he cast aside the dead man's digit. Caine scrubbed the ring clean in the snow and held it up to watch the sunlight glint on the silver. The ring felt heavy, charged with power. Here was the talisman the Red Man had spoken of.

Caine slipped it on, stood and breathed deep. He looked about the forested mountains. He felt he could count every pine needle and hear the footfalls of the small animals about. He fancied, too, that he could hear men at the camp calling for their missing comrade. That wasn't possible, of course, for Caine was too far away, but hear them he did. He turned and looked at the dead bandit. A man he saw, but at the same time something else, just for a moment. He saw a craven beast, a feral dog that ran wild at wanton slaughter. And it had met a wolf in Caine and suffered swift death.

Caine took a breath and the vision passed, but he still felt hyper-aware. He was lightheaded. In fact his whole body felt light, as if his feet just barely held him tethered to the earth. It didn't make him feel weak, however quite the contrary. He felt swift and cunning and nearly invincible. He had scouted and lain planning long enough. Now was the time for action.

A Nathaniel Caine Adventure

Caine strung up the bandit and loped off into the woods. He found a small cave where he dozed the rest of the day. He felt the searchers in his sleep, but they didn't trouble him even when they passed within a few yards of his den. Their eyes were clouded and his were clear.

That night's work went far easier than it had a right to. Though the night was dark, Caine had no trouble picking out paths swift and silent. He crept up on the camp and studied the barracks.

The building was a simple log structure, long and low to the ground with a shake shingle roof. The building seemed to have a faint nimbus of light that Caine found curious. It made the building easy to see and made the guards who thought they were hidden in the trees easy to spot.

Many things had been easy to see on this dark cloudy night, but Caine wasn't ready to question it. His new eyes would be an asset for the coming assault; better to take advantage now and question later.

He left the barracks for now and made his way to the tents of the miners where he discovered no guard. Whether they had been pulled for the extra duty at the barracks or the captors trusted to fear of the Grinder, Caine couldn't say.

So Caine just strolled among the tents, occasionally listening at the flaps. There wasn't much activity, but finally he stood before one lit from within by fire or lantern. The form was indistinct through the canvas, but Caine thought he saw an old man sitting near a small stove. He was carving a bit of wood with a sharp knife. The scraping of the blade paused for a moment, and Caine knew the man had become aware of him.

Caine lifted the flap and walked in. The only sign of surprise the old man gave was a slight widening of bright blue eyes. The man was old and spare, but not weak. Caine saw bright steel, like the knife in his gnarled hands.

"I'm attacking the barracks tonight," Caine said without preamble, "and I need someone to lead these people out of here."

"To what end?" the old man said. "The soldiers will just find us and round us up again. We have no arms to resist them and we can't outrun them."

"I'll keep their attention for a time," Caine said. "Is there someplace they can go?"

"What about the Grinder?"

"I'll face the Grinder after tonight's business," Caine said.

He didn't think the Grinder would be interfering tonight, but he didn't bother trying to convey this to the old man. The old man regarded Caine, ice blue eyes held flint grey ones for a hard moment. The old whittler passed a hand across his jaw and the calloused fingers rasped on the white stubble there. He nodded.

"I will lead them," he said. "There's a cluster of farms we can reach by morning."

"Excellent," Caine said. "You'll know when to move."

With that Caine left and made his way back to the barracks. He circled the building twice, marveling again that the guards lying in wait were so easy to spot and seemed so blind to his presence. If they had stood in pairs Caine would have had a big problem. He would have been forced to shoot and that would bring the men inside to the fight before he was ready. As it was, they stood alone where they thought they could see or at least hear each other.

Caine felt outside of himself as he crept up and cut the first sentry's throat. Caine had killed in the heat of battle, and a man could not afford to shrink from violence in the rougher parts of the frontier. This felt different, cold and predatory, and soon enough all the guards were dead. Caine stripped their weapons, stuffing pistols in his belt and stashing rifles at several different spots.

The barn was his next stop and his luck continued to hold. The barn was also a storage shed, and he found several tins of lamp oil and even some matches. Caine opened all the stalls and the gate to the corral before taking the oil to the barracks.

He decided to trust fully now whatever luck veiled the eyes of his enemies and allowed him such clear sight. His tread was soft, but he made no special effort at concealment, simply walked up and started pouring oil over the eaves. The few windows were shuttered and Caine resisted the urge to peer in the cracks. Though he suspected the men inside were trusting to the sentries, he yet sensed a wary watchfulness within.

Soon enough the oil tins were emptied and Caine struck a match. He set flame to the wood in several places, and it caught quickly. He retreated into the tree line facing the front door.

He drew a revolver and topped it off, so all six chambers were charged. He repeated the act with a second revolver and stood with both hammers back, so not even the sound of cocking pieces would warn his foes.

The flames licked and danced at the eaves. They caught and spread, quicker and quicker. The smoke was rising up, so the men inside did not yet know their predicament. The roof was fairly burning, and finally the shakes started to snap and crack. This alerted the soldiers, and there was some shuffling and questioning voices from within. The door opened.

One man stepped out, but Caine held his fire. The man held a rifle, and took a few steps out while scanning the night. Caine could see the man's eyes pass over his hiding place twice without seeing him. Finally the soldier turned and saw the roof. The man started, and still Caine held off.

"Fire!" the man shouted. "Get out of there, you fools! Fire!"

That was the word Caine was waiting for, and the panic was instant. As the rush of men reached the door, his pistols barked, both barrels taking the first soldier in the back. Caine let the pieces go like chain lightning and sent his bullets flying through the door and into the mass of frightened men.

The hammers snapped on empty chambers and Caine let them fall, circling around to the side where one of the Winchesters was leaning against a tree. He drew a bead on the shutters of the window. The men started firing out the front door and Caine started firing through the window.

There were yells and curses inside and Caine continued to circle, stuffing shells into the loading gate until he was even with the next window. Bullets started blasting through the first window and Caine emptied the rifle through this one. He let it fall and ran back to the front door. He had another rifle stashed and caught it up.

The door still hung open and lamps burned within. Caine actually laughed. Battles were chaotic things that made hash out of careful plans. This night's plan had been desperate, even a little mad, but not only was it working, it was almost easy. Caine had a fleeting and unchristian thought that some ancient god of battle was pleased with the slaughter and working toward his victory.

He took careful aim and put a hole through a soldier's head. He killed four more and managed to wound one before someone thought to close the door. Caine put the remaining rounds through the door for good measure.

His next move was to circle left to the other side of the barracks. He had two loaded rifles stashed together, and he gathered them now. He fell back further into the shadows of the trees to escape the growing ring of light from the fire.

The shakes were completely ablaze and the beams must be catching. The men inside must make a break for it soon or else burn. Caine positioned himself on an angle from the corner of the building. From here, he could cover the front door and the windows on this side and hope the bullet holes would discourage flight from the other side.

Caine was prepared for a panicked rush, but instead the front door opened a crack and then swung wide. No targets presented themselves, and Caine went to one knee, bracing the barrel on the tree trunk. After a long moment, Caine saw the brim of a trooper's hat poke around the jam, and soon the whole crown was visible.

It was a child's trick and Caine held his fire, for the hat undoubtedly sat on a rifle barrel instead of a head. The hat waggled comically before it was withdrawn, and Caine waited for a peeking head to take it's place.

Instead two men dashed out, one with a carbine and one with a pistol in each hand. Two more with rifles followed and the men formed a semicircle before the door. The men with long arms knelt, but the pistoleer stood. Dogs these might be, but someone had put sand in them and Caine laid his money, and his rifle sight, on the pistol-man.

This fellow called behind him, and two more men dashed out. Then two men filled the doorway, a trooper bearing up a wounded comrade. Caine chose that moment to fire, shooting first the man with the revolvers and then the men in the doorway.

All hell broke loose with the men outside shooting wildly, and the men inside crowding the doorway with the wounded soldiers. Caine stayed low and circled to a new tree. The man with the pistols had crumpled but now stood back up and was shouting orders to the soldiers. Caine shot him again and saw movement to his left; the shutters had been thrown and men were tumbling out. Caine swung his rifle at the knot of men but checked his trigger finger.

Two men were out already and Caine recognized them. They were members of Cullen's gang; the first had taken Caine's boots which the bandit was now using to run for the trees, not waiting for

A Nathaniel Caine Adventure

his fellows. Quick as rats from a burning barn, which Caine supposed was pretty accurate, they jumped out the window and ran for the woods.

Without pause for thought, Caine dropped the rifle and ran after them. The bandits were running all out, and soon the rifle fire behind was reduced to distant cracks and pops. Caine had a pistol out as he ran the dogs down. It was rough terrain, but still Caine gained, and he was less than twenty yards behind when they stopped.

Caine stopped as well, and dropped to his belly with his thumb on the hammer. The bandits, there were five of them, bunched up, panting with hands on thighs. None of them bore rifles and their pistols were all holstered.

"Which way to town?" gasped one.

"How the hell should I know?" came the answer. "I'm just running from that slaughterhouse."

"You think it was Red Men?"

"Had to be. Fucking savages'll have all them blue coats dead and scalped."

"We need to get to the fort. Which way to town?"

"I can't see moon or stars through these trees. I think it's this way. Let's keep moving and for Christ's sake stay quiet. No use getting away from the Indians to be kilt by the Grinder."

There were hoarse curses and furtive looks around at that. Several of the men looked directly at Caine, but he lay still as death and none of them marked him. They gathered themselves after a few moments and moved off single file at a quick walk.

Caine waited until he could barely see the back of the last man before rising. He stowed the pistol and pulled the black knife before setting off after them. In a few moments he had overtaken the rearmost bandit. Caine fell on him like a hunting panther.

He slit the thief's throat with a quick jerk of his blade, and the man hit the ground already dying. Caine looked up to see the next man stop and turn. Perhaps he had heard the body hit the ground; certainly there had been no cry, or perhaps he just sensed the danger.

It didn't matter, for Caine sprang before the man could fully make sense of what he was seeing. The bandit went for his gun, but the long fingers of Caine's left hand locked on his wrist like bands of steel.

The right hand stabbed over and over, a bloody blur. The man kept straining to get his gun out while Caine punched holes in him. The bandit let out a mewling groan, and the other three turned as well.

They drew pistols and called out, but didn't fire. Caine let the man he grappled with fall, but the others still held their fire. Their heads turned this way and that as they peered into the gloom. They reached out with their gun barrels as if the weapons could probe the dark night.

Caine realized the men couldn't see him well enough to aim. That wouldn't stop them from shooting, so he eased off the narrow trail to be out of the line of fire. There was one more call, then tense whispers. Caine circled around to the group's flank. He could feel the terror of the murderous rogues, and finally one of them cocked his piece. Caine sprang in the same instant the pistol cracked. The glassy black blade flickered and flashed in the cold air as Caine fell among his enemies. It was over in a few short seconds. There were no more shots.

Caine sat for a few moments to catch his breath. He regarded the corpses, and it was clear his coat, at least, was a lost cause. Even if he could get the blood out, it was full of holes.

After a moment's consideration he stripped it anyway, not to wear but to make a point of the man's crime. He took back his boots as well, but decided not to wear them either. The moccasins from the mysterious Indian allowed him to move silently, which had clearly helped him in this fight.

But it had to be more than soft footfalls helping him. Caine looked around at the trees. The bandits had cursed the darkness, but he could see quite well. The moon was out and the trees shone, silvery in the night. Caine looked high up in those trees, and thought he had enough rope to put yet more fear into the soldiers.

And to leave a calling card for Elisha Cullen.

The Fort

The fear had taken root well. Caine could sense it as sure as he heard the horses' hooves. It grew as the sounds of galloping slowed and stopped outside the saloon. He didn't turn his head, didn't have to. The fear of the men came to him as a palpable thing, and he could visualize the troopers. He sensed the furtive looks through the window and the nervous muttered conferences.

The creak of tack and whisper of leather told him they were dismounting and sliding weapons out of scabbards. They were trying to be quiet, but as the boot heels sounded on the boards, Caine could almost make out each separate man. He could feel their nervousness and the eager muzzles on his back.

Caine still kept his back to the front door and sat relaxed with both hands on the table. He could sense more men moving up to the back door. He heard their boots crunching in the still frosty mud, but none showed their faces through the open door there. The tension stretched out, and then came the snick of a hammer going back.

"Turn, you son of a bitch. I want to see your eyes before I send you to hell."

"That sounds like my Smith & Wesson, you thieving whoreson."

Caine didn't turn as ordered and he kept his tone conversational. This was mere theatrics; he recognized Elisha

Cullen's voice, not the sound of his revolver. He merely guessed that Cullen had his Smith, but it had the desired effect. He could feel the fear behind him grow.

"Have it your way, Caine," said Cullen. "You won't be the first man I shot in the back."

Caine laughed.

"Just the sort of boast I'd expect from such a cowardly mongrel."

"Hold your fire, Cullen."

This growl came from the rear door. A man appeared with pistol drawn, just a spare black shadow in the square of morning light. He stepped quickly through and to one side of the door to avoid making such an attractive target. The man's black eyes swept over the whole saloon in two quick passes before settling on Caine. The man waved the soldiers in and directed two up to the second floor. When they made to cross in front of the man's pistol, he gave a short growl and the men flinched before moving behind him. Caine watched them clomp up the stairs and poke about in the rooms. Finally they came out on the balcony.

"All clear up here, Sarge."

"Cut 'em down," the man said.

His eyes, and his pistol barrel, had never wavered from Caine while his men searched. They didn't waver now as the hanged men fell to the floor before him. The bandit who yet lived moaned and flopped as he tried to gain his feet. The sergeant spared one look for the dead man and one for the living, then walked forward to take a seat across the table from Caine.

"Sergeant Murphy, I presume?"

"It's quite the mess you've made for me, stranger," Murphy said. "I'm not a curious man as a rule, but I just had to get a good look at you before I killed you."

"Why would you want to kill me," Caine said, "when I'm here to help you?"

"Help?" Murphy said. "Was it help when you set to burning and slaughtering my men in the hills?"

"Your men were merely in my way," Caine said with a shrug. "It was Cullen's dogs I was after. I've a score to settle with them and their master. They ambushed me in the passes and kept me from my business. "

"Is that a fact, now?"

Murphy's eyes flicked over Caine's shoulder. Cullen still held the .44 trained on Caine. He lowered it now, but kept it cocked and gave a curt nod to the question in Murphy's look. "And what was your business before Cullen interrupted you so discourteously?"

"I came to kill the Grinder."

Murphy's black eyes narrowed for a moment, and then he started to laugh. His head went back and he laughed loud, but the heavy barrel of his Colt stayed steady on Caine. A few of the troopers laughed as well and Caine smiled. Behind Murphy, Smith was not laughing or smiling. He had worked the ropes off his hands with the help of a trooper and stood fuming. Now he strode forward.

"Don't listen to this bastard, Murphy" he said. "He killed Jones and hung me up like a side of beef."

Murphy's laughter stopped, and the fire was right back in his black eyes.

"Is it my fault the two of you couldn't defend yourselves against one man?" he said. "Shut up and back away. You stink of piss."

"He ain't here to kill that thing," Smith went on. "He's here to bring down the whole operation. He took my guns and my money and he was gonna take my horse. If you ain't gonna kill him, I will!"

Smith snatched at the Remington lying on the table. He didn't even get a grip before Murphy shot him. The big slug took him in the side of the neck, and blew an obscene hole out the other side.

Smith dropped as if a trap door had opened beneath him. He made one surprised woofing sound before expiring with a wet gurgle.

Caine regarded the corpse for a moment before turning back to Murphy. The smoking .45 was again pointed at Caine's chest and cocked for another shot.

"Now then, buck."

Murphy spoke as if the interruption had been no more than a barking dog, hushed with a swat.

"You would have me believe you came to kill our beastie? And you alone?"

"I was alone last night," Caine said, "and managed alright."

"You were alone in the passes when *I* took you," Cullen said.

"More empty boasting, Cullen."

Caine still didn't give the bandit chief the satisfaction of turning. He merely spoke over his shoulder. "For it wasn't you alone that took me but a whole gang. Two of that gang still lie on that mountain. But I made it off. And how many of your gang are left now?"

"Now who's boasting, Caine?" Cullen said. "You know, I'm going to enjoy it when I…"

"Bah!" Caine cut him off.

"When you what, kill me? You already had the chance to face me like a man and kill me yourself. Instead, you left me for the Grinder."

Caine heard the creak of a floorboard behind him, and knew Cullen was advancing on him. Caine gathered himself to leap out of the chair, but Murphy held up a hand.

"Cullen!" he said. "I said hold your fire and put up your piece."

There was a tense pause, and then the oily click of the hammer being let down.

"So it's true then?" Murphy said to Caine. "Cullen told me he bound you in the mountains after you killed his men."

"Oh, it's true," Caine said. "Bound and hanged on a wind swept tree."

"How did you get down?"

"No bonds can hold me, Sergeant Murphy."

"Well, that must come in handy," Murphy said. "So you slipped your bonds and traipsed about the mountains like a red savage for a few days before attacking our mine. By yourself."

"And now I'm here to face the Grinder."

"Well, of course there's that," Murphy said. "And did you have a plan for this encounter?"

"Well, with permission from Colonel Hayes," Caine said, "I thought I'd sleep in his house and let the beast come to me."

There was some muttering among the men and Caine looked around. The troopers had stopped covering him with their weapons. They held them slack and watched the exchange, enthralled. Caine was pleased with the effect, and thought he may have an unexplored gift for the theater.

"And come he will, bucko," Murphy said. "Then what? You'll shoot him with all those pistols? If it was that easy, the thing would already be dead."

"Well, if no gun will harm it, I'll use none," Caine said. "I don't need them."

This brought considerably more muttering from the men in the saloon.

"Then you won't mind if I hold 'em for you?"

Murphy waved his free hand and two men came forward to stand on either side of the Sergeant. Two more flanked Caine.

"I'll have to have the Remingtons back when I'm done," Caine said and cocked his head at the dead bandit by the table. "I purchased them as well as a rifle and horse from this man."

"Purchased? You have no money. What was the price?"

"His life."

The room erupted in laughter and Murphy joined in.

"It's madder than a shitehouse rat you are, Mr. Nathaniel Caine," Murphy said with a smile that almost touched the smoldering black eyes. "And you shall have your wish, I think. I'll take you to meet the Colonel, and then you can spend the night in his fine house."

"Don't be a fool, Murphy," Elisha Cullen said. "This bastard is slippery. Slippery as a snake and more dangerous. Kill him and be done with him."

"Settle yourself, Cullen," Murphy said. "Hayes will want to see the man that's caused all this trouble. The Grinder will get him tonight. We'll take a few precautions, of course."

The sergeant made a quick gesture and the troopers closed in. They were careful to stay out of the way of Murphy's pistol, but they took all the guns Caine had collected in his recent mischief. One ran his hands over Caine's leather shirt with quick pats. When he was done he backed away and nodded at Murphy.

Murphy's eyes narrowed and he made another gesture. Another soldier approached, and there was an atonal clank as he brought forth a pair of manacles. Caine tensed. It was slight, but Murphy didn't miss it and he tensed in response. The soldier felt the current between the two men and hesitated.

"I hardly think that's necessary," Caine said.

"What's the worry, Mr. Caine?"

Murphy gave his hard grin.

"No bonds can hold you, after all."

Well, that's what boasting will get you, Caine thought. *So much for my career in the theater.*

He kept the act up anyway by giving a shrug before holding out his hands. The soldier put on the irons and backed away in haste as if Caine was a dangerous animal. Caine knew Murphy saw, and offered a grin of his own.

Murphy didn't rise to that bait, just sat back in his chair and cocked his head. The movement caused a ripple of blue highlights to run down the raven feather in his hat. There was a matching ripple on the Colt's barrel as Murphy replaced the spent round. The feather made Caine think of Old Corbie and his friends.

"Right then," he said, "you can ride your new bought horse up to the fort and meet Colonel Hayes."

Murphy strode outside without a glance at Caine. Caine got up and followed. The group of men parted before him and closed in behind.

Tor Nielsen stood behind his counter with a stricken look etched on his face. Caine would have reassured him, but he was mindful the merchant's position was still precarious. He settled for a quick wink which just seemed to frighten the Swede more. Caine smiled and walked out the door.

"And which one is the gentleman's?" Murphy asked with sarcastic politeness.

He executed an exaggerated bow and gesture at the bandits' horses, and his men laughed. Caine wasn't sure which horse he had 'bought.' He looked quickly between the two horses, both decent mounts.

"That one," Caine said, and pointed at the one with the better saddle.

Murphy removed the rifle from its scabbard and tossed it to a soldier before giving the order to mount up. Caine mounted on his own, but when he reached for the reins a soldier snatched them away. Sergeant Murphy set off and the troop followed without order. Caine sat easy and rested his hands on the saddle horn.

The fort sat up on a hill, less than half a mile from town. Murphy rode fast, and Caine ignored the group of armed men about him to watch the building grow larger before him. From here, Caine could see no reason why the building should be such proof against the Grinder's night raids. It was like any of the other frontier holds the army was throwing up for Indian fighting. Small and stout, with a commanding view of the countryside.

Caine bowed his head and tried to put the new pieces together, but it just wasn't logical. He regarded the silver ring on his finger. Shaw's ring, though that wasn't possible. Not possible, and not logical, and yet there it was.

Caine fingered the bright silver and pondered the Latin motto: *See the truth.* The truth was that *none* of this was logical. Shaw's ghost had warned him not to cling to logic and trust instead to instinct. Easier said than done, for Caine considered himself an educated gentleman, not a savage.

He shook his head at that, for it was instinct that had him haunting the hills last night. Instinct that led him to abduct the bandit and cut off the finger that bore this very ring. Caine lifted his head and they were almost at the fort—and now it didn't look so plain.

It was still the same log fort, but it seemed surrounded with a nimbus of silvery light. He looked at the men around him, but he didn't think they saw the light. He remembered the same light in the forest last night. Then he had just thought it was the moon's rays on the snow and birch bark. It had to be more, though, for the bandits had been near blind.

As he gazed at the fort now, he could almost see a ghostly image of waving branches and quivering leaves. It was the timbers that made up the palisade! They still held some virtue that was theirs when they were living trees. That virtue must thwart the Grinder's rage.

Caine raised himself in the saddle and looked around with new eyes. The land around the fort was cleared, but in the distance he could see the trees of the forest and feel that same virtue. The stony mountains had their own power, but it seemed more hidden, deeper.

Shaw had said as much; veins of power he had called them. Caine didn't doubt that those veins of power ran along the same veins of gold that Hayes was delving. Hayes had opened those veins of power, but someone else had tapped into them.

Ana the aggrieved mother was, according to Tor Nielsen, from a tribe known for their magical practices. Caine could easily imagine the witch's curse growing, at first only grief and rage, but taking power from the bones of the earth until her vengeance took form and walked.

Grinder's Keeper

The real question was what to do about it. The wood obviously had great power to protect, but it wasn't enough to hide behind the walls. The beast must be faced.

Caine cut his thoughts short and brought them back to the now, for they were riding through the gate. There were more soldiers inside but not many, and Caine wondered at their small number. A colonel usually commanded a regiment, but there was barely a troop here.

Roarke had said as much when he had set out on this mad venture (ages ago that seemed), but it struck Caine harder to see it himself. It only took a few moments of looking around for Caine to see the truth. These men weren't with the Army, despite their blue coats.

Caine's own time in the War meant he had an intimate and almost instinctive eye for who was a soldier and who wasn't. It could be a small detail: the manner in which a man wore his hat or buttoned his coat or just the way he walked. Some of these men, most notably the sergeant, were doubtless soldiers at one time. But Caine was sure most of them had not been in the army.

He was just as sure that this fort was a sham. It made a good ruse for the settlers. What safer way to make your way in the frontier than under the direct protection of professional soldiers with the full authority of the government? Caine had to shake his head.

Who was this Colonel Hayes? It was clear the whole venture was planned well ahead of time, and the farmers had been caught in a pretty trap. But what kind of man would have the arrogance to set the trap under the guise of an Army Colonel?

A moment later a man in a tailored uniform dripping gold braid strutted into the morning sunshine. Finally Caine had his answer and he bit down an exclamation, for this man was known to him. Though not by the name of Hayes.

Caine kept his face schooled, but his mount sensed the rider's agitation and tried to shy and turn. The trooper holding the reins cursed at the horse and jerked at the bit. Caine kept his eyes on the Colonel.

"You've returned quickly, Sergeant Murphy," the Colonel said. "Was this all you could catch me, or was it indeed a single Indian?"

"That's the second time today I've been mistaken for an Indian," Caine said before Murphy could speak. "Perhaps I am in need of a haircut."

The Colonel started in surprise and looked again at Caine. Caine stared back, impassive and patient, but the Colonel showed no sign of recognition. Caine didn't think he looked *that* much like an Indian, despite his black hair and clothes. Perhaps it was more of the luck that had hidden him from the bandits last night, or perhaps the explanation was more mundane.

It was more than a few years since they had met, and Caine had been in a uniform himself then. Whatever the reason, Hayes didn't recognize him and that was fortunate. For in that case, Caine was sure he would be killed out of hand.

"It would take more than a barber," Hayes said. "You might try dressing like a white man. How much trouble did this trash cause me, Murphy?"

Murphy gave his report to Hayes in a few terse and unvarnished sentences. Hayes stood mute, though his face quickly went white with fury.

"Why the hell does he still draw breath?" Hayes finally broke in. "He should be swinging from a tree and kicking his way to hell!"

"Well, Cullen already left him hanging from a tree," Murphy said, unfazed by his boss's anger. "It didn't take. Our guest wants to meet the Grinder, so I thought you might want to oblige him."

"*Wants* to meet him?"

Hayes drew closer to Caine and looked longer at him.

"I've been over this with your Sergeant," Caine said. "I was coming here to kill the monster when I was waylaid."

"So you plan to face the bastard with no weapons?"

"I don't need weapons to vanquish my foe. And by all accounts, weapons harm him not," Caine said with a haughty jut of his chin.

Then he shrugged.

"Of course, that mangy half-wit mongrel who licks your boots has my weapons. If you want to give them back, I won't say no. If I get them back now, perhaps I won't have to kill Cullen as well as the Grinder."

"Oh, I think you have enough to worry about," said Hayes.

Hayes was clearly used to talking down to people and he spoke with contempt to Caine, but a quick look came over his face. It was a thoughtful look, and Caine feared recognition was tugging at the ersatz Colonel. That wouldn't do.

Caine lowered his eyes to his crossed hands on the saddle horn and moved them a bit so the chains clanked. Hayes shook his head in a gesture of swift dismissal and flashed a cruel smile.

"You're insane to face it at all, and as you say, weapons won't help you. But I'll tell you what. You kill this thing barehanded, and not only will you get your weapons back, but I'll give you a fortune in gold."

"A generous offer, but it's not gold I came for," Caine said. "I was to collect forty dollars in silver for delivering the post, but that didn't turn out so well. There is one thing you can do for me when I kill the monster."

"What might that be?"

"Let the farmers go."

"Is that all?" Hayes said.

He reached out and gave the chains a swing to set them clinking again.

"I think you're putting your cart a tad before your horse. When I see the Grinder dead, we can talk again. In the meantime…put him in the stockade."

Hayes turned his back and strode to his office. Murphy gestured to his men and they started to close on Caine. He dismounted before they could lay hands on him and walked on his own to the stockade. Murphy's black eyes regarded Caine's retreating back without blinking, and he made a sound in his throat, a low growl.

"Double guard on that bastard," he ordered and then stalked into Hayes' office.

Hayes was settling into his chair and plucking a cigar out of the box. He gestured at the box and started to cut his smoke. Murphy took the offered cigar. He bit through the cap and spit. He hit the silver ashtray dead center, and once his cigar was lit, paced from the desk to the window.

"You should kill that bastard," Murphy said.

"That's the idea," Hayes said.

"I mean right now," Murphy said. "Don't wait for the Grinder."

"What's your hurry, Murphy?"

Five minutes ago it was Hayes sputtering for the stranger's death and Murphy who had been calm. Hayes didn't bother pointing this out.

"Maybe you didn't notice it, but there's something strange about that man. I don't like it."

"He's just a piece of trail trash," Hayes said, "another drifter."

"You didn't see the shambles he made up at the mines, Hayes," Murphy said.

He made his way to the colonel's whiskey decanter and started knocking back drinks.

"He ain't just another drifter."

"So he's good with his guns," Hayes said. "We know guns won't help him against that damned beast even if he had them. It's precisely because of the damage he's done that I want him to suffer."

"Things are getting out of hand, Hayes," said Murphy. "Hadley's betrayal, the miners running off, Cullen's gang is all but butchered, the barracks burned, and a pile of men laid in the dirt. Most of that we can lay at Caine's feet. He's here now. I'll kill him now."

"Don't forget who's in charge here, Sergeant," Hayes said. "Things will only get out of hand if we lose our heads. Dragging him out and shooting him looks like we're rattled. We wait until tonight, and we send him to the Grinder like the others."

"He was left for the Grinder once already and slipped away."

"Cullen's work," Hayes said, "and we'll just have to do better. Though, as you say, his gang is much diminished and therefore, so is his usefulness. Perhaps we can turn recent events to our advantage."

"How do you mean?" Murphy said.

"Think of it as a bit of house cleaning," Hayes said. "A large operation means a large payroll. This stranger has caused us trouble, but he's also increased the size of the remaining shares. Once he's taken care of and the stray miners rounded up, perhaps we can trim the fat even further."

"And I'll do the trimming, I suppose," Murphy growled and puffed on his cigar. "Tell me Hayes, what's to stop you from trimming *me* from your operation."

"Well, that's simple, Murphy," Hayes said. "Don't stop being useful."

* * *

In the stockade, Nathaniel Caine stood in the center of his tiny cell. He had paced it off and inspected it for any means of escape. He had done it mechanically because it seemed the right thing to do. He didn't really plan on escaping, and in any case, the stockade was sound.

There was a window, but it was too small to squeeze through even if he could defeat the iron bars. He was glad he had eaten well at Tor's; he thought they might not feed him here. So he determined the thing to do was get some rest. There was a rough plank bunk with a straw mattress and woolen blanket. The mattress wasn't particularly soft and the blanket still smelled of horse, but they were both free of bugs, so Caine laid down.

"Psst. Hey in there!"

Caine got back up and moved over to the window.

"Who's out there?"

A face popped up in front of the window, pale and blue eyed with long blond mustaches. Caine had seen the fellow earlier outside the saloon. He had kept himself a little apart from the soldiers.

"Who are you?" Caine said.

"I am Swenson."

The blue eyes were cool, like a pool just before icing over, and they stared at Caine with keen regard.

"I am an Army scout."

"Indeed?" Caine said and laughed. "I might believe that if it was the Army out there."

"You see much, eh?"

Swenson leaned forward so his face was right up against the bars and his head took up the whole of the small window. His unblinking gaze looked Caine up and down, took in the cell and came back to Caine, who just stared back at the tracker.

"Who are *you*?"

"My name is Caine."

"Did you really come here to kill the Grinder?"

"That's what I keep telling people," Caine said. "I grow weary of repeating myself."

"Can you do it?"

"Yes."

Caine spoke without hesitation.

"How?"

"Well," Caine said, "that I don't know."

Caine went and sat on the bunk and the manacles made their music. He wasn't sure why he had been so frank with the man. He didn't trust him any more than the others, but there was certainly something different about Swenson. Caine didn't think he would be fooled or impressed by any of the theatrics he had performed in the saloon.

"What is it to you, Swenson?"

"I would see the thing killed," the tracker said. "Hayes thinks we can out wait it, but he's wrong. We can dig out every bit of gold, but as long as the Grinder walks we'll never get it off this mountain."

"And you want to get your share away, eh?"

"I've done my part and more in the fight." Swenson's tone grew hard edged and proud. "I've a right claim to my share of the fortune."

"A fortune scratched out of the mountain by your own people made slaves?"

"Fortune favors the bold, Caine," Swenson said without apology. "It is the bold and the strong who make their mark in the world. Hayes was bold enough to go after the gold and strong enough to keep it. But now..."

"Now what?" Caine said and he sensed opportunity. If he survived his night with the Grinder, he didn't expect Hayes to keep his bargain. In fact, he expected to be shot. If it wasn't for the townsfolk, Caine would have left this valley days ago, and Hayes be damned with all his men. But now it seemed the scout, at least, wasn't wholly Hayes' man.

"Now his boldness wanes," Swenson said with a shrug. "He hides in this fort like a badger in his hole. For now, the Grinder is kept out, but it's not enough to wait."

Swenson placed a hand on the rough-hewn timber. He gave it an appraising look, like a man assessing the virtues of a horse. It occurred to Caine, sudden and sure, that Swenson could see the same glow in the wood that he saw. Or if he didn't see the weird nimbus of silver, he at least knew it was some power in the wood keeping the monster at bay. Caine got back up from the bunk and went to the window so he was face to face with the cold eyed tracker.

"If you're such a bold man," Caine said, "why don't you face the thing yourself?"

"Do not seek to chastise me, Caine," Swenson said. "I have faced it. I waited in the house with the others. I pelted his stony hide with lead. I splintered a good knife on that hide, and he swatted me away like a horsefly. I was lucky to get away with three cracked ribs, for he turned many men that night to red ruin. As soon as I was able, I took to the woods to track him. Sometimes a bear will kill all the hounds set on it. That same bear can be taken in his den."

"If a man is bold enough to face him in his den."

"I don't know what I could have done different from the first fight," Swenson said, "and likely he would have just killed me. But it didn't matter, for I couldn't find his den. He leaves tracks a blind fisherman could follow, and I've cut his trail countless times. And countless times I've lost it. Sometimes it just ends in a snowy clearing as if he disappeared into thin air."

"A fine story, Swenson," Caine said, "but why come to me?"

"I've yet to meet my equal as a tracker," Swenson said, "and I can't even remember the last time I lost a trail. There is some power in these hills. I don't mean the Grinder. There's a power that protects him and hides him from my sight. You know, I was at the little fire you set last night, but I never saw you. I followed *your* tracks too, Caine, after your mayhem last night. I followed the track and lost it same as the beast."

"What do you know, Swenson?" Caine said. "If you want the Grinder dead, anything you tell me can help."

"The Grinder? Bah. He's but the lash, not the hand that swings it."

"Ah, now I begin to understand," Caine said. "It's the sorceress you want."

"Hayes has put a price on her head," Swenson said, "out of fear and anger at her defiance. He doesn't truly grasp the power she wields."

"And you do?"

"I will when I hold her head in my hands."

Caine was taken aback at the man's frank desire to murder a woman, but then he remembered the words of the Red Man in the cave. He had told Caine the quest wouldn't be over until the one who called the Grinder was confronted.

"You think I can find this woman."

"Yes! You move through the woods as the Grinder. You savaged Hayes' men just as the Grinder. I'll get you out of here and you can help me find her."

"No," Caine said.

"What?"

Swenson grasped the window bars as if he might tear out the window.

"Are you mad? Why not?"

"What's in it for me to help you?"

"Your life for one thing," Swenson said. "Even if you best the Grinder, you can't think Hayes will keep his bargain?"

A Nathaniel Caine Adventure

"Of course not," Caine said. "I know what sort of man Hayes is. Better than you might think."

"Gold then," Swenson said. "You can have the bounty. More from my own hoard."

"I came here to face the Grinder, Swenson," Caine said. "Such is my fate, so there's little point in running from it."

Swenson growled and sputtered, but seemed to accept this bit.

"I'll stash weapons in the house then, and stand the night with you."

"No," Caine went on implacably. "You know that won't do any good."

"Damn you! What do you want then?"

Caine went back and sank on the bunk. The chain of his shackles rang as they struck the wooden pallet. Caine looked up at the eager blue eyes.

"There is one thing you can do for me."

The Grinder

Caine might have found the bed more comfortable if he wasn't wondering how many men had died on it. Murphy hadn't given him a tour, merely marched him up the stairs to the bedroom which had become their execution chamber. That had been plenty to gauge the ruin the Grinder had made of men.

When Hayes stopped sleeping here, he apparently stopped cleaning here as well. There were signs of violence everywhere: bullet holes and strange gouges in the walls, but mostly blood. The house had once been fine, especially fine for the frontier. Now it was an abattoir. If Caine had ever thought the tales of the horror wrought by the Grinder to be exaggerated, he couldn't think that now.

With an effort, Caine put aside disgust for his surroundings and concentrated on freeing himself. Despite his word that he was here to fight the thing and not run, he had remained chained. Caine had expected no less, but he hadn't expected that the colonel's bed would be a stocks.

It was made as a four-poster but with large heavy timbers. The timbers were from the local forest, for they gave off the same nimbus as the palisade up at the fort. Caine looked hard at them and put his mind to work on how he could use them in the coming fight.

Those thoughts didn't get far before they were stopped by the sound of a Colt being cocked. Caine turned and Murphy's eyes were the same hungry black as the .45's bore.

"I trust the accommodations are up to the gentleman's standards," Murphy said.

"I've been sleeping in caves for days," Caine said.

Murphy had spoken in what passed for a humorous tone, but Caine couldn't match it. His lips twisted in a disgusted sneer at the gory bedclothes. He could smell the blood, a faint tang like wet copper, and he repressed a shudder at the thought of how this room would reek when summer finally came to the mountains.

"But I'd prefer the meanest cave to this shambles."

"I keep it that way on purpose. It adds to the terror of the condemned. Sure and it's bad, but his lordship the Colonel hasn't been here in a long time."

Caine didn't respond to this, but he caught something in Murphy's tone. The Irishman hated Hayes. Not that Murphy had acted too full of the milk of human kindness. He was a dangerous and bloodthirsty man to be sure. But there was something there. Perhaps a natural dislike of the poor for the rich, the soldier for the gold-braided officer. Caine tucked the info away.

"O'Brien is going to unlock your left shackle," Murphy said, "and thread it through that ring."

Murphy jutted his chin to indicate the ring. A heavy piece of black iron set into the post by an equally heavy staple.

"Do anything I don't like, and you'll miss your fight with the Grinder on account of your brains will be blown out."

Murphy didn't bother seeing if Caine agreed or understood, just nodded at a soldier. That soldier must have been O'Brien, for he stepped forward and caught the key that Murphy tossed him. O'Brien performed the operation, and soon enough Caine was lying supine with his wrists shackled above his head.

It wasn't particularly pleasant or comfortable, but with his ordeal on the tree so recent, Caine was able to stay philosophical. It could be worse. Murphy dismissed his troopers with one of his wordless nods, and when the stamp of boot heels had receded down the stairs, he came to stand at the foot of the bed. The two men regarded each other for a long and silent moment.

"No jibes?" Murphy finally said. "No boasts?"

"No, the boasts were mere theater," Caine said, "and a jibe now seems unwise. I think you want to kill me, despite the Colonel's orders, and it wouldn't take much of an excuse. I don't think you like following his orders."

"It's a sharp eye you have in your head, buck."

Murphy actually smiled and holstered his revolver.

"Any last requests?"

"You don't strike me as the sort of man to grant final requests, Sergeant."

Murphy shrugged.

"I didn't say I'd grant it. Let's hear it first."

"All right," Caine said after a moment's consideration. "Advice."

"How's that now?"

"My request is for advice."

"You don't strike me as the sort of man who takes advice," Murphy said.

"I didn't say I'd take it," Caine said, "but I will if it's any good. I want your advice on how to beat the Grinder."

"*My* advice?" Murphy said. "What makes you think I have any advice to give."

"Whatever else you are, you're no coward," Caine said. "I'm sure you were there when the beast was fought. If anyone kept his nerve, I'm guessing it was you. You must have seen something, some weakness. Anything might help me."

The Irishman thrust his hands through his belt and his lips twisted as he regarded Caine. The man lay shackled in the black iron, and still he talked of fighting the monster that would soon turn him to tripe. Murphy had no romantic tales of his ancient homeland such as Marshal Roarke on the other side of the mountains. Yet he still felt the Celtic admiration for a fighting man unbowed. Mad as a March hare, Caine must be, but you had to respect that kind of sand.

"Sorry, buck," Murphy said. "Even if you weren't in those bracelets, I fear it would be a one-sided fight. I've battled it as you say, but I saw no weaknesses. The thing was big as a grizzly bear and its roar more fierce. We fired on it from short range, and I saw the bullets splatter as if against rock, for that's what its hide is.

"Even so, I rushed the brute when I emptied my rifle. The gun splintered to nothing when I struck it. Not just the stock, but the barrel was bent and broken. The last time we met, I spent most of a day out cold from the buffet it gave me, and the headache lasted a week.

"I don't know what power the old woman called on to bring this thing forth, but it's stood proof against every civilized weapon I could bring to bear on it—lead or steel or even me *bata*."

He patted the iron bound club at his belt.

"Damn," said Caine, struck by the similarity between Murphy's account and the huntsman Swenson's. "That's rather less encouraging than I hoped for."

"That's the way it is, and I'm the kind to give it straight."

Murphy turned and started out the bedroom door.

"See you in hell, Nathaniel Caine."

"We'll see, Sergeant Murphy."

Caine muttered this softly, more to himself, for his mind was already working. He knew he would be manacled, but not to the bed in this manner. It would take some contortions to reach the key in his boot. The key was the favor he asked of Swenson, and the tracker had returned very quickly with it. The Swede, at least, thought Caine had some kind of chance.

First order of business was getting out of the irons. Caine twisted about on the bed, but couldn't get to his boot with his hands tethered to the post. Finally, he pulled up his legs and did a sort of backward somersault. It was neither dignified nor graceful, and the resulting squat had him perched awkwardly on the headboard. It also put his hands in reach and he fished out the key. He went slow, fearful of dropping it, and soon enough he had his hands out.

Caine at first was going to put the manacles back through the ring and close them. He intended to get rid of the key, and leave a mystery for Murphy when he found empty irons. But now Caine paused to examine the post with its unnerving phosphorescence. The bed was large and stout, but the construction was straightforward—simply built with mortise and tenon. Uncomplicated but well-crafted, rather like one of the hoary timber-framed barns back in New England. It was designed to stand a long time but could be easily broken down by knocking out pegs. The beginnings of a plan to fight the Grinder began to form.

The colonel's house was built like a hunting lodge similar to ones he had seen in the English countryside. The central feature was a huge stone hearth that opened to the sitting room on one side but went straight through to the kitchen on the other. The walls were hung with trophies, many of them spattered with the blood of the house's hapless defenders.

Caine eyed the balcony of the upper floor and the space below it, a short hall which led to the kitchen. From the top of the balustrade to the lower floor was about fourteen feet. Caine didn't know if it would be enough drop, but it was enough to give it a try.

He started moving fast, racing the setting sun. A tack hammer was all he could find, but it was enough to get the pegs out and the bed apart. Caine could find no rope in the house and so started shredding the colonel's bedclothes. He braided quickly and made some stout lines.

After he had his trap set, he stared at it, wondering if it would work, if the Grinder would fall for it. Caine thought of the malevolent eyes of the brute in the woods as the great head had sought its prey. Inhuman as it was, there was intelligence as well as malice in those eyes. So Caine tried to conceal his play. He was worried about time and so settled for simply covering the whole thing with a carpet.

After working so quickly, Caine steeled himself. It turned out he needn't have hurried. As Caine stood, tensed before the door, the long shadows grew longer. Soon the house was in all but darkness, and the Grinder didn't appear. Caine took a deep breath and decided to have a look around. He found a lamp and searched the house for anything useful.

There wasn't much. Food was what he really wanted; as he feared, the soldiers didn't feed him, and the pantry was bare.

Weapons would have been another comfort, and here he was somewhat luckier. There were no pistols or rifles, but he did find a beautiful fowling piece and some shells.

He also found an old saber in the Hussar style. It hung on the wall where it would have been crossed with another saber, but Caine couldn't find the mate. It had no scabbard, so he slid it through his belt.

During this little search, Caine kept his ears open, listening for the sound of the Grinder. He peered out all the windows, but he saw nothing. The town was dark, and if there was light at the fort, he couldn't see it from here.

The night was growing cold fast, but Caine didn't want to light a fire. He managed to find a thick, heavy quilt that must have belonged to a servant, for it seemed a bit homey for the Colonel's taste. He moved a wingback chair so it faced the front door and placed the lamp on the mantle. He turned the flame down low and sat in the chair, wrapping himself and the shotgun in the quilt.

Caine made a conscious effort to relax and breathe easy to be patient as he had been on the mountain, waiting for his chance at the bandits. Caine's long sleep in the stockade paid off now, for he wasn't drowsy. Time passed and Caine became more and more attuned to the surrounding night.

First the sounds of the Colonel's cursed house, the creaking timber, the skittering claws of a hungry mouse in the kitchen. Gradually his senses widened to the woods outside the walls. He heard the soft susurration of wind through the mountain's trees. Those winds picked up and made their music in the boughs, but died down suddenly so that sounds carried. Caine heard the cry of an owl that must be a half-mile off but clear as a bell. He sat watching the door and listening to the lonely hills until the moon rose. Slim tendrils of silver light started to leak into the silent house, and finally Caine heard it. Felt, at first, as much as heard the slow tramp of heavy footfalls.

The Grinder was coming.

Caine closed his eyes and let his senses stretch out. The Grinder was coming straight for the house. He couldn't say precisely how he knew this, but it wasn't the beast's nightly wanderings. It knew someone was here and was coming to kill.

Caine noticed something else as the rhythmic tread of doom grew unmistakably audible. He could hear animals making way, fleeing before the malevolence that Caine himself could feel. But the rhythm of the Grinder didn't sound wrong on the ground. In fact the heavy footfalls seemed to echo and resonate with the bones of the mountain.

Caine didn't have time to ponder what that might mean, for now he felt the malice of the thing reaching out like a questing hand. Caine drew back his own questing senses and let his head droop on his breast like a man asleep. He could still feel the thing's approach, like the pressure behind one's eyes before a bad storm.

Nearer and nearer the footfalls came until it must be right outside the house, and then there was tense silence. Caine kept his breathing low and slow, but his heart started to hammer in his chest. The silence held. Then there was the creak of wood outside as the front porch protested some great weight.

Caine closed his eyes to mere slits and watched the front doors. He had thrown the bolts even though he didn't expect them to be proof against the Grinder. Still, Caine was surprised by what happened next.

He had steeled himself for a mad bull's rush through the doors, instead he sensed a soft probing. He imagined nothing so much as a naughty child listening at a keyhole while adults talked. He sensed that probing reach into the room, and took care not to probe back. He tried to project the very essence of a man caught by slumber as he sat near the hearth. As Caine watched, the doors

A Nathaniel Caine Adventure

moved in their frame, slowly, by inches, until they met the bolt's resistance. They bulged and creaked under pressure from the other side. They settled back, and Caine watched the bolts slide back as if being drawn by unseen hands.

There was another of those unbearable pauses. Then the doors swung wide on darkness. Darkness and rage filled the open portal, and it was a struggle for Caine to remain still in the path of that formless wrath.

Two pinpoints of angry orange light flared and grew until Caine recognized the eyes he had seen in Elkhorn pass. He felt the same bolt of fear at the wrongness of it, the wrenching terror of seeing that malevolent sentience that was not human. Where in Hell did the old woman call this thing from?

The light of its eyes pulsed and grew, and Caine was dimly aware of the form of the thing. The ponderous bulk blocked out everything of the outside, and Caine wondered how it could fit through the door at all. No sooner did Caine wonder than a great rocky foot came into the room.

There was a stony creak of whatever passed for its joints as the Grinder...*folded*... himself through the door. It scraped wood off the frame as it passed its bulk through. It unfolded itself on the other side and was revealed plainly to Caine for the first time.

It stood on elephantine legs spread wide to carry the great hulk. It was manlike in that it stood on two legs and had two arms, but the impossible proportions made it an insulting mockery of man. The hide was a myriad of plates like an alligator, but grey and stony as granite. The craggy tor of a head sat on the bedrock of

Grinder's Keeper

shoulder with no discernible neck. Yet the head moved slowly to scan the room, and the bright light of its eyes made Caine think of a lighthouse beacon, back and forth on a lonely tower of rock. When those eyes had finished their scan of the room, they settled on Caine. He had to trust to the darkness of the room and the shadows of the quilt wrapped around him to hide his slitted eyes.

There was only the suggestion of a face—and the aspect all the more hideous for that. A wide black crack that must be a mouth and an irregular black triangle for a nose. Caine remembered pumpkins in his boyhood, carved into jack-o-lanterns for All Hallows Eve. Macabre beacons made by merry children that would light the way home in the autumn night. Whatever lit the Grinder's eyes blazed bale-fire now as it regarded the small and huddled man.

The Grinder came for him.

For all its ungainly bulk, the monster moved quickly. A few strides crossed the room, and the Grinder's long arms reached for him. The stony spires of its hand splayed out to grab him up. Caine waited until the claws were almost on him, then moved.

He sprang up from the chair and threw off the cloaking quilt in one motion. It was hard to read emotion on the Grinder's rocky face, but the mouth crack dropped open. Caine fancied he saw surprise.

Caine thrust the shotgun forth in one hand like a fencer lunging and jammed the piece in that gaping maw. Caine loosed both barrels, and the shotgun went off with a deafening roar.

A shock ran up his arm, more than the recoil of the twelve gauge could account for, and he almost dropped the gun. The Grinder took a step back, but that was all. The blast should have taken off his head or at least blown out the back. Instead the eyes glared and the beast roared, louder and longer than the gunfire, and it swung backhand at the offending weapon. The gun flew out of Caine's hand and splintered at the Grinder's touch. The barrels came free of their welds and clattered and chimed when they hit the floor.

Caine leapt headlong to escape the Grinder's next swing, an overhand blow as if it were squashing an insect. The chair burst into matchsticks and a few shreds of cloth. The floorboards cracked at the impact.

"Jesus Christ."

Caine breathed out the heartfelt oath, but fought the urge to use the open doors. He wanted the Grinder to follow him, but not outside. The Grinder turned its head and gave voice to a growl that made Caine's bones ache.

He ran through the hallway to the kitchen. He turned back and could see the Grinder peering down the hallway. He took the door in both hands and slammed it shut, then shoved at the heavy table until it was against the door. That wouldn't stop the monster, wouldn't even slow him down. Caine had planned as if there was intelligence in the inhuman hulk. He was convinced that was the case after looking right in those eyes, and the table now was some playacting.

Caine listened to the footsteps as the Grinder stalked down the hall, no longer playing at stealth. They came quickly and Caine stepped away from the door. He darted to the hearth and crawled through to the parlor. It was Caine's turn for stealth, and the Red Man's moccasins made not a sound as he edged up to peer around the corner of the hallway.

He was staring at the vast expanse of the Grinder's back. The splay fingered hands came up to touch the door, and Caine heard the latch click back, though the creature hadn't touched the knob. The Grinder pushed gently, and there was the scraping sound of wood on wood as the door rubbed against the table and stopped. The Grinder gave out another growl, not as loud but Caine still winced, for the sound was felt as much as heard, and it was painful.

Caine didn't fully understand what happened next. The Grinder put its other hand on the door but didn't shove at the barricade. Instead, the timbre of its stony growl changed and the door burst asunder. Caine flinched at the wave of power. His night eyes saw the door and table splinter into kindling. It was as if cannon shot had hit the kitchen.

The Grinder stalked forward and there was the sound of the brute stomping around the kitchen for its prey. Caine darted around the corner and snatched the trigger rope of his makeshift trap. There were a few more seconds of crashing sounds and then silence.

Once again Caine felt that unseen questing. It wasn't patient now but flailed about in frantic search. Caine didn't hide or pull back from it this time, but sent out his will like a bullet from a gun.

"Here, you son of a bitch!" Caine bellowed at the top of his lungs. "Here I stand! Come if you dare!"

The Grinder whirled in the wreckage of the kitchen and darted to the kitchen door. Caine didn't need to read expression off the featureless stone face. Hate and rage rolled down the hall like the leading edge of an avalanche. The Grinder held out its great hands and opened them slowly, clenched them just as slowly.

Caine suppressed a shudder at the flinty snap and crunch. The Grinder repeated the gesture a few more times, and its growl changed to a rough chuffing sound. Caine realized the thing was laughing, and now he couldn't repress the shudder, for that laugh was death.

Still, it wasn't the first time Nathaniel Caine had stared at death and stood fast. He gripped the hilt of the hussar saber and drew it forth. Caine waved the blade in a 'come on, then' gesture. He was rewarded with an answering bellow from the Grinder.

The beast stalked forward and Caine braced his feet with the saber held before him. He only had one chance and the timing had to be perfect. Caine didn't want to give away his trap by looking at it. He kept his eyes locked on the hellfire eyes of his foe.

On the Grinder came, and time stretched out as in a nightmare. It was only a few strides for the tall brute, but each one took an infinite agony to fall. Then the thing was almost on him and Caine heaved at the rope.

There was a quick scrape of wood on wood as the bedpost came off the ledge of the balcony. The blanket came away and Caine had an absurd moment where he felt like he was unveiling a new work of art.

The dead fall Caine had set wasn't particularly artful, but so far it was working. The post fell almost straight down until it reached the end of the manacle chain that fastened it to the railing above. Caine came the closest he had to praying in many a year.

Please hold!

The chain rattled and the railing groaned. But everything held and the drop turned into an acute arc. Whatever eldritch power that made the wood shine now made a silvery trail like a falling star.

The Grinder stopped and followed Caine's gaze just in time to take the beam full in the face at the bottom of its swing. The post split along its length with a crack like a pistol shot, and the Grinder went straight back on his heels. The Goliath tipped over and fell on its back.

Caine rushed forward with a wordless cry of triumph. He leapt on his long legs to land on the Grinders chest. The hard hide was like the stones of the mountain through his soft-soled moccasins.

Caine was already swinging the saber at the spot where neck and shoulder would meet if his foe were a man. It was a hewing stroke to open a body and let out the life. Caine knew the blow was true. But when it went home, the saber shivered into useless shards, and a shock went up his arm to the shoulder.

The Grinder's hand came up in a quick sweep like a man swatting at a gnat. Caine had never been hit by a charging bull, but this had to be close. He flew through the air, and everything went stark white for a moment when he crashed into the wall.

He rolled to a stop and got to his hands and knees, fighting to bring back his vision. He didn't think he could stand but made himself do it anyway. The house pitched and yawed until he managed to get one hand on the wall. The other hand still held the hilt of the ruined saber.

Through the haze, he could see the Grinder getting to its feet, and Caine shook his head to clear it. It worked and his vision cleared. There stood the Grinder, unhurt and unfazed.

It reached forward and grasped the bedpost. It had not been easy for Caine to wrestle the stout beam into place, but the Grinder easily took it in one hand. One tug and the railings cracked so that the chain came free, and the Grinder took it up in its other hand.

It glared at Caine and growled again, and the rhythm of that growl made Caine think there must be words in it. The rhythm and timbre changed and Caine's eyes widened. The black iron chain started to glow—cherry red, then orange, and then a shimmery yellow that was hard to look at. The metal melted and flowed and poured through the Grinder's fingers. The wood of the floor smoked and charred where the iron splattered.

Caine voiced another wordless cry, but instead of triumph, now it was despair. He had laid the trap carefully and it had failed. Now he had nothing but a bladeless hilt. Absurdly, Caine hauled back and threw the sword hilt, and just as absurdly, the Grinder brought up a hand to block it. It gave a dull clang as it hit the rocky paw, but Caine had already whirled, sprinting for the open doors.

The Grinder bellowed and in front of Caine, the doors swung shut. Outside, the shutters slammed shut hard enough to shatter the windows in their casements. Caine was running too fast to stop and crashed against the closed doors.

He wrenched and swore at the handle and bolts, but they were stuck fast. Caine whirled and the Grinder was right on top of him. Only sharp reflexes honed sharper by terror let him duck quick enough to evade the Grinder's swing. A fist like a river boulder hit the wall hard enough to make the house shiver. Some of Colonel Hayes' wainscoting popped loose from the walls. Caine tried to lean and roll out, but the Grinder's backhand still caught him on the shoulder and he went sprawling. Caine used the momentum to crawl away and scramble to his feet.

He had to stay on his feet and stay nimble. He couldn't withstand many more buffets from the beast and knew that if it managed to lay hold of him, it was his death. Caine looked around, frantic, searching for some way to escape the crushing monster.

The hearth!

Caine faced the Grinder and made himself stand before the next charge like a bull fighter. The beast reached out, and Caine feinted to his right toward the shuttered windows. The Grinder fell for it and swatted, but Caine was no longer there.

He sprinted for the hearth, and remembering the quick backhand, dove headlong. A good thing, for he felt the wind of the passing blow, and now he was scrambling over the cold hearthstones. He was halfway across and could see through to the kitchen. He could also see the broken windows and closed shutters. Whatever spell had barred the front had done the same in the back and likely every opening in the house.

All but one, Caine thought and gathered his legs beneath him.

There wasn't time to look before he leapt, and if there was a flue then the game was up. Caine's long legs uncoiled like springs and he shot up into the chimney. His head hit no flue, and he flung out all his limbs with desperate strength.

He glanced down between his feet and saw the Grinder's groping hand shoot through the opening. Caine thought of a cat pawing at a mouse hole and bit back a curse. The giant stone arm was thrust through to the kitchen, and when the beast's shoulder hit, the chimney shook and swayed alarmingly.

Caine looked up and started crawling for the top. He could see stars in a rough square, the opening of the chimney and escape. He kept his eyes on it as he struggled upwards. Below him the Grinder thrust again with his shoulder, and the stone chimney again shuddered. Caine kept his eyes up and kept crawling.

The tumult beneath him ceased for a moment, and then he heard the scrape of stone on stone. The beast must have withdrawn its great arm. Then Caine felt what he had felt earlier, mere minutes ago though the fight felt longer. He felt the unseen questing of mind and senses, felt it wash over him and radiate from the very stones he grasped.

There was no hiding from it this time, and Caine heard the rumbling roar of the Grinder's chant. Caine reckoned he was just past the second floor and made himself keep climbing. He tried to block out the horror of the Grinder's song, but it seemed to rattle off the stones of the chimney.

No, the stones were vibrating and Caine tried to put on speed. As he watched in growing horror, the star-filled opening above was getting smaller. The stones were shifting. It should have been impossible, but they were moving—moving at the command of the towering hulk that waited below.

Caine kept going, but it was hopeless. The chimney top closed with a crack, and soon the chimney itself was too narrow to pass. Caine beat at the stones, but they didn't obey him, only his foe. The stones rumbled and slid, and the gritty sound of mortar coming out of joints was the sound of sand running out of a glass. Caine braced himself against the shaft, but the stones pressed, inexorable.

He looked down, awkwardly, for he was now being crushed into a near fetal position. There had only been a dim light leaking through the hearth below, and that was now blacked out. The monster must be crouching to look in.

That made Caine think of the first time he saw the beast in the mountain cave. Caves and stone had been his sanctuaries in these mountains, but now it looked like they would be his funeral cairn. He thought again of that first cave where he had dreamed of, or been visited by, his friend Shaw. The thought made him look at the silver society ring that seemed to shine out, even in the Stygian blackness of the closed chimney. The Latin motto 'See the Truth' whispered in his mind, and it was no surprise that it was Shaw's voice he heard. He remembered the paintings that had danced in that nighted cave, and finally Caine *did* see the truth.

The tiny man at the top of a volcano who wrestled with a monster. That monster, or one like it, now reached a hand into the chimney to grind the life out of Caine. That was why the thing had such power over the stones, they were of the same elemental essence.

It wasn't rational, but Shaw had warned him against clinging to rationality, as he was clinging to the very stones trying to crush him to death. It was instinct that let him decimate the soldiers singlehandedly, not rationality. It was rational to try and fight the Grinder with lead and steel, even though he had been warned against that as well. The Red Man had told him plainly that white men's weapons would avail him not.

Rationality started draining out of Caine. Instinct took over. The instinct that made him a wolf in the hills. The instinct that made him conceal the Red Man's knife in his tall moccasins before he went into town. The soldiers had taken the arms he bore openly but hadn't found the knife. As the Grinder's hand scrabbled for Caine, Caine's hand scrabbled for the hidden blade. Rationality said to hang on as long as possible, and cling to every last second of life. Instinct said that a man couldn't run from his fate, even if it be death. Better to leap headlong and show fate what you're made of.

Nathaniel Caine's lips skinned back in a feral grin, and a growl started in his throat. He managed to get his hand in his boot top. Caine's long fingers felt and then closed on the bone hilt of the gifted knife.

The Grinder's groping fingers were almost on him as he drew forth the weapon. Even in the sooty black of the chimney, light gleamed off the glossy black blade. He had it point down like an icepick and that's how he struck. Instead of shattering like the tempered steel saber, the stone blade bit and the hand flinched back.

Caine let the growl loose as he dropped. The Indian knife grated on the Grinder's hide, but it pierced. There was no room for proper blows, but that also meant there was no way to miss. Caine's strikes were short chops of the forearm, and he managed a flurry before the beast pulled out its arm.

Caine dropped and landed on his back hard enough to drive out his breath with a *whoof*. The Grinder also barked in pain, and that made his own worth it. He kicked out and managed to scramble back on his rear through the hearth and into the kitchen, where he rolled into a crouch.

Caine looked through, and the Grinder was on the other side in a crouch, unconsciously mirroring its foe. The Grinder held its wounded hand close to its chest. Its attitude, incongruous for its size, was almost childlike; a youngster just learning the hard lesson of why mother told it not to touch the stove.

The cuts bled in their fashion. The rent hide seeped and the thick blood glowed the same forge fire orange as the beast's eyes.

Caine had never seen a live volcano, but this must be the same stuff as lava, molten rock from who knew what depths.

The blood, unimaginably hot as it must be, cooled quickly. It scorched briefly where it fell on the floor planks, but no flame leapt up and not much smoke. Instead, the magma blood gelled and turned black and glossy. Glossy and smooth as glass, for he realized that's what it was. Obsidian, just as the shard he held in his hand. Nathaniel Caine started to laugh. It wasn't a pleasant sound.

The Grinder heard it and looked up, and it lunged forward to glare at Caine through the hearth. Caine didn't flinch. Pain and hate he saw in the thing's eyes, but something else as well. Not fear, Caine thought, but doubt, and that would do well enough.

"Hurt your fingers, eh pup?" Caine said and laughed some more. "I'm thinking it's naught but a schoolyard bully you are. All bluff and bluster when you harry the defenseless. Not so game when someone fights back and you take a trifling hurt."

Bale-fire blazed from the Grinder's eyes and he snarled, but Caine waved a dismissive hand.

"Don't bother, you coward. You're not facing some scared farmer chained to a bed tonight."

Caine's voice grew into a hard shout, and his own eyes blazed back at the monster.

"You've tried for me twice already, and still I draw breath. I see what you are, and I know what you're made of. I hold your bane in my right hand! Come on!"

The stony maw split wide and the Grinder's roar belched forth like a blast out of hell. Caine stood before it, though his skull felt like it would crack from the unearthly bellow.

When the Grinder struck, it was quick as a rattlesnake and Caine was almost caught, even though he was ready for it. He hurled himself to one side, and the Grinder's hand shot past. The beast plunged up to the shoulder with enough force to dislodge the mantle. It hung up on one end and a few stones rolled loose.

Caine grasped the free end and pulled so hard he could feel the muscles in his gut start to wrench. The oaken mantle flew out in a spray of mortar dust. It was finally more than the battered chimney could take. More than a ton of mountain stone dropped on the Grinder's outstretched arm. Caine pounced on the pinned limb and plunged the obsidian knife up to the hilt. The Grinder screamed and Caine could hear it, even through all the rock. He added his own savage scream and matched it with savage slashes to his trapped foe.

The stony skin split and burst and the lava flowed. The Grinder's screams grew in volume and terror and it thrashed on the other side. Caine could hear hammering blows, the monster must be beating at the pile trying to pull free. Caine felt the arm moving beneath him and braced his whole body to try and keep it pinned. He continued to hack, and he thought the whole house might collapse at the bellows of the beast.

Then there was a lurch beneath him and a sickening crack and Caine fell back. He kept his grip on the Grinder's hand, though it was like wrestling a tree trunk. The fingers had stopped trying to

A Nathaniel Caine Adventure

crush him, and Caine looked at the hideous wound the Red Man's knife had made.

He had managed to hack almost all the way through the Grinder's arm; it hissed and smoldered with foul smelling vapors. Caine reset his feet and plunged the knife once more, pulled at the arm, and then it was free. He staggered back and fell under the weight of it.

The Grinder screamed louder yet, though Caine didn't know how that was possible. He dropped the knife and clapped his hands over his ears, rolled in pain at the fury and terror of that cry. Finally, the volume lessened and Caine opened his eyes. He hadn't realized they were shut tight. Caine scrambled about until his hands found the bone hilt. He took a breath and forced himself to his feet. He would have used the table to steady himself, but all the furniture was shattered. Caine lurched to the wall and used that instead.

He went through the kitchen door and past his failed trap. Cold mountain air was streaming in through the wide open front doors. Caine drew in huge draughts of it. The parlor was in even worse shape than the kitchen, but the monster wasn't there.

The fresh air was bracing, and by the time Caine walked through the front doors, he was walking almost normally. He walked out on the porch and it sagged a bit, but then so did he. He looked out into the nighted woods and listened. Far off, he could hear a howl that might almost be a wolf.

But it was no wolf.

The Grinder had fled.

The Grinder's Mother

Swenson moved always with unconscious stealth. He was a scout and a hunter, and it was second nature to walk with careful footfalls and smooth movements to avoid drawing eyes and ears. So when a man like Swenson was purposely trying, as he was now, to be quiet and unseen, it may as well be a shadow in the woods.

Swenson made himself into that shadow, and it took all his self discipline to do it. He wanted to hurry. He had heard the screams and bellows; hell's fires, hadn't they shaken the whole valley? But he didn't know what they might mean. He had seen fate's mark on the dark stranger, to be sure, but he still found it hard to believe the Grinder could be bested by one man. Yet he had seen the Grinder in battle, and the bellows of his murderous rampages were different from the desperate shrieks he and the soldiers had heard on the palisade.

The Irishmen had crossed themselves and clutched their carbines and shrank back on the ramparts. Swenson leaned out into the night, peering at the Colonel's house, though all was in darkness. He tried to read the tale based on what he could hear, but of course little could be known for certain.

"Sure and the Grinder's sendin another soul to hell tonight," one of the troopers said.

Swenson wasn't so certain. The mere fact that the noise went on for so long spoke for a fight, not a one-sided slaughter. Of course the Irish thought the stranger was chained, but Swenson knew better. He had placed a key in the stranger's hand himself. He knew the man could get free of his bonds, but was less sure of what he would do after. The stranger had given his word to face the monster, and Swenson knew now that Nathaniel Caine had stood by those words.

The sounds of the clash reached a crescendo with a world-shattering shriek that hurt Swenson's ears. More than one of the soldiers on that wall clapped hands over their own ears and sank down on the platform. The shriek came again further off, and again further still, until it might have been mistaken for the howl of a wolf.

The silence that flowed in was, in some ways, more disturbing. There was no wind or bird call, just the heavy quiet of a starry night in the chill grip of Spring in the mountains. Swenson swore in Swedish and swung a leg over the parapet. One of the troopers grabbed at his tunic.

"Are ye feckin mad, man?"

"Take your hands off me!" Swenson said. "I am going to find out what happened."

"How will you get down there?"

Swenson just snorted and dropped off the wall like a cat. To the troopers, it seemed the white-haired scout just disappeared into the black night.

"It's your funeral," the man said and crossed himself. "Ye feck, ye."

The need to hurry burned in Swenson, a desire to pelt down the road and run in the front door of Hayes' house. But he was a scout and a damned good one, and he made himself approach with caution. He forsook the road, but stayed close enough to see any that might pass on it. He moved from tree to tree, stopping every twenty paces or so to listen and watch.

Swenson came on the house from the forest side and slowed his pace even more. He went down on all fours and used deliberate movements that would not draw the eye of any watchers. From the great clashing noises they'd heard at the fort, Swenson was half expecting the house to be a pile of rubble and matchsticks, but it stood whole and sound.

Well, maybe not whole. Swenson saw some of the shutters hanging at odd angles, and it looked like the windows were broken. He moved in a sideways shuffle to make a wary circle around the house, and something else looked wrong.

It was the chimney. Or rather it *wasn't* the chimney. It had been a wide tower of local stone that jutted proud from the roofline, but it was no longer there. Swenson let his eyes sweep over the ground around the house. Since there was no huge pile of rocks outside, logic dictated the chimney was all inside the house.

Swenson abandoned his woodsman's discipline with a curse and stood up. He cocked his rifle and stalked around to the front of the house. He could see some flickering light from inside and it drew his eye. It almost made him miss the figure on the steps, and Swenson was almost upon it when he did notice.

He jerked back a step and shouldered his rifle. The figure was a man, sitting on the crooked steps and leaning against the post, but more Swenson couldn't say. The shape was black in a black night, and only the faint lamplight through the doors showed it at all. Swenson used the night-hunting trick of not looking directly at it. It was a rangy framed man with long legs, the stranger Caine.

Swenson lowered the rifle and moved closer. The man was still as stone with eyes closed and mouth open. Dead then. But why did the Grinder leave him? The corpse's eyes flashed open and gleamed in the low light. Swenson jumped and the rifle came back up, finger on the trigger.

"Good evening, Swenson."

The voice rasped and the man coughed and spat. He tried again and it was still rough, but better.

"I don't suppose you have anything to drink?"

"Christ Jesus, Caine," Swenson said. "You near scared the life out of me! I came a whisker away from shooting you for it."

"After the fight I just had, that would be disappointingly mundane," Caine said and gave a weak gesture toward the scout's tunic. "The flask?"

"How did you know...?"

Swenson's hand went to his chest, where he had a leather flask of brandy in an inside pocket.

"I knew there was *seidr* power on you Caine. You see much."

His hand brought out the flask and tossed it to the dark figure.

"My thanks," Caine said and unstoppered the leathern flask. He sniffed at it before taking a draught. Caine gave an appreciative gasp.

"Brandy! And a fairly good one. Again, I thank you."

Caine took another drink before passing it back.

"Yah, everyone drinks whiskey around here, but I don't care for it."

Swenson took a swig himself before tucking the flask back in.

"Now Caine, what happened here? Did you kill the Grinder after all?"

"Well..."

Caine levered himself up with an effort and beckoned for Swenson to follow into the house.

"I won the fight, at least, and laid a fearsome wound on him. I'm not sure if he'll die from it. He's a fell thing."

Swenson went to the lamp and turned up the flame. He gaped in silence at the aftermath of the battle. He shook his head as well at the figure of Caine. He was battered and blackened, and it was no wonder Swenson had taken him for a corpse. His thoughts must have shown, for Caine's teeth flashed white in his sooty face.

"I look worse than I feel," he said. "The brandy helped. Have a look at this."

Caine led him into the kitchen and Swenson knelt beside the great stony hand. He laid his rifle down and ran his own hands over the ridges of rock.

"Well, that's quite a trophy," Swenson said. "And quite a story I bet. Sometime you'll have to tell it, but not now. Dawn's not long off, and then Murphy and his boys will be about. I don't want to be here then."

"Our bargain."

"Yes, Caine," Swenson said. "My aid in exchange for the sorceress. I gave you the aid. Now you must find her for me."

That was true enough. Without the key Caine would have been manacled and helpless when the Grinder came. What's more he knew he *could* find the sorceress, for he expected the Grinder to run right to her. The woman must answer for her actions, but Swenson wanted her head, literally. It wasn't Caine's way to offer harm to an old woman. He said as much to Swenson.

"This isn't some innocent girl, just come in from the morning milking, Caine. This is a she-wolf, and we're going into her den. She'll kill both of us if she gets the chance, and she won't stop her feud with Hayes or the people you risked your life to help."

"Perhaps," Caine said. "At any rate, the bargain was I'd lead you to her, and that I think won't be difficult. Let's be about it."

"One moment," Swenson said. "A good scout leaves signs for the army. Let's leave a token for Murphy and his blue coats."

Swenson bent and grasped the Grinder's hand. It scraped as he dragged it across the floor, and Caine moved to help him. The thing was heavy, but the two men managed it and got it out the front door. Swenson pointed with his chin, and he and Caine grunted as they lifted the limb to the lintel. They got it hung over the door and Caine gave a hard grin of satisfaction, for it made a barbaric trophy.

That work done, the men set off. The Grinder's black blood gleamed in the moonlight, and Caine could follow the track easily. They moved at a lope like a pair of lean hunting wolves. If any were there to mark their passing, they would have thought the men quite similar, despite their different coloring. Both were tall and rangy, and they moved with a long limbed grace. Both had bright eyes and sharp features that burned fierce with the hunt. The Indian style tunics added to the similarity.

The sign showed a headlong flight with a great deal of blood, and Caine began to hope that the wound was mortal. But mile after mile went by, and there was no body.

The great gouts of blood turned to splashes and trickles as they moved down closer to the valley floor. The blood trail continued to diminish until it was just widely spaced black marks. Easily seen on the patches of snow, but nearly invisible on the bare ground.

Or would have been invisible. To Caine they gave off a slight sheen in the moonlight, but he didn't think Swenson could see them. Without discussing it, they adopted the tactics one would use for dangerous game. One man read sign and trail, the other followed just behind and to the side, scanning ahead with weapon ready.

The blood stopped altogether as the mountain pines closed in, and Caine had to follow footmarks. The huge splayed craters of the Grinder's initial flight were also gone. Caine saw long furrows as the beast dragged it's feet, and he knew it must be spent.

Caine stopped and peered into the trees ahead where they marched along the escarpment of the mountain's walls. There was no wind, but still the woods seemed to whisper. Caine just stared, and finally Swenson could take it no longer.

"Why do you stop?" he murmured in Caine's ear. "Do you see the beast? Or its mistress?"

"No," Caine said and kept his voice as low as the scout's, "but we're close."

He pointed into the trees.

"There? I've been up and down this valley many times, Caine, and never found either of them. These pines go right up to the bones of the mountain."

"There will be a cave. The Grinder's strength is all but gone, and as I thought, it runs right back to its dam."

"Dam?" Swenson said. "You mean that thing has a mother?"

"You said it yourself, huntsman. You named her she-wolf and its her den we approach. A she-wolf with a wounded cub."

Caine watched Swenson's face as he worked out the meaning of Caine's words. After a few minutes the look hardened.

"And now you've warned me," he said, "but my resolve has not wavered. Lead on."

As Caine thought, it wasn't far. The trail went into the copse of scrubby mountain pine. As the trees grew closer, so did the darkness. Oddly, there was almost no sign here. He expected a swath where the beast would have bulled his way through. There were a few fresh broken branches, but no more than any large forest creature might make.

A Nathaniel Caine Adventure

After fifty paces or so, the trees ended abruptly in a glen, itself about fifty paces wide. The far side was the rocky wall of steep rising cliff. The cliff faced west and showed the last light of the moon, which was ready to set. A gurgling freshet came from above head height and made a tracery of silver on the exposed rock to fall in a small round pool.

"Damn it!" Swenson said. "It's as before. The track simply ends!"

"No," Caine said.

His eyes had gone instantly to the small tarn and lay there now.

"It leads to yonder pool."

Swenson cast about on the ground, but saw no sign. Caine walked over to the rocky edge and stared into the water. Swenson followed, but he could not see any sign and he threw Caine a look, half question, half accusation. After long moments, Caine met the look.

"Can you not see it?"

"See what?" Swenson said. "All I see is a pool of mountain water. I've been here before, and never seen her or any sign of her."

"You're blind then," Caine said.

His right hand went to the silver ring on his left, and he twisted the silver a few times, as a man might worry at a good luck charm. To Caine, the trail was clear and led directly to the edge of the water, but that wasn't what made his eyes wide with wonder.

The water fell gently down the rocks, not enough to churn the pool, but instead the surface danced and wavered and shone in the night. It wasn't moonlight, but a bright silver shimmer from within. It was beautiful, but cold and fell like jewelry on a pagan queen.

"There's a cave. In the water. The woman waits within."

Swenson took a step back, chilled at the quiet singsong of Caine's voice. He clutched at the man's arm.

"Snap out of it, man! There's no cave. You speak as one bewitched."

Caine smiled at him. It was not reassuring.

"It's a witch you seek, is it not, huntsman?"

The scout straightened and lifted a defiant chin.

"I'm not afraid, Nathaniel Caine."

He dropped his rifle on the ground.

"If you say we must go in the water, Sven Swenson won't balk."

He took off his hat and made to shed the rest of his gear, but Caine put up a staying hand.

"I'll go alone I think, Swenson," he said. "The woman's in there. She knows you and hates you, I'm sure, as she hates the others in this valley. She doesn't know me. Perhaps I can talk to her."

"What makes you think she'll bear you any love?" Swenson gestured at the knife Caine bore.

"Doubtless you're right, but I'll try anyway," Caine said.

He set a foot in the water then drew it back.

"Still."

He took the knife out of his belt, sheath and all, and tucked it into the leather of his tall moccasins. No sense in openly displaying the weapon that had dealt such a fearsome wound.

"I still don't see any cave," Swenson said. "This had better not be some kind of trick."

"Well, lately I've been playing tricks a good deal more than I'm used to," Caine said with a shrug, "so I won't take offense. But I tell you there's a cave, and the Grinder went in there. I feel some other power in there as well."

"The witch," Swenson said. "Very well, Nathaniel Caine. I will wait for you here."

Caine nodded and stepped into the water. It was cold as only mountain water could be, and he fought against holding his breath. The rocks on the basin's bottom shifted here and there as he made his way to the center where the water was about waist deep. Caine took a deep breath and sank in one movement beneath the water.

From here, the cave's entrance was plain to see. It wasn't large. In fact he would have said the Grinder couldn't have made it through. Then he recalled the strange way the beast had…*folded*…himself through the doors of the Colonel's house.

Caine stood back up and dashed water from his eyes. He didn't know how long the tunnel was. Better to walk over and take a deep breath before trying it.

Caine took a step, and the rock beneath his foot gave way. His ankle twisted painfully, and Caine shot under the water. He tried to push himself off the bottom with his hands and get his feet under him, but he was moving along the bottom. Some unseen current dragged him across the rocks, and it was growing stronger.

Caine snatched at the stones, but they all gave way as he was pulled toward the dark mouth of the cave. His feet went in, and his arms shot out in a desperate attempt to catch the edge. But the rock was worn smooth as glass by eons of the water's passing.

In a flash, he was sucked down the narrow tunnel. He could see the silver shimmer of the pool drawing away at a rapid pace. The current swirled, and Caine was twisted and battered on the rock walls. He thrashed and struggled, trying to break the surface and get air, but it was no use. Either the tunnel was wholly filled with water, or the current was too strong to break.

Caine's lungs were already burning, and the desire to take a breath was overpowering as white flashes began to appear in his eyes. He couldn't tell up from down, or if the tunnel took any turns.

There was only the beating of rock, the rushing of water, and the hellish need to breathe. Then there was a violent twist, and his head cracked against the tunnel wall. The rest of Caine's hoarded breath went out in a cry of pain and blackness seized him.

* * *

When Caine came to, everything was still black as a Stygian tomb. He blinked his eyes rapidly to assure himself that they could open. For a few panic-stricken moments, he thought he had gone blind. Thought took over and he reasoned he was probably just in a cave, and at night to boot. Apparently his newfound night vision wasn't working.

Caine was wet and chilled, but now he felt a sharper cold on his hand, and he fancied he could see the gleam of Shaw's ring in the inky blackness. Fancy grew to a certainty, and gradually his surroundings were revealed in a pale silver light.

He lay propped against the wall of a largish cave, and his hands were tied with rope. He couldn't have been out long, for he was still wet enough that his clothes and hair dripped on the floor. As the light strengthened, or his eyes grew accustomed, he could make out a form before him. No, two forms.

The Grinder lay on his back next to a pool of water. The open eyes stared at the ceiling of the cave but no longer glowed. All the hateful fire had burned out. The arms were crossed at the breast, and one great hand lay flat next to the ugly stump of the Grinder's death wound.

The Grinder was perfectly still, but another figure, much smaller, rocked and swayed beside him. Its back was to Caine, clad in shapeless rags with its head covered. Low muttering and mewling sounds came from it, and they were in a woman's voice.

The sorceress.

As she rocked she would sometimes reach out a hand and touch the Grinder's chest. It was a delicate movement, a tender gesture that confirmed what Caine had suspected about the creature. Caine held up his hands and looked at the cord wrapped around his wrists.

Damn and blast. Bound again, he thought. *That's happening far too frequently these last few days.*

He had a strong and uncomfortable feeling that this time was the most dangerous yet. Caine examined the rope in the silver-grey light and started to work and flex his wrists. The bonds felt tight, but they had been tighter when he hung on the tree. The thought of the tree made Caine think of the Red Man, and suddenly he could feel the skeins of rope starting to loosen.

The small and raggedy woman ceased her mewling. Though her head was covered in a shawl, Caine knew she was looking back at him. She gave a harsh cry and sprang up. She had been squatting on her haunches but wasn't much taller standing. She covered the distance between her and Caine in a rush and reached beneath her ragged clothing.

"None of that, now!"

She drew out a short length of wood, just a branch with the bark pared away. She thrust the point through the strands of rope, and they snapped tight like a sprung snare. Caine hissed at the pain.

There were two or three inches of twig showing and the old woman snapped it off. Caine wondered why for a moment, and then realized she had broken it so he couldn't pull it out with his teeth. As Caine watched, the ropes seemed to shift and tighten a bit more, and now he couldn't see the twig at all.

He looked up at his latest captor and repressed a shudder with an effort of will. The woman's face was haggard, skin drawn tight to show too much of the skull beneath. She was unwashed and her hair, unbound, fell in lank and limp tendrils. The too thin face made her blue eyes bulge and they smoldered with madness.

"A little rowan will stop your tricks, Old Wanderer," she said.

"I'm not sure I take your meaning, Mrs. Jorgensen."

"Oh, my. Listen how polite and how charming you talk to me."

The woman spoke with a singsong accent similar to the Swedes in the valley. But where they flattened and drew out their vowels, Ana Jorgensen's came out in a high trill, almost like a woodwind instrument.

She made a gesture with her hand on her cheek that Caine thought was supposed to be coquettish. The effect was spoiled somewhat by the skeletal aspect of her fingers—knobby jointed with long cracked nails. The effect was then spoiled wholly when she swung that hand like a cat's paw and raked those nails down Caine's cheek.

He recoiled and grunted at the pain. The crone nodded with eager satisfaction. The wound stung and Caine could feel blood flowing, but he stopped his hands from going to the hurt. Instead he ignored it and returned the woman's look of glee with one of impassive regard. The woman drew herself up and put hands on hips, and despite her short stature, managed to look down on Caine. After a moment, she tossed her head and turned her back.

"All very interesting," she said and walked slowly back to the stone corpse. "It seems the grand Colonel Hayes has gotten himself a higher quality of hound."

"I'm no man of Hayes'," Caine said.

He drew up his knee and started digging in his boot top for the knife.

"No? Then why are you after me? Why did you kill my dear one?"

"I'm not after you," Caine said.

He tried to keep his voice calm, but his fingers were eagerly questing.

"I was raised not to offer violence to women. Your dear one was trying to kill me. I was only defending myself."

"Defense?" Ana said.

She didn't look at Caine while she spoke, only stared down at her 'dear one,' but there was a hard and venomous edge to her voice.

"And when he ran from the hurt you did him, what then? Was it defense that set you on his trail? That made you follow all the way to our home?"

At the word 'home,' Caine looked around the cave. It was littered with an array of items that must have come from the empty houses.

There was a mattress, filthy and with no frame, that must be the hag's bed. There were crates, and barrels, and other odds and ends, but one item drew Caine's eye. At least some of the plunder came from Hayes' house, for leaning against the wall was a saber. It was a wide, broad Hussar blade, the twin to the one he had broken on the Grinder's stone neck. But he couldn't use it with his hands tied, so he went back to fishing for the stone knife in his boot.

"Is this what you are rooting for?"

A Nathaniel Caine Adventure

Ana turned, and she held the Red Man's knife in her hands. She waggled it teasingly at Caine, as a cruel man might waggle a bone at a hungry dog. She drew the blade from its leathern sheath, and the obsidian gleamed in the witch-light. "Did you think you could slip this black shard between my ribs?"

"I sought only to cut my bonds," Caine said with a shrug. "I told you, it's not my habit to harm women."

Rage twisted her face. Again she rushed at Caine.

"But you *have* harmed me!" she screamed in his face, and Caine winced at the fetid breath. "You harmed my poor dear boy! He could barely crawl when he came back and he howled as he died!"

"I'm sorry for your loss, but I can't take it back."

"Sorry?"

The woman was coming even more unhinged and froth flew from her lips.

"I can make you very sorry, indeed!"

The blade flashed at Caine's face. He jerked his head back to crack painfully on the stone wall. The bodkin point hovered in front of his eye. He could see the facets on the inky surface of the blade.

"I should take your eye! Then you'll match your Terrible One."

Caine had no idea who the Terrible One was, but he had little choice other than let the mad woman rave. The knife came down and she held it to his right wrist. Her whole body trembled with rage and insanity, so that the razor sharp blade started to draw blood from Caine's flesh.

"Or maybe I'll hack off your hand and maim you as you did to my dear one. You can get out of the ropes easy enough then."

She was trying to scare Caine, trying to make him squirm at the promised torture. Caine *was* scared. The woman's mind was unmoored, and he had no doubt she would do as she promised and worse. Caine could still fight with his hands bound. But not well and not without risking injury from the knife, even against a smaller opponent.

Caine took a deep breath. He had been advised not to rely on brute force and strength of arms. Both the Red Man and the visitation from Shaw had warned him expressly not to fall into that trap. Caine let the breath out in a long sigh.

"Mrs. Jorgensen," he said. "Ana. You have to know that is no longer your son. Your son died more than a year ago."

"It *is* my son," she hissed, but wouldn't meet Caine's eye. "It's part of him. Enough."

"Enough for what?"

"For vengeance. Hayes and that devil Murphy treated my boy worse than a dog."

"Yes. I heard. And no one could fault your desire for revenge," Caine said. "but it's killing you. Jesus Christ, woman, your vengeance is eating you alive!"

"Christ?"

Ana turned her head and spit.

"I have no more use for him. My husband was a good man and a follower of Christ. For him I gave up the old ways, the secret ways. My dear boy was good too, but Christ did nothing to help either of them."

"Christian or no, your son should rest in peace," Caine said. 'What you've done to him isn't right."

"What do you know of it?"

"I know that Hayes' mining opened veins of power in the mountains. I know that the thing you called on is a destroyer. The Indians put it to sleep here centuries ago, millennia perhaps. Now it uses your son's body to walk in mayhem and murder."

"It's not murder," Ana said. "It's justice."

"Vengeance and justice are not always the same. Hayes wronged you certainly, as did Murphy, but what of the townsfolk, Ana? How many innocent people have been ripped to shreds for your vengeance?"

"Innocent?" said Ana. "They're not innocent. They stood by while my dear one was murdered. Not one of them raised a hand, or even a word of protest, while my son's flesh was lashed from his bones."

"What would you have them do, woman?" Caine said. "Against Murphy and his goons? They were unarmed farmers against professional killers with guns. None of them as brave as Willem. None of them as powerful as you. And they with their own children to think of."

The old woman looked back at the Grinder that had once been her son. Her face worked and Caine thought she had truly not seen any of it in that light. He could tell also that it wouldn't be enough.

"I care not."

She made a dismissive gesture with the hand that held the knife, and the black blade almost cut Caine's face. "They all made their choice. All they have to do to escape the curse is forsake their gold and leave."

"Ah, yes."

Caine ignored the flailing knife with an effort and held Ana's eyes.

"Just run off into the wild on foot with no food and children in tow. Even if the troopers didn't hunt them down, they'd never make it more than a few days. I ask you again; give up your revenge before more die. Before it consumes you."

"You are full of fine talk, Wanderer," she said, "like any poor preacher."

"I don't take your meaning."

"Bah! You are all but a warg in the woods these past few nights," the crone said. "Ana hears and sees, even from her cave. What drives *you*, but vengeance? What would you do to kill the man that hung you on that tree?"

Caine blinked, taken aback. How the woman knew so much was a mystery, and he opened his mouth to deny. He closed it with a shrug and surprised them both by laughing.

"I suppose you have a point, madam," he said. "I was coming to this town to help people. It's true I've done much since for revenge, and much of it was not in my normal character. But when the time came, I put aside my vengeance. If you like, Ana, we can do it together. I will forswear my vengeance against Elisha Cullen if you forswear yours against Colonel Hayes."

"It is easy for you," she said. "A few hurts and wounded pride, but you yet live. My Willem died, and blood must pay for blood. Hayes must die."

"Aye, there's the rub. Hayes yet lives while townsfolk die. Strong as your curse is, it hasn't touched the man himself. His luck holds."

"What do you know of such things?"

Sudden fire rekindled in Ana's eyes, and the knife flashed to Caine's throat. He could feel the keen edge with every pulse of the artery in his neck, but he remained calm. There was little choice else.

"I know him better than you think," he said. "I know that there is some virtue in the timbers of his fort that protects him. I know he didn't plan it, was merely lucky. He's always had that kind of luck. The luck of a fox that steps in a trap, but pulls its leg out just before the snare closes. And I know this. His name isn't Hayes."

Ana's demeanor underwent another mercurial change. Where before she had blazed with the fires of rage, she now went icy cold. The knife came away from Caine's throat, though she still held it ready. Her other hand reached out slowly, and tendons creaked as fingers twisted in Caine's buckskin tunic. The woman pulled and despite her small stature and emaciated frame, she drew him away from the cave wall until they were close enough to kiss.

"I will have none of your tricks, Grim Man," Ana said.

Caine felt the cold of her as a physical thing. He thought to pass it off as his wet clothes, but he knew it was more. Being pulled close to the witch felt like being lowered into a deep well. Her breath streamed white in the air as she spoke.

"The King in his fort is not named Hayes? And you know his real name?"

"I know his name and his work," he said. "This isn't the first time he's killed innocents for wealth. This isn't the first time he's escaped justice."

"You still want justice, but I still want revenge."

"I said they weren't always the same," Caine said.

He was fighting not to shiver in the chill coming off the mad woman.

"But sometimes they are."

"And so, would you trade your vengeance for mine?" she said. "Bring justice to the man?"

"I would," Caine said. "I came to help the townsfolk. They won't be safe until the Colonel is dealt with."

"More than you know."

Ana let him fall back and turned to look at the stony heap that had been the Grinder.

"You said that isn't my son, but it is. His body at least. My poor Willem. You say true that there is a power imprisoned in these mountains. I drew that power out to make my son into a slayer, but the thing itself is still bound.

Every day those murdering bastards dig out the veins, they gets closer to that prison. If it gets out it, will take more than a few pricks of this pretty piece of glass to defeat him. Everything in this valley will perish."

"Then we must stop him, Ana."

"Easy to say," she said. "A fox you call him, but more like an old badger in his hole. How will you get him out of his fort?"

The old country must be full of badgers, thought Caine, for Swenson had described the colonel just as Ana had. He bowed his head as he ran through options in his mind.

"Well, I don't think I can," he said after a few moments. "So I'll just have to walk right in and deal with him there."

Ana turned her eyes of frost and stared long at Nathaniel Caine. Time seemed to stop, and even the dripping of water in the cave felt suspended. Finally, the sorceress moved. Her hand shot out and the black knife flashed. Caine's bonds fell away and time started up again. The old woman stood and turned her back.

"I'll need to borrow your shard, Wanderer," she said. "Fetch me the King's steel there."

Caine stood and rubbed his wrists where the ropes had bitten, rubbed at other hurts. He went to the untidy heap of goods that she indicated, looked again at the dirty bed. There were bits of unfinished food, bread crusts and fish bones, strewn about. Even though Caine's face still stung from Ana's attack, he felt a great pity for the woman. He pushed it down for, old woman or no, she was dangerous. Far more dangerous than the colonel thought and even more powerful than Swenson dreamed. Her power filled the cave, and Caine could not sweep it aside with rational explanations.

His course was set. He must see it through.

He took up the old saber and gave it the quick inspection that was the reflex of any fighting man. The hilt and guard were attached solidly to the blade with no give, and the wire-bound leather grip was still supple. The steel flexed well in his hands, and the edge was keen with no nicks or pits. Caine brought the sword to the old woman and presented it to her, hilt first. Ana's bony hand wrapped around the weapon and she thrust the point skyward. The steel flashed as she brandished it, and then Ana Jorgensen began a slow dance.

Caine stared at the ragged and wizened form as she shuffled and paced with saber clutched in both hands. There was a pattern to it, but he couldn't make it out. Nor could he guess at the meaning of the strange words she began to chant. They had the same singsong rhythm and musical hoots, so he guessed it was her native tongue.

Gooseflesh rose on Caine's arms, for it was a fey figure she cut. He pivoted to watch her as she described a circle around them with the Grinder's body at the center. Her chant rose and fell and reached a crescendo as she came back to the spot where she began.

She lowered the sword and placed it so the naked blade lay flat across both palms, and turned to face the monster she had made of her son. Her gait now was slow and stately as a funeral march. Caine again felt the chill of her as she passed.

Ana knelt beside her son and laid the sword on his breast, adding to the funerary aspect. She grasped the dirty black rag of her shawl and drew it up so that it covered her head. The hood took away humanity. Ana Jorgensen was no more. All that now knelt in that ancient cavern was sorceress, fell and terrible.

She began to chant again and the voice seemed disembodied, coming as it did from the black depths of the crone's cowl. Power was building in the cave. Caine could feel it mounting like a coming storm. The pressure of it intensified as Ana chanted her weird song.

Presently she drew forth the Red Man's knife and plunged it into the Grinder's chest. Instead of snapping on the stone it sank to the hilt, and the power that was building began to flow. Caine could feel it through the soles of his feet, a deep and terrible throbbing, and he took a step back, then another.

Don't break the circle!

This was no whisper in his mind's ear. It was a voice clear as a bell, and Caine would swear any oath that it was his lost friend, Gibson Shaw. He stopped his feet with an effort and then, with a greater effort, made them take him back to stand behind the witch-woman.

She was bent almost double so her hooded head hung over the dead monster. She swayed to and fro over the steel and stone, and her constant chanting filled the chamber until the rock itself seemed to be singing with the sorceress.

The chant ceased abruptly and Caine winced at the silence. The song was over, but the throb of power still reverberated through the mountain's bones. Ana grasped the stone knife and pulled it forth so that the point hung downward, almost touching the saber. The hood shifted slightly, and though Caine couldn't see her face, he knew the witch was looking at him.

"Now then, Wanderer."

Her voice was a raspy whisper from the depths of the hood.

"Give me the name of my son's murderer."

He gave it to her and the knife started moving. Noises came from the hood, but not the full throated chant. Instead, Ana sang to herself in a buzzing whisper as the knife scratched marks into the steel. Letters from an alphabet Caine didn't recognize, but he could see the power of them. They glowed dull red with the forge fires of bane and hate.

The witch scratched and mumbled until the blade was scribed with a long line of runes. She flipped the weapon over and scratched until that side also bore the fiery writing. Finally she fell still and sat back on her haunches.

She sheathed the black knife and held it out for Caine, who tucked it into his belt. The white fingered hands drew back the hood, and once again it was just a wizened old woman. Haggard she was before, but now she looked all but a corpse. Caine almost reached out to her, but he didn't know how she would take such a gesture.

"I have worked a strong magic here, Wanderer."

Her voice quavered a bit, but still her words had steel in them.

"But it is for you to finish it."

"What must I do, woman?"

"Take up the King's steel and strike me down."

"What? Are you..."

Caine bit off his words.

"Mad?" Ana said and shrugged. "I was, but as you said I can't take it back. I suppose I still am, but among my people, madness comes from the gods."

"Among my people, a man should not murder an old woman," Caine said.

He dropped to his knees by the tiny figure.

"I went through all of this to avoid killing you, Ana. There's plenty of people out there who are trying."

"None of them could find me," she said. "Even now. Even Swenson who's waiting, oh so patiently, outside my door."

"I'll take the sword and deal with the colonel, but I won't harm you," he said. "You've suffered enough, Ana."

"Yes and my suffering is almost at an end," she said. "You *must* do it, for the spell depends on it. Blood will pay for blood."

"Ana…"

"You will do as I say."

Ana Jorgensen turned and held his eyes with her own. The witch's eyes were cold as a glacier and just as implacable.

"You owe me a debt, Nathaniel Caine."

Long he held that icy gaze, but no words came to him. Finally, he just nodded. Caine reached for the hilt and the blade scraped on the Grinder's skin as he stood.

Ana tugged off her ragged shawl and pulled aside the lank white strands of her hair to expose her thin neck. She put a hand on the Grinder's chest—Willem Jorgensen's chest. She gave the misshapen mouth a tender kiss but remained leaning over him.

"Make it quick."

He thought to ask her how she knew his name, but it seemed trivial.

He drew back the saber, and the steel sang through the air as Caine struck.

Accounts are Settled

Swenson didn't know how much longer he should wait. When the stranger had gone under, Swenson had gone in after him. Caine was his key to the witch, so he had dropped his rifle and plunged in.

The pool at its deepest only came up to his chest. All the more puzzling, then, that he couldn't find Caine. Swenson splashed about in a frenzy but finally calmed himself. He made a systematic search, feeling with hands and feet, and plunging under the cold water. The pool wasn't that large, and in five minutes or so, he had covered it with no sign of the stranger. Swenson searched it again with the same result.

Then he combed the banks for sign to make sure Caine hadn't slipped past him in the water and sneaked off into the woods. The only tracks were the ones going in, so Swenson searched the pool a third time.

Caine had spoken of a cave as one bewitched, so Swenson searched every inch of the cliff wall, going so far as to probe the rocks with his knife. There was no cave. Well, Caine had to have gone somewhere. So there was a cave. He just couldn't find its entrance.

Swenson slowed his breathing and used his knife to scratch marks on the rock. They were runes that his grandfather had taught him, and the words he hummed softly were also from his grandfather: a charm to reveal hidden things.

He had used the charm successfully before, but all he got tonight was colder. The witch's power was too great.

No matter. Soon enough Swenson would take that power from her.

He backed out of the water and decided to wait. It was all on Caine now. He had taken the Grinder, so perhaps he could take the hag. After a brief inner debate, Swenson decided to get a fire going. The risk was small and far outweighed by the real danger of freezing to death from the icy water and wet clothes.

Swenson took dry wood from the nearby pines. Always he kept one eye on the pool. Once the small fire was burning, he allowed himself one stout sip from his flask. Then he settled into the patient watchfulness of the hunter.

He sat near the fire but didn't look into the flames, lest he ruin his night vision. The sound of the spring burbling would have beckoned drowsiness and sleep, but Swenson had many tricks to stay awake. And so he watched and waited, but now the night sky was starting to grow pale. Once dawn broke, Murphy and his soldiers would ride out and know the Grinder was vanquished. With the slayer gone, Hayes' men would round up the farmers and go back to mining. The yellow gold would flow, but Swenson didn't care about that. His share was already a fortune and with the bounty for Ana, he could live like a king anywhere he chose.

His grandfather had given him a glimpse of the power a man could wield, but Swenson wanted more. Ana Jorgensen was a maker of great power. With her head, Swenson could be a maker as well.

That depended on Caine surviving against the old Finn, of course, which was by no means certain. The stranger had been reluctant to kill a woman, though that might change when he faced the witch. She wasn't some cheery granny with biscuits and fresh cream. If Caine didn't kill her, he would likely perish at her doing.

Still, Caine's luck had held out so far and he was, Swenson believed, the best chance. Other scenarios occurred to Swenson. Whether Caine knew it or not, whether he wanted to admit it or not, he had the marks of power on him. More than the cunning of a skilled soldier and arms-man. He was new to it, to be sure, but he had tasted it as Swenson had tasted it.

If Caine got the same hunger, he might want to keep the Finn's power for himself. Swenson was prepared to kill him if he showed the slightest sign of breaking their bargain. Perhaps Swenson would take Caine's head as well and see what power truly lay within the man.

A sound intruded on these thoughts. Gradually, so that Swenson was aware of it unconsciously before his mind put a name to it. It was the sound of water dripping.

He turned to his right and there stood Nathaniel Caine. He was soaking wet and loomed over the scout. Swenson actually started and caught himself just before he cried out.

"*Uff da*, Caine," he said. "How the hell did you get past me?"

Caine said nothing, and Swenson didn't like the look of him. The power was on him, even stronger, and he had a fell aspect.

That aspect was not softened by the broad-bladed saber in his right hand.

In his left was a bundle of black cloth. It was soaked, as was Caine, and it was the water dripping off of the bundle that had alerted Swenson to his presence. Caine lifted his head and turned it this way and that, apparently looking at the sky. When he moved, the bundle swayed and the weight of it could only be one thing.

"Is that..."

He fought to keep the greed out of his voice. Caine nodded, but when Swenson reached for it, he pulled back his hand. Swenson's left hand lay near his rifle, but it would be far too slow to bring to bear. He carried an old Colt with the butt forward, and his right hand twitched toward the piece.

In the blink of an eye, Caine stepped forward and brought the saber to Swenson's neck. He could feel the eager edge in the hollow of his throat.

"We had a bargain, Nathaniel Caine."

"That we did, Sven Swenson," he said. "The bargain was you gave me the key and I would help you track the Grinder to his lair. That I have done."

Swenson bent his head to look at the sword blade, even though it pressed the weapon into his skin. He could see the long line of runes, cunningly wrought. He glared at Caine.

"So you mean to take her power for yourself, you bastard?"

"There's no need to be rude, Swenson," Caine said and he held up the bundle. "If you want *this* we can make another bargain. There's something I need you to do for me."

"What? Name it and I'll do it."

"First, I need a drink from your flask," Caine said and lowered the curved sword. "But for this dainty, I'll need you to be my messenger."

* * *

Elisha Cullen sat his horse and watched the grey dawn creep over the palisade. He was riding out with Murphy, and he hoped this morning would be better than the last one. Just as before, Murphy was in the lead and leaned forward in the saddle, eager for the gate to be open. And as before, Cullen was the only one ready to follow when the gate was wide enough for a horse and Murphy dug in his spurs.

Ready as Cullen was, Murphy's horse was fast and he applied his quirt to keep up. He had been angry at the Irishman for not letting him shoot Caine there in the saloon and put an end to it. He had chuckled when Murphy himself was thwarted by Hayes from putting a bullet through the stranger's skull.

Normally the Grinder would have been sure death, but Caine had already escaped that death once. Cullen intended to inspect Caine's death bed with his own eyes. He suspected Murphy had similar reservations and similar intentions this morning.

The town wasn't far, and Cullen was just drawing even with Murphy as they approached the big house. The Irishman hauled back on the reins and his mount skidded to a stop. Cullen cursed, and his own horse crow-hopped as he fought to stop it.

"What the hell is wrong with you, Murphy?"

The sergeant's head whipped back and forth as if looking for foes. He turned the horse and stood in the stirrups to address the troopers who were just catching up.

"Rifles out and surround the house," he yelled.

His men obeyed without question. The group split into a vee that rode around Murphy and Cullen to circle the house.

"Murphy, what are you…"

Cullen's voice trailed off as he looked at the house. The eastern sky was turning red with the morning, but the valley was still in shadow and the front door in even deeper shadow beneath the porch. But he could tell the front doors were open, and he could see something hanging in the doorway. "What the hell is that?"

"I don't know," Murphy said and swung out of the saddle.

He wore his Colt's butt forward, but he didn't have them in the usual cavalryman's flap holster. He jerked both pistols out now and snapped back the hammers.

"Four with me. The rest stay here and keep your eyes peeled."

Cullen dismounted and followed Murphy up the steps, drawing his own revolver. The shutters were hanging and, in some cases, ripped off completely. The front porch was littered with broken glass which crunched under the boot heels of the troopers. Murphy stood in front of the door and Cullen walked up beside him.

"What the hell is that?" Cullen asked again.

"Isn't it obvious?" Murphy said.

He reached out with a pistol and tapped the object hanging there. The steel barrel rang dully on stone and Cullen took a step back. It was the stony skin of the Grinder.

The great fingers were curled, and someone had hung the gruesome thing on the lintel to block the doorway. Murphy now gave it a push and it swung a little, like a ham in a butcher's window. Cullen just stared for a moment, wondering who and why, but it could really only be one thing: a trophy. That meant it could really only be just one man.

"Caine."

"Aye," Murphy said. "Two on the ground floor and two with me."

Murphy moved in and went straight upstairs. Cullen shouldered past the soldiers to follow Murphy. Curses came from the soldiers downstairs as they wandered through the wreckage.

Murphy and Cullen stared at the disassembled bed while the soldiers made a quick search of the upstairs. They had nothing to report, so they went back downstairs. There was little else to be learned there.

There had clearly been a fight, though he was damned if he knew how Caine got out of his irons. But if the Grinder had been the victor, where was Caine's corpse? The Grinder sometimes took men off, true, but there would be blood.

Red human blood at least. Murphy thought the black stains on the floor might be the Grinder's blood; it had certainly taken a wound last night. But if it was fatal, where was the body?

He shrugged.

"What the fuck do you make of it, Cullen?"

"How in hell should I know?" Cullen said. "It looks to me like that bastard got away again, but I can't tell how from this wreck. I'm not a tracker like your scout."

"Where the hell is Swenson?" Murphy said to the soldiers. "He was in the fort last night."

"He left, Sarge," said one trooper.

"What do you mean, he left?"

"Collins told me. He was on watch last night, and Swenson was on the walk with 'em. There was a great ruckus, screams, and howls, and all. Swenson went over the wall after it was over."

"Well, fuck me. Isn't that curious?" Murphy said. "High on my list of things to do today, is to find that squarehead bastard and have bit of a chat."

"That works out well then, you drunken Irish whoreson."

They all whirled to the door and pointed weapons. Swenson was standing in the doorway. He looked up at the Grinder's arm and patted it. He walked in and set it to swinging as he passed, the dead fingers making a slow scraping sound on the lintel.

"I would chat with you, as well," he said. "Private like, although you should join us Cullen. Nathaniel Caine has a message for you as well."

* * *

When Colonel Hayes awoke that morning, he was in a bad mood. He had been in a bad mood every morning that he had been forced to wake up in his quarters here in the fort instead of in his house. The quarters were as comfortable as he could make them—indeed by army standards they were sumptuous—but that wasn't the point.

The point was an old woman was keeping him from sleeping in his own house. A house he had designed and had built from the ground up as a symbol of his wealth and status. Every night he had to hide behind the timber palisade was an affront to his leadership.

Hayes had done well turning the situation to the best advantage possible, but while the monster haunted his town and his house, his grip wasn't complete. That grip must tighten into a stranglehold.

Today.

He would start with having Cullen and the rest of his bandits killed. Their task was to keep strangers away, and they had failed miserably. Bad enough the black-haired stranger had been allowed to pass, but the man had wreaked havoc on the mining operation. No matter, for the scum would be hours dead by now.

That thought improved Hayes' mood, for he hadn't cared for the ruffian's manner. Not only wasn't he suitably afraid in Hayes' presence, but he had looked down on him as if *he* were the superior. It had been insulting and overly familiar, as if Colonel Jonathan D. Hayes would associate with such ragged trash.

For a moment, the thought of that cold grey gaze brushed at the back of his mind, some memory. He pushed it aside with the cheery thought of him screaming while the Grinder ripped him apart. Hayes thought about the rest of his plans while he attended to his toilet.

After Cullen, he had to deal with the workers. Some of them may have tried to run, but most of them would probably be huddled on their farms. Thanks to the recent depredations, his overseer staff was greatly reduced.

Hayes decided to take the women and children and keep them in town as hostages. That should keep the squareheads digging, and anyone who got out of line could watch his wife or his daughter be given to the soldiers for sport. That thought made him positively jolly, and he grinned at himself in the mirror while he inspected his shave.

That's the easy part, he thought as he put on his uniform.

The hard part was still the old witch and that thing she had unleashed on this valley. There was the matter of a new system to keep strangers out.

Then there was Hadley. Hadley and his planned treachery were bad enough, but Hayes thought the filthy moron had done more subtle damage. More subtle, but more dangerous.

The erstwhile hero had heard about their local mascot before he came. That meant Hadley or his drivers were letting secrets slip. Most folk would discount the monster stories; Hayes himself would have mocked such a tale a year ago. Gold, however, was a different matter altogether. The slightest rumor of gold would bring hordes of greedy trash, and no monster would keep them away.

Yes, Hadley was a problem, and he decided that was a priority over the mad woman. He would send Swenson. Murphy was a fierce fighter and cunning in his way, but Swenson was the choice for a manhunt.

The Swede was more subtle. Patient and relentless as a hound on a trail, Swenson was the obvious choice for tracking down the traitor. But more than that was the cold and mercenary drive in the man. Hayes didn't just want Hadley dead. He needed to know who he had talked to and how much he had spilled.

For the right price, Swenson would find Hadley and ask those questions in a manner that assured they were answered. Hayes meant to keep this quiet if he had to kill a thousand men. This was his gold, and no one was going to take it from him.

All that decided, there was a jaunty rhythm to Colonel Hayes' steps as he walked from his quarters to his office. The sun was just coming over the palisade and the fort was still relatively quiet. His secretary was at his station. The word was just a title. Though some of these men had been soldiers once, none of them were more than hired thugs now, and this one could barely read.

He sent the man for breakfast and when that was finished, he ordered coffee. Hayes lit a cigar and smoked while he waited for Sergeant Murphy to report. He should be up from the house soon with confirmation of the stranger's death. Once Hayes gave him his orders, he thought he would send down to the saloon for a couple of girls and share his good mood.

The door to his office banged open and Murphy stomped in in his usual manner. He gave no salute, no greeting at all. He merely stalked over to the whiskey decanter and poured himself a shot. He didn't offer Hayes any.

If this had been the real army, such behavior would have warranted a whipping at the least. But even when Hayes *had* been in the real army, he had seen the value in men like Murphy. As much as he loved the status of being an officer, it paid to let some of the niceties go in order to nurture the savagery of a natural killer like the black-eyed Irishman.

"So," Murphy said.

That was all and he took another shot. The raven feather in his hat glinted as he tipped back his head for the whiskey. Hayes took a slow draw on his cigar so he didn't look impatient.

"Your report, sergeant?"

"I saw something this morning. Something…unexpected."

"Oh," said Hayes, "and what might that be?"

"Well, I'll tell you what I didn't see first," Murphy said. "I *didn't* see the bloody corpse of the dark-haired stranger."

"What?"

Hayes leapt up from his chair.

"He escaped?"

"No. I don't think he escaped."

"Damn it, Murphy!"

Hayes threw his cigar in the ashtray, and came around to the front of his desk.

"Start talking."

A Nathaniel Caine Adventure

"Caine wasn't there, but I don't think he escaped," Murphy said with a shrug. "He got out of his irons somehow, but I think he faced the Grinder just like he said he would."

"Well, then he was mad and must have died."

"There was no body and no sign he died. I don't believe he did die."

"Nonsense," Hayes said. "You've seen it in action. It would take a field piece to even dent it. One man couldn't face it and live."

"Well, face it he did," Murphy said.

He poured another drink and paused. He shook his head slowly.

"He faced it, and I do believe he lived. In fact, I think he bested the thing."

"Horse shit!"

Hayes could feel his good mood receding rapidly. "Why would you think that?"

"He left a trophy, Hayes," said Murphy. "The Grinder's hand, hacked from its body, and hung from at the door for all to see."

"You lie!"

Murphy slammed the glass down on the board and amber liquid spilled.

"Careful now, *Colonel.* I'm not one of your fish-eating clod-hoppers that you can bully."

The black eyes blazed with anger, but then settled just as quick.

"Still, it's a wild tale, no? That's why I brought the arm back with me so you can see for yourself. It's in the courtyard."

Hayes swore under his breath and stalked for the door. He knew something was wrong the instant he threw it open. A fort, even a small one like this, tended to bustle. But all outside was quiet. It only registered as annoyance though, not danger, so Hayes walked right out onto the boardwalk in front of his office.

All the soldiers were gathered in knots around the courtyard, which was left open. The arm was indeed lying there as Murphy said. And standing over it was the dark-haired stranger.

He stood, calm and impassive, with feet planted wide. His hands rested on the hilt of a saber, point down in the dirt of the yard. Hayes had a moment to be angry when he recognized it as one of his own.

He started to turn to order Murphy to shoot down the thief.His head barely made a quarter turn before he heard the four clicks of a Colt's hammer going back. An instant later, he felt the hard cold circle of a pistol barrel at the base of his skull.

"Good morning...Colonel."

The man in the courtyard spoke calmly in his slow Yankee twang. His voice was even pleasant.

"Unbuckle your belt," Murphy's growl was anything but pleasant, "and walk forward down the steps."

"Murphy," Hayes said softly, "what do you think you're doing?"

"Please do as the sergeant says," said the stranger.

"You're not in charge here!" Hayes said. "Murphy, shoot this trash!"

"Captain Avery Merrill!"

A Nathaniel Caine Adventure

The man didn't shout, but his voice had grown hard and carried easily.

"I am calling you out!"

Hayes started violently at the sound of that name. But there was command in that voice that would not be gainsaid. He unbuckled his belt, and the clatter of his weapons hitting the boards fell heavy in the silence. He marched forward down the stairs and took three steps into the courtyard.

"Who in hell are you?"

"I think you came close to recognizing me yesterday, Merrill," he said. "But all you saw was 'trail trash,' someone beneath you. When last we met, though, we were equals. In rank, if not in virtue."

His voice was in complete control, but there was no disguising the contempt and cold rage. Hayes, or rather Merrill, grimaced as he racked his brain for where they had met. Recognition sparked at the face, something about those hard grey eyes.

"Yes, you almost have it, Merrill. My name is Nathaniel Caine. Formerly Captain Nathaniel Caine."

"Caine…with the 4th, under Colonel Banks."

Full recognition bloomed and with it fear, but Merrill found the cheek to laugh.

"Have you been chasing me all this time, Caine?"

"No, Merrill," Caine said. "We chased you enough in '66 and '67, when we should have been going home to our lives. I and others didn't think you died in that fire in Sweetwater, but enough did."

"Then why are you here now?" said Merrill.

"Perhaps it's mere coincidence," Caine said with a shrug. "Or perhaps it's justice catching up with you. You'll remember I was at your court martial, and you'll remember the sentence was death. You deserted your men to *their* fates. The traitor's rope for some, and forty years hard labor for the rest."

"Nobody put a gun to their heads," Merrill said. "All my men were willing and cheerful participants in the venture."

"Well, then they got what they deserved," said Caine. "And now you'll answer as well. You are a war criminal guilty of high treason, profiteering, looting and raping, murder and slaughter of civilians, desertion, and conduct unbecoming an officer and a gentleman. Clearly you haven't lost your taste for such pursuits. So here I am. Call it fate."

"So…what," he said, "you're going to have Murphy here shoot me?"

"A fine idea, for what does one do with any mad dog?"

Caine's smile held no mirth.

"I said your men got what they deserved, but you will get better. You'll get a chance to face your fate on your feet."

Caine lifted the saber and it flashed in the morning sun. Merrill flinched back from the glare, and a cold fear bit at his nerves. The saber was his, but it looked different. Caine held it steady, but it seemed to Merrill it was moving slightly on its own. It looked to him like a poison serpent, poised to strike and swaying slightly, relishing the moment of venomous release to come.

"Among your many crimes is the murder of Willem Jorgensen," Caine said. "His mother marked this steel with your bane and charged me to wield the weapon. It's in my mind that I'll end your luck today, Avery Merrill. Just before I end your life."

"Murphy!"

Merrill turned his back from Caine to beseech the grim-faced sergeant.

"Murphy, you can't think this is a good idea. Kill this bastard and let's get back to work. I'll promote you to captain and give you a share equal to mine!"

"So you can desert me as soon as it's convenient?" The black eyes were hard as obsidian.

"I think I'll promote myself. Colonel sounds better than captain."

Merrill turned his head about like a beast at bay, scanning the circle of men. There was Elisha Cullen, standing among the few remaining members of his gang.

"Cullen," Merrill called to him. "You're smart enough to see sense. Help me and you can have Murphy's place. No more cold camps in the woods waiting for trail trash to walk into a trap. You'll have a warm bed and warm whores. I'll increase your share."

Cullen ran a hand through the wild strands of his beard, and turned to glare at the lone figure of Caine. The bandit stepped out of the circle and crossed the courtyard. Caine didn't move as the man drew near, even when one of his hands dropped to his gun, the gun he had stolen from Caine.

"Thank god someone is seeing sense," Merrill said.

Cullen's other hand went to the knife that had also been robbed. He drew them both forth, but not for combat. Pistol and blade were both in their scabbards and he held them out grips first. Caine nodded and indicated the Grinder's hand before him. Elisha stooped and placed the weapons near the gruesome thing.

He stood and looked Caine in the eye.

"Our feud is ended, Nathaniel Caine."

"Agreed."

Cullen crossed back to his men and spoke to Merrill as he passed.

"Did you think I would just wait until you 'trimmed' me with the rest of the fat?"

Cullen didn't break stride, but he spit on the ground at Merrill's feet before retaking his place in the circle. Merrill's face twisted with rage and the fear.

"What was the price?"

His calm was cracking and he was starting to yell. "What was the price, you treacherous dogs? Did he give you thirty pieces of silver, or promise you all of my gold?"

"It's not the gold, Merrill," Caine said, "as I told you before. The price was the farmers and townsfolk. The bargain was a fair fight, and after I kill you, any who want to leave this place can come with me."

"Fair fight?"

His voice had returned to normal, but Merrill still looked like a cornered animal.

"You might not be a gentleman, but *I* am," Caine said, and again moved the saber to make it gleam in the sunlight.

"We haven't the time for a formal challenge, I fear, so you won't get to choose weapons. We'll face each other with sabers."

"Fine!"

Merrill spat the word, and turned to walk to his sword belt, which also held his holstered pistol. He only got a few steps when Murphy raised the Colt to stop him.

Murphy nodded at a trooper. He bent and Merrill's sword made a slow scraping sound as he drew it from the metal scabbard. The soldier held it awkwardly as he trotted it out to Merrill, and then returned to the circle of men.

Caine watched carefully. Many of the officers in the war were West Point graduates and well versed with the saber. Many more came from wealthy families that still upheld the dueling tradition.

Though the pistol was preferred for such affairs, a gentleman's education would include training with the sword. He was certain Merrill had killed many with his blade, but cutting down the defenseless from a saddle while you sacked a town wasn't the same as a fight against an armed and ready opponent.

There was no awkwardness to Merrill when he grasped his weapon, and no awkwardness as he began to stalk across the open yard. Caine smiled and was surprised to find he was pleased Merrill had skill. Despite the stakes and the price he had paid to get here, Caine realized he was looking forward to this fight.

He stepped over the severed hand and walked to meet his foe in the center of the courtyard. The time for talk was passed, and Caine expected neither a salute nor a call of *en garde* from Merrill.

He was not disappointed.

When only a few paces separated the men, Merrill went from a walk to a run and lashed out. Caine evaded the first two cuts and parried the third on the flat of his blade.

Merrill danced back out of range, and Caine's counter cut whistled in the air. Both men stood light on their feet, blades in an easy guard.

Caine made a feint, which Merrill ignored. Caine beat his opponent's blade off line, and delivered a descending cut to where shoulder met neck. Merrill made a hard parry and struck with the hilt of his sword.

Caine ducked and received a vicious kick to the side which sent him sprawling. He was rolling up and out as soon as he hit the ground and caught the next slash as he rose. Caine stepped in to lock the hilts. The men stood nearly *corps a corps*, and he smiled in Merrill's face. Such behavior in a duel would have immediately raised cries of foul, but there were no seconds here, and the circle of watchers saw only a brawl to the death.

"No time for the formalities," Merrill said, "eh, Caine?"

"As you say."

Caine snapped his head to smash his forehead into Merrill's nose. He drove his shoulder forward with the whole weight of his body behind it to break contact.

Merrill flew back, but recovered his balance quickly and parried Caine's flurry of cuts. Soon enough he was able to ignore the pain of his nose and started counter attacking. The steel rang as the men exchanged blows, but neither gained the advantage.

They parted and circled, each man starting to breathe heavily from the exertion. Caine felt the subtle vibration running through his blade. He looked at the runes which, to his eyes at least, still pulsed with dull orange bale fire. The blade felt eager, hungry to bite Merrill's flesh, but he must master the impulse. Brawl or no, he would not be able to take his foe with brute force.

For his part, Merrill was glad of the heavy breathing. Caine was taller than him and had the reach, but his blade was also heavier, designed for shearing cuts. Merrill could see those great cuts coming from a mile off. As long as Caine kept cutting and missing, he would tire first. When that happened, Merrill would stop parrying and his foe would over swing and leave himself open.

Merrill's own blade was not Army issue but a fine saber from Britain. The blade was slimmer and lighter, but supple enough to withstand the broad-bladed Hussar assault. It was also straighter, better suited to the thrust. When Merrill saw that opening, he would ram the fine Sheffield steel through Caine's heart.

In the meantime, he couldn't let Caine recover his breath. Merrill swung a few short cuts from the elbow at Caine's face to make him parry. The more he parried, the quicker his sword arm would fatigue.

He changed levels and slashed at Caine's legs. The man stood in a squared stance like a boxer instead of a fencer. It let Merrill attack both legs to keep him moving. The more he moved, the quicker his legs would fatigue.

Merrill pressed the attack as much as he dared, for Caine still managed to defend and counterattack. He knew it couldn't last. The man had spent the last two nights fighting in the woods, and that must tell soon.

Caine backed off, puffing like dray horse, and Merrill bit back a grin. He let his enemy retreat a bit, then ran forward with a wild cut. Caine parried, but grunted with the effort. Merrill quickly disengaged, and gave a quick thrust on the high line. This wasn't parried so much as swatted away, and the tip nearly caught in the buckskin shirt.

Merrill stepped back, and relished the look of grim worry that came into Caine's eye. The taller man snarled and renewed his attack. Merrill parried and started to give ground. He could feel his opening coming.

Caine bit back a grin of his own at the sly look in Merrill's eye. He now knew Merrill's game. The murderer stood with his right foot well forward and the knee bent, the classic fencer's pose. The stance was well suited to the piste and designed as the perfect engine for driving thrusts.

Caine kept waiting for those thrusts and grew suspicious when they didn't come. Caine had been worried about fatigue himself, but despite his recent and current exertions, felt his wind would hold up just fine. He had exaggerated his breathing and made his parries more and more wild to draw Merrill out.

That plan had worked, and Merrill gave himself away with that last thrust. Caine drove him forward now with slash after slash. Merrill gave ground and with every attack, increased the distance between them a little more.

And now Caine had him.

Giving ground meant Merrill would not try a stop-thrust, but was waiting for an opening to lunge. Caine continued to drive at him, so Merrill moved back in a straight line. Mostly the game of swords was chess, but the final move often became a throw of the dice.

Caine threw them now with a great looping cut from the shoulder on a descending line. He was open for the windup, but Merrill drew back and Caine let the slash go. Merrill danced back and his muscles bunched as the steel split the air in front of him.

Caine's sword now came completely off line. The force of the blow bent and twisted him until he was almost on one knee, with his off hand on the ground. He looked off balance to everyone there, but especially to Merrill, who sprang forward in a picture perfect lunge.

But Caine wasn't off balance.

His hand and forward leg uncoiled like springs, and he leapt up and off the line of thrust. Don Octavio would have been proud of the dancelike grace that Caine used to spin around his opponent's blade and raise his own over his head like a matador. He dropped and brought the saber down in a descending hook thrust.

The saber's point struck Merrill in the meatiest part of his thigh, which was exposed from the lunge. What began as a cry of triumph turned to a cry of agony in Merrill's throat. Caine jerked out the blade and turned the motion into an ascending cut. Merrill threw himself backward trying to evade it. He succeeded, but the man's injured leg betrayed him and he lost his balance.

Caine's next cut was a simple hack to split the skull. Merrill managed to get his own blade up, but it was a desperate and inelegant parry. Merrill went sprawling from the force of the blow and threw out a pleading hand to stay Caine's upraised sword.

"Quarter, Caine!" he shouted.

"Quarter, I beg of you!"

"I'll give you no quarter, dog," Caine said, "this is to the death. But I'll let you rise. On your feet and let us finish this."

Caine backed up a few paces but kept his weapon in the guard. Merrill pushed himself up with his free hand and struggled painfully to a standing position. His sword hand shook as he slowly started to bring his weapon to *en garde*. Then he moved suddenly, snapping his left hand forward to throw the dirt he had gathered in Caine's face.

A child's trick, but it almost worked. Caine saw the movement and instinctively turned his face away. He stepped back in the same instant so that Merrill's slash only scored the flesh of his upper arm. Merrill pressed forward swinging wildly. Caine parried and gave ground, letting Merrill advance on a straight line.

Don Octavio's teaching was a very old Spanish style that relied heavily on geometry. Don Octavio taught him that straight lines were simple attacks for simple minds. And here was Merrill trying the same game that had just failed him. Caine waited patiently while his opponent gave slash after slash. Finally, Merrill thought he saw his opening and thrust straight at Caine's heart.

But Caine was ready.

He stepped off line and pivoted in a neat little arc, avoiding the attack entirely. His blade made a similar arc and flashed through the air to sever Merrill's sword hand neatly just above the wrist.

Merrill gasped, a sharp inhale of air, and stared for a long, mute moment at his saber lying on the ground. For that long moment, he couldn't reconcile his sword in the dirt, for he was quite sure he hadn't dropped it. He wondered whose hand that was wrapped around the hilt, and then the pain raced up his arm. Merrill let out his air in a long and high-pitched scream.

"You bastard!"

His voice wavered and he clutched his sword arm, driving the stump into his breast to try and staunch the bleeding.

"What have you done to me, you whore-loving bastard?"

"I've cut off your hand," Caine said. "Now try and gather your dignity and I'll finish it."

"You go to hell, Nathaniel Caine!"

Merrill turned and tried to run, but his injured leg only allowed a limp. Caine stepped forward and swung his sword to hamstring the whimpering man. Merrill went to his knees with a curse.

He thought about crawling away, but a shadow fell over him. He looked up to see the slim form of Caine looming over him with eyes of flint. The sun flashed silver on the steel blade before him, and it looked even hungrier than before.

"It's got a taste of me now," he muttered in a small voice, but Caine heard him.

"Indeed. And it must be fed. Blood will pay for blood."

Caine swung the sword in a flat arc. The broad Hussar blade bit deep, crunching through the spine and slicing through the tissue of neck and throat. Merrill's head fell with a thump in the dirt, and his body made a heavier thump a second later.

Silence gripped the courtyard. All stood frozen in a grim tableau. Caine looked at the man he had killed, and then raised the saber to look at it. The blade was a good one and showed no damage from the fight.

As Caine watched, the blood on the sword began to move in a strange fashion. Instead of flowing to the edge and dripping off, the blood swirled and flowed up the blade. It poured over and into the furrows of the runic scratches and began to smoke and steam.

With a sudden crack that rang like a gunshot in the silence, the blade shattered into pieces and Caine was left holding a hilt with four of five jagged inches. The hellish glow of the letters was gone; they were now just scratches in the steel. Caine let the hilt fall by the body.

It was done.

Merrill's blood was still pooling in the dirt when he turned and addressed Murphy.

"The fort and the town are yours as agreed, Sergeant Murphy," said Caine. "Or Colonel, if you prefer. The farmers and any folk that wish to leave are mine."

"Less any gold, Caine," said Murphy. "As agreed."

"I don't think that will be an issue," he said and beckoned to Tor Nielsen who stood in the circle.

"I plan to leave quickly. I'll be at Mr. Nielsen's place if you need me."

He nodded cordially to Murphy and strode out the gate. Tor Nielsen gathered Caine's weapons, and fell into step beside him.

"That bastard got what he deserved, Mr. Caine," Tor said, "but I didn't enjoy it as much as I thought I would."

"That speaks well of you, Mr. Nielsen. It was indeed an unpleasant task, but now it's done. We need to move apace. Let's go straight to your saloon, where I must prevail on you for a room. The exertion, it seems, has finally caught up with me, and I feel like I could sleep right here in the ditch."

"Why didn't you use the fort?"

Tor's tone was worried, for now that Caine mentioned it, he looked drawn and haggard, ready to pass out.

"Bargain or no," Caine said in a low voice, though they were already out of earshot of the fort, "Murphy can only be trusted so far. I'll sleep in your place and ask you to keep watch."

"Sure, Caine. You can sleep in my own bedroom," he said. "I've been sleeping in a tent since the witch's curse. Another night won't hurt."

"I'll need you to help gather the folk, as well," Caine said. "Tell them the bargain. None of the gold from this mine can leave with them. Make sure everyone knows."

"They'll leave it and be glad," Tor said. "That gold is cursed."

"Indeed," said Caine. "When I was in the mining camp, there was a man. He was old, but still strong. Blue eyes and a white beard. He was carving wood."

"That sounds like Olaf Swenson."

"Swenson? Is he related to the scout?"

"No, Caine," Tor said with a chuckle. "There are a lot of Swensons in Sweden."

"I see. At any rate, this fellow had steel in him. I told him to be ready to get the farmers out during the attack, and he didn't ask a lot of useless questions."

"Yah, that's old Olaf. He's sharp, he is."

"Good," Caine said. "He was to take the folk and hide on the farms. Get word to him and help them get ready to leave as soon as possible."

"It might take awhile," Tor said. "We'll need to get wagons together and supplies."

"I understand, but take just enough to get back over the mountains. I'm eager to be out of this valley."

"I can imagine."

"It's not just what's passed," Caine said. "I can't shake the feeling that danger still threatens."

Tor looked like he wanted to press for details, but he refrained. Caine was grateful, for as palpable as the feeling of dread was, he had no details to give, just the feeling.

When they arrived at the saloon, Tor showed Caine to his own bedroom against Caine's protests. Caine plucked at the tunic he had worn for so many nights and asked if Tor could have a bath drawn. His host agreed and left to see it done.

Caine remembered sitting on the bed and taking a deep breath, but he had no recollection of lying down. Of course, that wouldn't be unusual since he was quite literally asleep before his head hit the pillow.

* * *

Bright sunlight lanced through the window, and Caine's eyes snapped open. Someone had covered him in a warm quilt and he threw it back. He was still fully dressed and realized he must have simply passed out and slept the day away. But no, this window faced east and so the light was from morning sun.

He shot to his feet with the realization that he had slept all day and through the night. Caine went to the door and threw it open. A great din poured through and he stepped to the rail to find the saloon below bustling with activity.

There were folk coming and going through both doors, sometimes carrying bundles. Some folk were eating and many of them did it while standing, shoveling food down in quick forkfuls to get back to their business. Others simply stood in small knots talking and gesturing in animated discussions. The whole place buzzed with nervous energy, but it didn't feel panicky. Caine mentally shook himself and went to the stairs. Tor Nielsen saw him and raised his hand in greeting.

"Good morning, Mr. Caine."

Tor was speaking with a tall white-haired man who now turned to look. It was the old man Caine had charged with evacuating the mining camp. Olaf Swenson was his name, and he now turned and called to the room.

The buzz died away as Olaf spoke in a loud voice. Caine didn't understand the language, but he caught his own name at the end. The assembled folk turned to him with wide eyes and began to applaud and yell. Those who were seated stood up and Caine stopped, surprised at the clamor.

He had a sudden urge to turn and flee and actually took a step back. He stopped himself and raised a hand to the folk before coming down. The applause stopped, but there was much handshaking and backslapping as Caine made his way to Tor and Olaf.

"Good morning, gentlemen," Caine said and looked around. "Hartsburgh looks different with people in it."

"*Uff da.* There used to be more," said Olaf with a grim look at the room. "But thanks be to God for those we still have."

"You must be hungry, Caine," Tor said. "Or do you want that bath first?"

"Business first, Mr. Nielsen. We have to get these people ready to go."

A Nathaniel Caine Adventure

"We're nearly ready, Mr. Caine," said Olaf. "We should need another two hours I would say."

"What? How the hell did that happen?"

"You said we needed to be quick, Caine," said Tor, "and I took you seriously. Olaf here has not been idle."

"After we last met, I got the folk to the farms," Olaf said and then shrugged. "It was clear that we couldn't huddle there waiting for the Grinder or the soldiers. Whatever our chances, we had to make a run for it, and I didn't know if you would survive to come for us as you said."

"*I'm* still not sure how I managed it," Caine said.

He spoke quietly, more to himself than anyone, but the other men nodded.

"We got as many wagons as we could from the farms and gathered supplies," Olaf went on. "Mostly food, for I didn't really know where we would go."

"I went to find Olaf myself yesterday," Tor said. "He was pretty much ready, so we brought everyone back here. We got the rest of the wagons from the soldiers and have them all assembled and pretty much loaded. We have enough mules and oxen to pull them, but not many spares, so we'll have to go easy on the beasts. But they'll pull us out of this damned valley."

"The gold?"

"Most of the folk were happy to be rid of it," said Olaf. "A few wanted their share and a few even want to stay. But only a few. We let Murphy search the wagons and he's satisfied we have none of it."

"Well, gentlemen," Caine said, "you've done better than I could have hoped. I wasn't sure how we could get them all out."

"Don't judge us too harshly, Caine," Olaf said leaning close. "Whatever spell of terror was on them is broken. They're still afraid, of course, but their good sense is back. They're tough people. Good people."

"I'm sure you're right, Mr. Swenson, and I meant no offense," said Caine. "In fact, I'm very impressed. And since all is in hand, I believe I'll have the bath before I eat."

The bathhouse was set up outside in back of the saloon. It was simply a board platform with canvas roof and walls, barely a tent, but there was water on the stove already, scalding hot.

He stripped and stepped into the tub, and had a moment to reflect on the nature of luxury. On occasion back east, he had stayed in hotels that could only be described as sumptuous. But as he lowered himself into the hot water in that tin tub, and his breath steamed in the still cool mountain air from a sigh that approached ecstasy, Nathaniel Caine swore that if he lived to be a hundred, he would never experience anything so luxurious.

Caine took up soap and brush and scoured away the weeks of living in the wild. He was bruised and bloodied here and there from his recent fights, and he cleansed those as well as he could. He was able to relax a bit knowing the townspeople were almost ready to go, but still there was a nagging sense of danger. He let the heat sink through his skin and into his bones for a few moments, and he tried to let go of the hurts and aches.

"Good morning, Mr. Caine!" came a chirruping call as the tent flap was thrown back with a snap.

Caine started and there were more chirped greetings and a staccato stamp of shoe heels as a group of young women stormed in.

"Ahh...."

Caine managed to stammer out a good morning as the girls started to bustle about his tub. One bore towels and another a bundle of clothes, and they chattered to one another and to him, seemingly all at once. Caine's head swiveled trying to follow the conversation, if such it could be called.

"Here, let me scrub your back!"

"I brought you clothes!"

"Oh! Let me get the tangles out of your hair!"

Caine was no Puritan, but neither was it his habit to bathe attended by some chattering seraglio. They ignored his stuttering protests, and he could do little to fend them off with his hands over his privates.

"You need a shave, darling! Let me strop a razor!"

That did the trick. The girl handled the razor like she was ready to harvest cane. The pun was not lost on him, and he gave up modesty to grab the young woman's wrist.

"Ladies!"

It came out a harsh bark and the girls froze. Caine took a deep breath and got a good look at them. They were the prostitutes he had shooed out during the trouble with Cullen's gang members. Pretty young things all, and they all had the same look now. It was the look of an eager puppy waiting for a kick, but not understanding why it would come. Caine gently removed the razor from the girl's hand and softened his tone.

"Ladies, I thank you very much for your attentions, but I was very nearly done. Time presses, you see. We need to leave this town quickly, and I still need breakfast."

"Of course!"

"You're probably starving, you poor man!"

"I'll get it ready!"

"No, *I'll* get it ready!"

The soiled doves flew the coop in the same flurry that they entered. Caine could see their shadows cross on the white canvas as they went into the saloon and argued about who exactly was going to get breakfast ready. Caine sat holding the razor and looking around, wondering dazedly what exactly had just happened.

He did in fact need a shave, so he did it quickly and dressed. He was surprised to find that the clothes were his own. Tor Nielsen must have gotten them back from Cullen. They had been laundered and the bullet hole in his shirt had been mended. Caine pulled on his belts but paused before leaving the tent.

He went back to the pile of buckskins that lay on the floor. The obsidian knife lay on top in its beaded leather sheath. He took this and tucked it into his belt before going into the saloon.

The room had cleared out somewhat, but there was still plenty of coming and going as folk consulted with Olaf and Tor. The men had clearly fallen into the leadership role for the townsfolk.

A Nathaniel Caine Adventure

Caine could see through the windows all the wagons lined up in the streets. Most of them had beasts already in the traces, a mixture of mules and oxen with a draft horse here and there. There were a few soldiers watching, but they bore only pistols and kept to the other side of the street. Caine only managed a few steps into the room before he was again accosted by the whores.

They frog marched him to a seat at a table where he was plied with enough food for three people. Among the ceaseless talk they tried to tell Caine their names, but he couldn't tell which belonged to which girl. He was reduced to calling them all dear ('Thank you dear', 'Yes, dear, cream please'), but he didn't think they noticed.

Caine was famished and it was a good thing. The food was abominable. The eggs were fried black on one side and were tough and leathery on the other. The potatoes, on the other hand, were nearly raw despite the fact they were swimming in hot bacon grease. The bacon itself was more like jerky, and there wasn't enough sugar to take the sting out of the coffee they kept pouring in his cup.

He kept murmuring and smiling politely while he choked it down, and noticed Tor and Olaf watching him. The men grinned at each other and Caine glared at them. Finally Tor wandered over and shooed off the young women.

"Go on now, girls," he said. "Mrs. Nielsen is seeing to some final arrangements. Go and help her."

His voice was stern, but he was smiling as they bustled off, looking over their shoulders at Caine.

"How was your breakfast then, Caine?"

"I had hoped to leave hardtack behind when I left the Army."

Caine dipped a rock hard biscuit in his coffee to make it safe for human teeth.

"That was some of the worst food I've had in years."

"Yah, it's pretty bad," Tor said laughing. "But they made it themselves you see."

"I hope they're better prostitutes than cooks."

"*Uff da*," said Tor, "that's no life for a woman."

Caine had taken the phrase *uff da* for some mild oath from Tor's homeland. The merchant shrugged at Caine's questioning look.

"They weren't my girls to start, you see," he said with a shrug. "I just took over the saloon when the former owner was killed. I wasn't much of a saloon keeper and an even worse pimp. But I figure I'm responsible for them now, so I took them in. I told them I would find them husbands."

"You're a good man, Tor Nielsen," Caine said and raised his coffee cup in a toast.

He grimaced as he swallowed the foul brew.

"And you have your work cut out for you."

Tor ducked his head at the praise but laughed at the jest.

"Come," he said and gestured at the counter. "I think I've recovered most of your belongings from Cullen's gang."

Caine went to the counter where several weapons were arrayed. Caine's knife and whip were both there. He inspected them carefully for damage and found them sound. His Smith and

Wesson was there as well as several other pistols. He picked up the Smith and broke the action.

"Do you have cartridges for this?"

"Yah. For all of them."

"Good."

Caine snapped the action closed and handed it, butt first, to Tor.

"I want you to have this. It will serve you better than that .36."

"Thank you," Tor took the proffered gun. "but what about you?"

"I made a deal for these," Caine picked up the brace of Remingtons, "as well as a rifle and horse. I would be grateful if you could give me ammunition, though."

With that taken care of, Caine and the two men went outside and checked the wagon train. As promised, the people were nearly ready to go, and everyone was about their tasks. So Caine checked that his own mount was ready for travel. That task done, he merely stayed out of the way and smoked his pipe. Soon enough it was time to go.

Caine mounted and rode with Olaf, also ahorse, to the lead wagon which Tor was driving. Before they could give the call to roll out, the sound of galloping hooves came. Murphy was riding into town and didn't stop until he ran the length of the train and reined in before Caine. He had a handful of troopers with him, but their carbines were in their saddle scabbards.

"Leaving without saying goodbye, bucko?" Murphy said.

"I didn't mean to be rude, Murphy," Caine said. "I merely thought you'd be anxious to have us gone."

Murphy leaned forward in his saddle. The black eyes passed over the convoy, glaring, and his fingers tapped on his saddle bow.

"What's on your mind, Murphy?" said Caine. "I thought we had a deal."

"We had a deal, right enough. But it's in my mind you can't hold up your end."

"The Grinder's dead, as is the one who called him down," Caine's voice grew hard, "as I promised. These people have given up their promised share of the gold, as agreed."

"It's the very existence of the gold I'm worried about," Murphy said. "You can't promise me all these squareheads will keep their traps shut."

Caine opened his mouth to speak, but Olaf nudged his horse forward until he was right next to Murphy. Several troopers let their hands stray to rifle butts, but Murphy held up a hand.

"We've taken council," Olaf said. "and I speak for all. Every last one of us is quit of you and your gold. We won't talk of it outside this valley, and do you know why?"

"Enlighten me."

"That gold is cursed, Murphy," Olaf said. "Or this ground is, but it comes to the same thing. I tell you so you'll believe me, we don't want anyone else coming here to suffer from this evil. But I also tell you for yourself and your men. Stop digging for this *blodguld*. It will be the death of you."

"I'll take my chances, granddad."

A Nathaniel Caine Adventure

Murphy laughed and called to his men.

"Let them pass boys."

Murphy dug in his spurs and rode off, and his soldiers followed as best they could. Olaf looked at Caine. Caine nodded, Olaf just shrugged and looked back at the train.

"Alright then!"

The old man's voice rang out like a trumpet.

"Let's get them rolling."

A wagon train moved slower than a lone man, but they were still far away from town and climbing into the mountains when the sun was high. That sun, for the first time, brought real warmth as it shone on Caine's face. The nights would stay chilly for a while yet, especially in the passes, but he knew the worst of the snow would be gone.

He turned his ring around his finger as the knowledge came to him. He could go back and forth over how he had managed to survive and triumph in the battles just past. If he tried hard enough, he could rationalize his luck with the soldiers and the Grinder, explain away his visions in the cave, and his night sight that let him move about like a wolf in the woods.

But he couldn't explain away the ring. Shaw's ring. He knew it had given him the edge, allowed him to see the truth of the Grinder, his weakness, and how to talk to his mother. He also believed it had kept him in touch with whatever power ran through these hills, and that's how he had overcome so many adversaries alone. He also believed that power was fading.

Perhaps the connection with Shaw was fading, or perhaps the power faded as he rode further from the hills, or maybe it was just over. But it wasn't over yet. It wasn't a rational thought, but he couldn't shake it.

Caine was taking them back over Elkhorn pass. He didn't think they'd make the pass before nightfall, but there was a bit of a plateau in the next few miles. There was a stream, so they could camp there and water the beasts and try the passes in daylight. His horse snorted and tossed his head, and Caine's own head came up. There ahead in the middle of the trail was an Indian on horseback.

"Call a halt, Olaf," Caine said quietly.

The older man looked up and swore, grabbing at his rifle. Caine shot out a hand and stopped him.

"No! He's not alone. Call the halt and keep them calm."

Olaf called for the halt and rode back along the line speaking in Swedish. Caine had to trust the man was keeping them from their guns, for he dared not turn his head from the warrior before them. Caine let his own horse continue forward at a walk while the Indian eyed him warily.

He had long black hair and his dark eyes blazed as he looked up and down the wagon train. Caine didn't have any professional scouts at his disposal, Swenson had apparently disappeared sometime last night. But he had Olaf pick the best hunters to act as outriders, and Caine wondered where those men were.

The Indian lifted his head and gave a few high pitched cries like the bark of a coyote. In a few moments, the entire trail was boiling with mounted warriors. Caine had heard of the red Indian's skill at moving in the wilderness, but this was shocking.

There were close to a hundred men, and Caine had heard no sign of their approach. More came pouring over the ridge. The first man gestured, and Caine knew what had happened to his scout.

The man was alive but terrified. They had his arms bound behind him and a hard gag in his mouth. His head was in a rawhide noose which one of the Indians kept tugging at. He rode forth with a few others and joined the first man. Caine let Olaf catch up before he rode to meet them. He kept his horse to a walk and his right hand up with the palm out.

The fierce aspect of the savages was not diminished as they drew near. They all wore paint on their faces, and most had feathers arranged in their hair. The weapons were mixed. Caine saw many rifles and a few pistols, but also a few bows, and they all had knives and clubs. The first man who had seen them had his face painted all white but for a black stripe across his eyes. He spoke a few harsh words and nodded at the man who held the scout's noose.

"Black Wolf speaks," the man said. "My name is Three Bears and I will tell you his words. He wants to know who is in charge of these...cart riders."

"I am Olaf Swenson. I can speak for them."

The warrior, Black Wolf, started speaking again and gesturing with his hands. Caine didn't need a translator to know that Black Wolf wasn't inviting them to Sunday dinner.

"All of this valley is holy land to my people. It is death for the white man to set foot here. All of these white hairs dig in the ground for the blue coats. They will all die."

"We don't dig for the blue coats," Olaf said. "Not anymore. We are leaving this valley and just want to pass. We don't want any trouble with your people and haven't fought them."

Black Wolf started speaking again and appeared to be working himself into a frenzy. Not that Caine could blame him. He scanned the main body of Indians, hoping that the Red Man who had healed his wounds from the tree was there.

Black Wolf would be more apt to listen to one of his own people. He couldn't see the Red Man, but then it would be hard to pick him out since all the faces were painted. No, not all.

Caine noticed an old man regarding him. As he watched, this man nudged his horse forward. He had a beat-up Henry across his saddle but wore no paint or head dress. His hair was steel gray and fell in two long plaits over his shoulders. At the end of each was an eagle feather.

He calmly took his place among the group of speakers but never took his eyes off of Caine. Black Wolf finished his current tirade by pulling a rawhide loop from his belt. It was threaded through a fresh scalp. So fresh that the blood was still glistening, and he shook it over his head before shaking it in the white men's faces. Olaf shrank back, but Caine just looked closer. The hair was long and greasy and sandy blond.

"I'll be damned if I don't recognize it," he said.

"Black Wolf says…"

A Nathaniel Caine Adventure

"Let me guess," Caine interrupted. "He doesn't care whether or not we work for the blue coats. He's going to kill us all and take our scalps to add to his collection."

"Who…"

"Tell me," Caine said. "Did he take that one from a smelly fat fellow with a dirty hairy face?"

Caine held his hands up to his own face to mimic a beard and Black Wolf looked nonplussed.

"How do you know this?" Three Bears asked.

"I know much. I know that man was a coward and a snake and he deserved what he got. But these are good people and peaceful. They were digging in the ground, but the blue coats were forcing them. All they want to do now is leave in peace."

Black Wolf put Bill Hadley's scalp back on his belt and moved his horse until he and Caine were face to face. Caine took a moment to be impressed with the man's horsemanship. They used neither saddle nor stirrups, and Black Wolf hadn't even touched the reins to bring his horse up. He now gazed hard at Caine.

"Who are you, grey eye?" Black Wolf said.

"My name is, Nathaniel Caine. I understand your anger. There's a great power in these hills, but also a great evil. The chief of the blue coats dug it out as he dug for the yellow metal."

"What do you know of this evil?"

"The Stone That Walks," Caine said and a few of the Indians clutched at small leather bags around their necks. "He was awakened by the blue coats and killed many people."

"And now you run?" Black Wolf said.

"I do not run. I fought the Stone That Walks and killed him."

There were outright gasps at this, but Black Wolf threw back his head and laughed.

"And then what, Grey Eye?"

"The chief of the blue coats still wouldn't let these people go," said Caine. "So I fought him and killed him."

"The Stone That Walks cannot be killed so easy."

The old man spoke quietly, but all eyes turned to him.

"He took a man's body for his own," Caine said. "The power still sleeps in the mountain, but I killed his Walker and broke the spell. There are no blue coats among us. Let us pass."

"Where are the blue coats then?" said Black Wolf. "Did you kill all of them too?"

"I killed many. But not all. They are still down there. They were warned about the evil, but they will keep digging."

"Why should I believe any of the words you have spoken, Grey Eye?" Black Wolf asked. "Your kind will say anything to save your own skin. Even if they have to cry like a woman."

Caine considered for a moment and then nudged his own horse. He rode away from Black Wolf and moved the few paces to the old man. Caine reached under his coat and a few warriors raised weapons, though the old man himself seemed unconcerned.

Caine drew forth the obsidian knife and held it out. The Indian's eyes widened and his hands shook as he took the knife. He ran gnarled fingers over the bead work of the sheath before drawing it. He stared long at the black facets before looking back to Caine.

A Nathaniel Caine Adventure

"I defeated the Stone Walker," Caine said, "but the wound is still in the earth. There was an old woman. She said the digging was nearing the source of power. The roots."

The old man straightened and held up the knife. He spoke in his own language and pitched his voice to carry to the main body of men. Black Wolf rode over and the two men appeared to be arguing. The two men shook their heads at each other, and eventually Black Wolf broke off with a growl. He rode back to Caine.

"You would give us your own people?"

Caine shook his head.

"The blue coats aren't my people. *These* are my people, and they've done you no wrong."

"Take them and go then. But hear me Grey Eye. If I see them on my people's land again, I will kill them slow."

Black Wolf wheeled on his horse and began shouting orders at his band. They started riding down the trail, streaming along the wagon train on both sides. The grey-haired Indian handed the knife back, but Caine held up his hand.

"It was only a loan," he said. "I'm happy I have a chance to return it."

"This is a great gift and it is a Great One that gave it to you," the old man said. "I wish we had more time to talk, Nathaniel Caine."

He tucked the knife in his belt and took up his reins.

"Grandfather, wait," Caine said. "When you heal the wound you have to put all the yellow metal back. You must never let white men know it's there, or they will keep coming and digging."

"Why?"

Caine shrugged.

"The metal drives them mad."

The grey haired one looked puzzled, but he nodded his head before he galloped off. Olaf waited until the last of them had gone. He looked at the wide eyes and white faces of the convoy and saw many people crossing themselves or openly praying in thanks giving.

"Jesus Christ, Caine," he said. "I thought we were goners. Looks like you saved us again."

"It was the old wise man," Caine said. "If he hadn't been there, we'd already be dead, I imagine. Come on, let's get them rolling."

"But what about Murphy and all those others?"

"Any white man in that valley by sundown won't live to see sunrise," Caine said in a flat voice. "I expect the lucky ones will go quick."

"Christ," Olaf swore softly.

"They were all warned, Olaf. They had their chance to leave."

Nathaniel Caine turned his mount's head back to the passes.

"And now it's done."

The End

A Nathaniel Caine Adventure

Thanks for reading Nathaniel Caine's latest supernatural adventure! If you enjoyed it, please rate it and review it on Amazon or Goodreads. Or drop me a line at ericbahle@backwoodsbard.com. And don't forget to keep an eye on the Eric Bahle fan page on Facebook for updates on upcoming Caine stories and other projects. If you're a first time reader, be sure to check out Caine's first appearance in West of Dead.

72036860R10166

Made in the
USA
Middletown, DE